Tethered Kites

a novel

by

Devlyn D'Alfonzo

ISBN: 9798990166707 (Hardcover)
ISBN: 9798990166721 (Paperback)
ISBN: 9798990166714 (Ebook)

Library of Congress Control Number: 2024904212

This is a work of fiction. Any references to historical events, real people, living or dead, places are used fictitiously. Names, characters, and places are products of the author's imagination and any resemblance to people, living or dead, places or events is purely coincidental.

Front cover image by Julie McLain
Cover design by Lynn Andreozzi.

Printed in the United States of America.

First printing edition 2024.
Broken Tree Press, LLC.
Brokentreepress@gmail.com

Dedicated to:

Joan Brooks Sulzbach Young

and

Shirley Mae Mitchell D'Alfonzo

who both passed before

I could know them as women

and not simply as Grandma.

Eleanor

The resonant tone of my father's old grandfather clock filled the space around me with its familiar sound. Four times it rang out. Now I knew the time. If only I knew how I got here.

I sat in my old wingback chair, its pale blue fabric fraying and faded from years of use. Nestled in a bay window with a view of the mountains to the west, this chair was my favorite spot. Neal called it my command center. I called it heaven. Through the wavy old glass of the window, the mountains were a pale blue line that blurred the difference between land and sky. Normally, this was the place where I felt the most at ease. When Jo was small, we'd read books upon books in this chair, her favorites always about horses. In the evenings Neal and I liked to sit here across from each other and talk as we watched sunsets over the mountains, each one a unique display of color, light and shadow. At the moment, I only felt disoriented.

I remembered my grocery trip and loading the groceries into the car. A bag had fallen over, sending a can of green beans rolling across the floor of the trunk. I'd chased it back into the bag, then driven home. While driving, the sun had flared in my eyes and I'd reached up to pull down the sun shade. Now here I sat, with no memory of the rest of my trip home. In front of me stood Hobbit, one of our two cats. She stared at me with unblinking green eyes, grey coat soft and inviting, tail twitching slightly. I stood, causing her to hiss and run away. She should

* * *

have been winding herself around my legs at this hour, begging for food.

The food.

I hurried into the kitchen and opened the fridge to check inside. The groceries weren't there. There were no bags on the counter, and no sign that I'd even brought them into the house. I went to the front windows to check the car, sure that the trunk would be popped open, groceries sitting within. It wasn't there. Our driveway sat empty, curving around the ancient magnolia in front of the house.

I was supposed to meet with my daughter Jo, my mom, and possibly Neal, depending on his shift, for dinner at seven o'clock. I needed to call Jo. I went to the oak hall rack by the door to find my purse and phone. Neither were there. I caught a fleeting glance of myself in the patchy silver of the old mirror. I was devoid of color from stress. Without a phone or car, I was adrift, stranded in my own house. I went back to the kitchen and stood without purpose. The cat-shaped clock on the wall ticked away, its plastic eyes flicking back and forth in time with its tail, telling me it was now six o'clock. The shadows on the slate kitchen floor had grown long and dark. Only a moment ago it was four.

What was happening to me?

My body felt disconnected and light, like it did when I took cold medicine. My hands clung to the edge of the smooth soapstone island as I tried to ground myself in my surroundings: worn wide floorboards in the dining room, Jo's framed watercolor of the fields at sunset hanging on the wall beyond the walnut dining table. To the left, through a wide arched opening, was the living room. The ornate mantle on the far wall held a framed photo of Neal and me at our wedding. Evidence of the vibrant lives that filled this space with chaotic joy. I blinked and the house was plunged into twilight.

The clock in the front hall chimed again, seven times. The mountains were now a deep purple undulation back lit by the orange glow of the setting sun. Again, I went to the front

• • •

windows. The looming magnolia was now just a black mass, devoid of the luminous white blooms it would hold this summer. Darkness poured in from my periphery, and I struggled against the weight of unconsciousness, agonizingly aware that my attempts were failing as the world slipped out of view.

• • •

Neal

I was finishing up records when the call came over the pager system. I checked my watch. 4:00pm on the dot. Depending on what this case was, I *might* still make dinner with Nora, Jo, and my mother-in-law. The receiving area hummed with the anticipatory readiness that I loved about emergency medicine.

Mike, one of the EMTs, rattled off the details as he wheeled in my patient. "Eighteen-year-old female, apparent head trauma from a collision with another vehicle. That driver was dead on the scene, probably an aortic dissection or something. This one was luckier. She has small lacerations on both hands from airbags and got pretty banged up in there." My patient was strapped on a backboard and had an IV catheter running fluids. Triage was underway. Now for some diagnostics.

I turned to Jenn, one of the ER nurses. "Pull blood for full labs and get her signed up for an MRI while I do my exam."

Her vitals were okay, with blood pressure, heart rate, respiratory rate all stable. However, she had not regained consciousness. With the time of the accident reported as three o'clock, it was not a great sign. Her severely swollen face was covered in blood from a likely broken nose and showed severe bruising, but there was something about her that seemed familiar.

Focus, I thought, snapping myself back into clinician mode. Her pupils were slightly dilated but symmetrical and constricted as they should be in response to my penlight. Nothing happened when I used my forceps to brush the bottom of her foot, but when I lightly pinched a brightly painted toe, her foot recoiled as it should. Her hand twitched, and her facial expression changed ever so slightly. Good, she was not truly comatose yet.

The rhythm of her heart was nice and steady, with no murmur that I could detect. Her lungs sounded clear, and while things could change within a few hours, so far so good. I headed to the treatment floor and found an empty computer station to type up my notes.

A few moments later, a police officer strode into the main treatment area. He walked directly to my station and filled my vision with his carefully impassive face.

"Excuse me, Dr. Brooks?" He inclined his head and raised his eyebrows at me.

"Yes, I'm Dr. Brooks." The words came out soft and tentative.

"I need you to come with me for a moment." He turned and gestured toward the elevator. I took a sip of tepid water and tried to find my voice.

"Can I ask what this is about, officer?"

"Don't worry, you are not in any kind of trouble, but I'd prefer we speak in private." My stomach lurched, and a soft ringing started in my ears.

The elevator doors opened a moment later, and we stepped inside the cramped space, which smelled of the officer's cologne mixed with sweat and stale coffee. My stomach turned again. I hadn't eaten since breakfast with Nora this morning. We'd had her favorite, toasted sesame bagels and honey walnut cream cheese.

"Sir, I must inform you that we have identified the driver of a vehicle involved in an accident on Hoover Rd this afternoon as Eleanor Turenne. Can you please confirm to me that Mrs Turenne is your wife?" The floor fell away as the elevator began to move down several floors, the ringing in my ears now a steady throbbing hum.

"Yes, Dr. Turenne is my wife. Is she injured? Can you please tell me what is going on?" My arms were tingling, and the elevator felt like it was spinning rather than falling.

"I regret to inform you that your wife, Eleanor Turenne, was found deceased when officers arrived at the scene." With a jolt, the elevator stopped and the doors opened. I stood as the officer held the elevator door open.

"We need you to please help confirm her identity." He stared at me for a moment before stepping out into the hallway, his face grotesquely impassive. Nora was meeting me for dinner. *This* was not happening. I forced my legs to carry me forward.

We moved through the labyrinth of hallways in the bottom of the hospital, toward the morgue, a familiar cold room that smelled of bleach, death, and formalin. As doctors, we all rotated through here. I found myself suppressing the urge to turn and run out.

A vague shape in a body bag rested on the steel table. A technician stepped forward to unzip the bag, revealing the body within.

It was Eleanor. But it wasn't.

Her features were muted by death. Her lips, once full and rose-colored, were pale and slack. Her green eyes stared up at the ceiling, dull and without expression. Her silver-streaked black hair pooled around her face, revealing the birthmark in front of her left ear. I kissed her there each night before bed. Yes, this was my wife's body, but she was gone from it. My mind went completely blank. Gripping the table until my knuckles went white, I looked down at Nora again. Tears streamed down my face, and I wiped them away to reach for her hand. Cold.

"Dr. Brooks, is this woman your wife, Eleanor Turenne?" The question came disembodied and failed to register.

My hand rested on hers. Her unpainted nails were trimmed neatly, wedding set on her finger. I touched the crook of her thumb, calloused smooth from riding horses her entire life.

"Sir, I am so sorry. I know this is difficult. Is this woman Eleanor Turenne?"

"Yes." A wave of nausea. "Yes. This is her body."

Her body.

Just her body. No more Eleanor. My Nora, gone. Just this mass of tissue left. Even as her body lay in front of me, physical and solid proof of her death, my mind still placed her at home, feeding the animals in preparation for meeting up for dinner tonight.

"Thank you for the identification, sir. Thank you for your cooperation, and I will be in touch. I'm so sorry for your loss." He handed me his card and walked out of the room.

I turned away from Nora's lifeless body, letting my hand fall away from hers. I took a deep breath and steadied myself. I needed to call Jo.

Josephine

L ockers slammed shut as everyone around me hurried to exit the school building. "Only three months left," I said to Nate as he rummaged through his locker next to me.

"Three months too many." He groaned, slammed his locker, and shuffled away down the hall.

I plopped my books in my locker and checked my phone. I had one voicemail from Mom, which I ignored, and a text from Cece: *mt u at R's*. If she wanted to meet me instead of riding together, that meant she was with Micah, her boring new boyfriend. Ugh. His family owned one of the biggest farms in the county, and lately Cece spent all her time with him. I texted back *don't be L8* and headed out on my own.

Outside, warm sunshine touched my face. I savored it. After a long cold winter, it was nice to savor this moment of warmth, especially since it would likely be followed by a return to bitter cold.

I walked in the door of Royston's ten minutes later and was enveloped in the rich scent of coffee. I approached the worn wood counter and saw that Luke was working.

A familiar warmth spread over me as he smiled, his brown eyes crinkling at the corners, subtle dimples in his cheeks.

"The usual, Jo?" The register beeped as he entered my total.

"Yup. Thanks, Luke."

The coffee machine hissed as he made my usual order of Chai tea. He handed it over and his hand brushed against mine.

I flushed and awkwardly turned away to sit in my usual chair by the window, tripping over a chair on my way. *Smooth.* Cece would have brushed her finger against his and smiled. *Dammit, why am I so stupid around him?* Luke nodded and smiled as I sat down and the door dinged. He kept his eyes on me as he helped the next customer.

Cece and I both had a crush on Luke, but she was the only one with the nerve to flirt. He was always quiet when she talked to him, so Cece insisted that he must be gay. Most guys fell all over themselves talking to her. Maybe she was right, or maybe she was jealous. When it was slow, he always chatted with me about whatever art project I was working on, and he told me about his. He was one of the few people in town I could talk to about art other than Memere, my art dealer grandma, but she flitted between here and her home in DC.

Mom would never understand. She was always so scientific. She was a radiologist, which meant she read x-rays, MRIs, ultrasounds, and other images for hospitals all around the country. She said it allowed her freedom, and she even told me once that she saw art in it.

To me, it looked like lots of hours sitting in a dimly lit room, staring at a computer. I wanted to be out in the world, where there was more sound, and color, and life, not trapped in a cave.

Mom always said I was free to do what fulfilled me, you know, all that crap, but it never seemed like she really meant it.

My pencil scratched on the paper of my sketchbook as I finished a drawing of my coffee cup and notebook. I checked my phone. Just about three o'clock. Typical Cece. She was going to make me late for dinner. I texted, *where r u?* Cece texted, *c u in 15 otw.* Of course.

I needed to leave soon to have time for a pre-dinner visit to Memere's new gallery exhibit in Charlottesville. I tried calling Cece's phone, but it went straight to voicemail. I waited another twenty minutes and then shot her a text to let her know I was leaving, snatched my bag, and walked out to my car.

● ● ●

I was nearly in Charlottesville when my phone rang. I was surprised to see Dad's name. I was expecting Mom, wondering where I was and getting on my case about timelines and responsibility as usual. I hit *Answer* on the car console. Dad's voice was softer than usual but filled the car with its familiar comfort.

"Honey, can you meet me at home? Dinner for tonight isn't happening." His voice definitely didn't sound right.

"Well, I'm almost in Charlottesville. I was going to head to Memere's gallery first. She has a new exhibit up. What's going on?"

"You're almost here, huh." He paused. "Okay, can you meet me at my office then?" His groan reverberated through the car speakers.

"Sure, Dad, why?" Last minute changes of plans did not happen often in my family.

"Just be safe." He paused. "Wait, you're talking to me while driving?" His voice was higher-pitched and shaky. He was worried.

If he wasn't my stone-cold, cool-headed dad, I'd swear he was almost panicked.

"Dad, I've got you on Bluetooth. It's fine. I'll be there in like ten minutes. Have you talked to Mom? I keep getting her voicemail." There was a soft sound, and Dad's breath fluttered through the speakers.

"Just drive safe. We can talk when you get here."

"Okay, Dad, I'll see you in a bit. Love you."

"Okay. I love you too." The line went silent.

I was shaken by the phone call. I tried Mom's cell, but it went straight to voicemail again.

I left a rambling message that I hoped would make sense when she got it, then drove down to the hospital, keeping my playlist on low.

The odor of microwaved food followed me down the small hallway to Dad's tiny office. His office door was covered with taped-on comics and stickers from various students, interns and coworkers. I knocked lightly, trying to avoid damaging any of them. Dad opened his door, then leaned on his desk and ran his hands over his head. It was the same motion he used when I was in trouble and he was about to lecture me about something. Ugh. Had I done something to piss them off?

"Hey, honey." His voice was shaky and he looked terrible, his face pale and his eyes bloodshot. Tissues were sticking out of his pockets. Had he been crying? I'd never seen my Dad cry, even when we'd put our old dog down when I was younger. *What happened?* The question kept pulsing in my mind. I sat down on the sagging office chair behind me, lightheaded, sweat already pooling under my arms.

"Hey, Dad." Arms of tension had wrapped around my chest, causing the words to come out small and clipped.

"Jo. I need to tell you something. I'm not quite sure the best way to do this, but I'll try." The room hummed around me as I waited for his next words.

"Josephine, this afternoon your mother was involved in a car accident, and as a result of that accident, she has...she...passed away. She's...gone." His eyes brimmed with tears, and he fell to his knees in front of me with his hands on mine. Everything around me became dull and muffled as though I had been wrapped in a heavy blanket. I curled up into the chair and closed my eyes. *No.*

At some point, Memere came in. I could hear their voices as they spoke, but it just sounded like background noise. A haze of numbness surrounded me. Memere came over and held me tightly. I could smell her perfume and feel the scratch of her wool coat against my cheek. I just couldn't seem to feel anything else.

We were driving home when I saw it.

Highlighted in the beam of the car's headlights was a piece of Mom's car. The bumper. Her stickers were all over it and it was lying on the side of the road. Just left there in an empty ditch. No one cared enough to even pick it up. Dad cursed next to me in the driver's seat.

"Shit. Why did I take this way? I'm sorry, honey, I didn't think."

All at once, I was very much *aware*. The comforting blanket of denial ripped away by a black piece of plastic. I choked and heaved on my tears, nearly vomiting in my lap.

Mom. Gone. Dead.

What was the last thing I said to her? Did I say I love you? Was she in pain when she died? Was she afraid? Did she feel alone?

Oh god, she died alone, alone on that cold piece of road, with no one familiar around her. She should have died as an old woman, in her warm bed, comfortable and safe under her beloved handmade quilts. She was supposed to pick colleges with me, watch me graduate from high school. She couldn't be gone. I shut my eyes and clutched my knees to my chest, my whole body hurting. I wanted my mom.

Eleanor

I heard the sounds I had been longing for: car tires on gravel, the squeak of the screen door, a jingling of keys and finally the click of the lock and groan of the heavy old door as Neal and Jo walked in. Relief. Neal stood for a moment in the foyer, his hand resting on the ornate wooden newel post. He was staring at the staircase and pictures hanging on the wall along one side.

I rushed up to him, disturbing whatever reverie he was stuck in. "Oh, I'm so glad you're home! I passed out. I was scared, and my phone is gone. I don't even know where the car is. I had some kind of time blank." He gave no acknowledgment and they moved through into the kitchen as if I wasn't there.

"Hello? Guys! Did anyone try to get in touch with me? I'm assuming you just ate dinner without me." Neal leaned against the soapstone island in the kitchen and rubbed his eyes.

Jo's face was blotchy and red as if she'd been crying and Neal bore his careful ER stoicism. Sure, I'd missed dinner, but I had a damned good excuse. If they were so upset, why had no one checked on me?

I stood right in front of Neal. He just kept looking straight ahead.

"Look, I know I didn't show up for dinner, but you can't be *that* mad at me. I passed out for goodness sake!" Neal still said nothing, so I reached out to grab his shoulder, but my hand slid away. "I was scared, and there was no one here." He just shivered in response.

"NEAL!" I yelled his name, but still he ignored me. I turned to Jo, who seemed much more upset than he did. I put my arms around her to hug her with no ability to feel her against me. She didn't lift her arms to hug me back, as if she were devoid of sensation too.

"Daddy, I can smell her perfume. It's like she's right here." Jo broke down in heavy, racking sobs, and Neal put his arms around her.

"I know. I wish she was too, but we'll get through this. You and I, we can do this. I know we can." His voice carried the monotone note he used when he offered platitudes to families receiving bad news.

Wait a minute, what was this? What were they talking about?

"I'm right here, and this is not funny." Looking at their faces, I knew deep down this was not a practical joke.

No, I couldn't be. Shit.

Was I...dead? Holy Hell. Or not, as it appeared.

The thought made me burst out in laughter at the absurdity of the whole thing. Ah, yes, laughing at inappropriate times. Of all the traits to transcend death, that one would hold up.

Perfect.

I focused again on Jo and Neal. I waved my hands in front of them, shouting a few more times, but nothing changed.

I tried to pick up something, *anything,* a mug off the counter, the paper towel holder, but my hand didn't interact with anything solid at all.

Neal was trying to calm Jo down and failing miserably. He never was very good at tears. He came off as cold and detached. As a practice of self- preservation, Neal was adept at closing down his emotions on a regular basis. Working in an emergency room does that to people. When it is your responsibility to be in control of everyone else, you certainly can't lose control of yourself. It was hard for him to shift out of that mindset. I was the one who dealt with emotions in this family, and now I could do nothing but watch, helpless and hollow.

● ● ●

If I really was dead, I was leaving Jo motherless. I was leaving Neal a widower. I was failing them both. I couldn't comfort them in this awful moment, their worst moment...a moment I evidently caused.

Again, I tried to hold them, but it was like holding freshly fallen snow. My hands grasped them lightly, then slipped away as I gripped harder, leaving only empty space.

Was that all I was now? Empty space? Just energy, a consciousness, floating around my house? A goddamn ghost?

Always stoic and practical, Neal started feeding the cats. Grimalkin and Hobbit twined themselves between Neal's legs and mewed angrily while Neal cursed them for nearly tripping him. I heard the tinkle of kibble filling their ceramic bowls, followed by the crunching and grunting of the eating cats. Neal was doing what he always did in the face of tragedy, pushing through and making sure someone was doing what needed to be done. He never did fully connect to his own pain until later, when we'd talk quietly in bed, safe in each other's arms. Who would he confide in now?

My mother came in a few moments later and began to bustle about, putting a kettle on, setting mugs on the counter. She'd pulled out Jo's favorite. A blue mug shaped like a cat. She told Jo to go sit in the living room and, with quiet efficiency, took over the emotional stewardship of the house. I was glad she was here and tried to focus on her, but there was something moving between us that glared in my eyes like sunlight on water.

It drifted toward me and when it touched my hand. I became aware that this was my father. I could smell the cigars he smoked, the leather of his favorite chair and the cognac he always drank in the evenings. Then I got images: my mother in her wedding dress, the sun filtering through the chiffon of her skirt to reveal the shadows of her legs underneath, myself as a child running through a lavender field, the fragrance rising through the air as I brushed my hands against the blooms. I became lost in my father's memories until my mother's crisp voice pierced the air and he began to dissipate, leaving me back in the reality of the moment.

Mom was on the sofa next to Jo, where they were drinking tea. Mom set her mug down on the side table, grumbling that she couldn't find a coaster. The table was one of

● ● ●

my favorites. It was a small table with twisted legs and leaves that folded up if needed. I remember buying it at an estate sale and the feeling of victory when I lifted the tag for it just as another woman started looking it over. Mom should have found a coaster.

The smell of bergamot filtered through the air in the steam of their cups. Earl Grey, my favorite. I listened to the rise and fall of their voices, wishing my own could join them. Jo curled with her head in Mom's lap and let herself cry. Hard sobs left her body, her tears hitting the patterned silk of Mom's skirt. Mom stroked her strawberry blonde hair and I longed for my daughter. I wanted to hold her and comfort her, smell her shampoo as I kissed her on top of her head. Jo now routinely grumbled and pushed me away when I attempted such affection. I always comforted myself with the thought that she'd come around eventually and let me be close to her as she did when she was little. Mom kissed the side of her head, leaving a smudge of pink lipstick on her brow. A physical reminder of her love, something I could never give her again.

Neal

The engine ticked and popped as I stood beside the car, for the first time in my life reluctant to enter my home. I looked at it for a moment, delaying the inevitable.

It was our dream home. A brick federal-style home built in 1854, it stood abandoned and empty for years before we bought it. I thought back to the day we found it, still and damp with disuse. Despite the decaying plaster, it retained original ornate oak trim and multiple fireplaces with hand-carved mantels that sat unchanged from the day they were finished. The brick exterior displayed tall walkthrough windows with the original glass still intact on most. The porch was wide and stretched across the entire front facade with hand cast iron railings and trim. Vines clung so copiously to the ironwork when we bought it that it was nearly impossible to make out what was iron and what was Virginia creeper. It was surrounded by stunning views of Hebron valley with the mountains rising up to the west behind it. Even abandoned and neglected it looked like a postcard, from a distance that is. Up close it was admittedly a bit of a mess, but it was our mess and we had both fallen in love immediately.

Over the years, we'd breathed new life into this home and made it ours. Normally, golden light from within spilled out onto the porch in welcoming pools. The darkened windows that stood before me now made it look every bit the haunted house our friends teased us about when we bought it. Since then, nearly

● ● ●

sixteen years ago, it had been a place of joy and life. We planned on growing old and dying here. Just not like this. This was too soon.

We walked in the front door and stopped for a moment in the foyer. I leaned on the gentle curve of the banister and looked up the wide, worn stairs leading up into the darkened hallway above. I was struck with a bright flash of a memory: Nora cursing as she stripped and sanded a good ten coats of paint off of the handrail. After her painstaking work, she drank a beer and proclaimed that it had been worth it. It had. People always commented on the warmth and beauty of that banister. Everything she touched seemed better because she put forth the effort that others neglected.

I thought of Jo's face in my office earlier, normally animated and lively, so much like Nora despite their difference in coloring. How she recoiled from me. I had seen it before in patients' families, but it broke something inside me to see it in my own daughter. I watched her receding, hiding herself away where nothing could find her. I wanted to pull her back to me, hold her close as I did when she was little, and make everything okay. It was so much easier then.

Once, when she was a child, she touched the oven door right as I opened it. I remember her looking up at me with her blue eyes filled with huge tears that soon rolled down her flushed cheeks. She looked at me as if I had betrayed her, recoiling from the physical pain. Recoiling as she had in my office. However, this pain couldn't be fixed with ice water, burn cream, and hugs. This pain was deeper, and I knew that I couldn't fix it for her. I wasn't sure I could even fix it for myself.

I let a typically jovial Mrs. Norris out, and then started to feed the cats. Pouring myself into physical tasks that I could complete.

Celestine came in the front door a bit later and immediately saw what needed to be done. The smell of the tea wafted through the house, its scent making me want Nora with a brighter intensity. Earl Grey was always her tea of choice, her comfort food.

"I'm going to shower," I called out as I left the kitchen, then walked down a small back passage to our bedroom where

● ● ●

I sat on the bed, my hands brushing against the soft quilt folded neatly at the foot.

Our bed. Creaky and old, as was everything Nora loved. We'd lugged this heavy brass bed everywhere from college onward. Typical Nora, she'd found it at a garage sale weeks before we moved into our first apartment together.

My gaze kept returning to an old photo of us from our early days in undergrad sitting on Nora's dresser. In the picture, Nora was sitting on a rock, I stood beside her, and behind us the land fell away to reveal a stunning view of the valley below. I remember setting up the shot, carefully placing the camera on the hood of my old, battered Toyota. We both looked young and fresh, smiling at the camera. The light hit Nora's face in just the right way, illuminating her eyes, highlighting their true bright green color. She was smiling and reaching her hand toward my knee, fingers outstretched on the way to me. Just after the camera clicked, she nearly toppled off the rock, and we laughed hysterically, wondering if we would just get a picture of her feet in the air as she fell backwards. I remember the anxiety while waiting for the roll to develop, and the excitement when we got them back and they came out so well.

How was I going to keep things together without her?

Grief always ended for me when the family left the hospital. It was an abstract idea that was discussed at continuing education conferences. I read articles about it, how to counsel families, how to help them cope. Grief was a clinical condition. Something to be looked at through the filter of medicine. Now that filter was being torn down, and I was exposed, vulnerable, and at a complete loss as to what to do next. I always told grieving families to "take things one day at a time." How trite those words sounded now, when the past few hours had felt like an eternity.

Josephine

I awoke the next morning with a heavy weight on my chest. I opened my eyes to see Grimalkin, our big old tabby cat, purring away happily, eyes closed. I scratched him behind his scarred ears as he started rhythmically kneading my chest with his huge white paws. The house was still bathed in a murky blue, and shapes were hard to pick out. For the briefest moment, everything seemed normal. My favorite paintings and drawings were taped up all over the purple walls, and my clothes were piled in front of my old pink hamper. A picture of Cece and me from a family trip to the beach sat on a shelf with my books. Signs of the life I'd lived before last night. Normal and happy.

The empty, churning sensation in my stomach reminded me that everything was not normal, and things were never going to be the same. It would make things so much easier if last night had all been some terrible nightmare, if I could just walk downstairs and find Mom puttering in the kitchen, making breakfast for Dad and me. I pushed Grimalkin off of me despite his grumbles of disapproval and reluctantly got out of bed. The house was filled with Mom, even with her gone. I couldn't be here too long. So I pulled on some jeans and a sweatshirt, put my hair up, and headed downstairs to put on my coat.

I quietly slipped out the back door and walked down to the barn. The air was still cold, and my breath followed me in trailing puffs as I walked down the path, gravel crunching underfoot as I went. As the ground sloped toward the barn, the

● ● ●

land opened up, away from the giant magnolias, oaks, and boxwoods that flanked our house, nestled in the center of the pastures, their borders defined by cedars and stone walls. The ever-present mountains were a pale blue, and a light fog hovered in the valley just past the barn. The sun was just rising over the ridge to the east and cast a pink glow over the bare trees and frost-coated grass. I got to the barn and with effort slid the heavy wooden door open. Tiny icicles dropped from the wooden beam above the door and crashed against the brick aisle. Inside the barn, I was met with the clean, sharp scent of pine shavings and the earthy musk of horses. It was my favorite smell in the world.

I opened the grain bins and inhaled the sweet molasses scent as I delivered grain to the stall feeders. The horses ambled up and nickered hungrily at the opposite door, blissfully unaware of the gaping loss that had just happened. I opened the door and let the horses in for breakfast. They filed in and went straight to their stalls. All I had to do was close the doors behind them. I stood in the aisle for a moment and listened to the rustling, grunting, and chewing sounds of horses at feeding time. I heard Mahalo, Mom's retired dressage mount, squeal and kick the wall of his stall. Callie, my mare, was in the stall next to him eating her grain, placid and sweet as usual.

I let myself into Callie's stall and leaned against her mahogany neck, burying my face in her soft winter coat, breathing her in. She turned her head and nuzzled my pockets, looking for treats, which I gave her. I looked across the aisle at our other two horses happily munching grain. All was right in their world, and I felt sheltered in this bubble of peace. I could almost pretend everything was okay. Almost.

Once they were done eating, I opened Callie's door and let her out, then the others as well. After throwing hay out for them, I closed the far barn door, checked the water troughs, and headed back up to the house. When I walked in the door, the smell of coffee filled the house and I heard Dad rustling around in the kitchen. I went in to say hi to him, and when he turned to look at me, he offered a weak smile that didn't reach his eyes.

"You've been down at the barn, I see," he said as he picked a stray piece of hay out of my hair.

● ● ●

"I woke up early and figured I'd feed them before anyone else got up."

"That's good. I'm afraid it's going to be a bit crazy today, what with planning everything to do with your mom." His voice broke as he said it. He turned away and put another piece of toast in the toaster for me.

"I know. I'm not sure what to do, but I want to help if I can," I lied.

"Well, just start by eating a bit, then go take a shower— you smell like the barn. My parents are coming down this evening, and the rest of the family arrives for the service tomorrow." His voice sounded tired, and there were dark, puffy circles under both of his eyes.

"Where is it going to be?"

"I think we are going to have the service here. Your mom wanted to be cremated, so there isn't really going to be any sort of a burial service. Just a reception here at home. I think we will most likely do an open casket. It's traditional. My family has always done it that way. Is that okay?"

My mind filled with images of Mom's dead body. "Yeah, I guess, I don't know—I don't know if I want to see her that way or not." Fear and sadness were both creeping in, the buffering effect of the morning in the barn rapidly wearing off.

"Memere and I are going to meet with the funeral home this morning to talk over options and details," he said, then raised his eyebrows as he watched my face. "Do you want to go with?"

"No," I replied quickly. "No, I think I'll call Cece and go talk to her, if that's okay."

"Yes, of course, that should be fine. I don't know that *I* am even really prepared for this, to be honest." It was rare for him to show any weakness. "I miss her, and I can't help but feel that she would have been better at all of this than I am."

"Sorry, Dad, but that's probably true. Do you remember when we tried to plan that surprise party for her when I was six?"

It was a disaster. Dad forgot to order the cake from the bakery, then tried to scramble to make a cake while I decorated. Due to my height at the time, it made for an interesting look.

● ● ●

"How could I forget that?" He smiled weakly. "Remember how, when she walked in, she just laughed until she cried at all the waist-high streamers?"

"Yeah, and when all the guests were crouching down hiding, I remember thinking that they were looking at my decorations."

"Your mom could always find humor in situations other people cringed at," he said, the smile disappearing. Then, almost under his breath, he said, "I miss her so much."

"I do too, Dad—I do too," I said, tears beginning to well up behind my eyes. The toaster popped up, and I took the warm, toasted bread out and began to butter it.

"Alright, honey. Are you sure you will be okay by yourself after I go?" No. No, I wasn't sure.

"Yeah, I'll be fine."

"Okay, I'll have my phone on me, so just call if you need me. Love you." He picked up his keys and gave me a kiss on the head.

"I will, Dad. I promise. Love you too." He walked out the door, shoulders slumped.

I took my toast up to my room and crunched on it while grabbing clothes out of my drawer. I stood for a moment, trying to find comfort in my room. Ribbons from various horse shows hung from a cord attached to the crown molding. They were ribbons won at shows with my mom, hung up in my room by my dad. All my life I'd enjoyed love from both of my parents, and now one half of that love was gone, leaving a gnawing emptiness behind. I didn't know what to do with this pain, but I knew I couldn't do it alone. After a shower, I got dressed and sat on the bed to call Cece. I wanted to talk to her, but I also didn't want to have to say the words out loud. It went straight to voicemail. I left a message for her to call me back and then looked at the time. It was close to nine o'clock by this point. Of course. She would be at school. It was Friday, after all, and everyone else was living a normal life today.

I went through the bathroom connecting to the studio my parents had set up for me while I was in middle school. Since we didn't need it as a bedroom, they'd cleared it out, installed cheap carpet I could ruin with paint, and gave me free rein in there. Other than the barn, it was my favorite place. I sat down

• • •

on the paint-splattered chair at my work table and looked out the window. My favorite window. It was on the southeast corner of the house, which meant sunlight poured in through the big old windows, especially mid-morning. I could see down to the barn, with its tall gothic roofline and deep green board and batten walls.

The horses were grazing nearby, surrounded by the now-lifting morning fog. Two turkey vultures sat on the roofline, wings spread, warming up in the sun before a day of eating the dead. Dead, like Mom was dead.

I got up from my seat and tore out of the house down to the barn. I screamed until my throat felt ragged and dry. The vultures flew off, chattering angrily. I collapsed on the ground in front of the barn and punched the clay until my knuckles were raw and bleeding. Eventually the senseless rage started to subside and I was able to breathe. It wasn't the vultures' fault I felt this way, and now I felt bad for chasing them off. I wiped the tears from my face and picked myself up from the cold ground.

Now that I was down here, there were plenty of chores to be done. Maybe I could do what Dad was doing and just stay busy. I wiped my bloodied knuckles on my pants and got to work.

In the tack room, I plugged my phone into the radio and turned it up, allowing the music to silence the noise in my head. I completely reorganized the tack room, swept the old brick aisle, and added fresh shavings to the stalls after stripping them of the old. By the time I was finished, it was around three in the afternoon and close to feeding time, so I called the horses in, turning my playlist off as I did. There were no calls or texts from Cece. Some friend she was turning out to be. Now that we were about to graduate, Cece was following Micah around instead of looking at colleges with me like we'd always talked about. She was so distracted by him that she was nowhere to be found when I needed her most. I pushed aside my anger at her as the horses approached the barn, at least they were dependable.

They ambled in and each went to their stall to eat. After she'd finished her grain, I pulled Callie out to groom her in the aisle. I brushed her, trying to tame her winter coat which, at the moment, was thick and a bit scraggly, as it had just started to shed for spring.

● ● ●

I was lost in the task when I heard a car on the drive and looked up to see Grandma and Grandpa arrive. Back to reality.

I let Callie off her cross ties and put everyone back out in the field. Briony, my normally bombproof old 4-H pony, spooked at something in the aisle and nearly knocked me over. I wanted to run out into the field with her and never come back. Instead, I wiped my hands on my jeans and dragged myself out of the barn to go up to the house.

Eleanor

Neal sat on our bed in his boxers, his body curled and smaller than I'd ever seen it. His straight shoulders and excellent posture were normally a beacon of solid, quiet strength. Neal was always capable, but the strain of this process was clearly wearing him down.

I longed to touch him, to hold him and feel the warmth of his body next to mine. His hair was streaked with silver now, and his face held little creases at the corners of his brown eyes. They were the marks of a happy life, earned from smiling or squinting in the sun outdoors. His coloring was the same dark Mediterranean hue as his mother, but his shape was completely his father's wiry Irish frame. His parents would be here soon. That would make for some interesting voyeurism, I was sure. To say that my mother and Grace, Neal's mother, did not get along would be something of an understatement.

Before our wedding, Grace had declared that she was concerned for her son's soul. She considered my family to be godless heathens and was convinced we were going to drag him into the fiery pits of Hell with us. I suppose there could be a Hell, but as I had a totally different view of the natural world at the moment, I felt pretty safe assuming there wasn't.

Neal's parents were both Catholic, his mother the more devout of the two. Neal had separated from the Catholic Church

● ● ●

long before I met him in college. He went with his parents out of duty until he moved away, then never went back. This caused some friction with them, but he still loved them. Sam helped immensely with the renovation of our house, and as long as we avoided religion or politics as subjects, we all got along pretty well. They were devoted grandparents who attended every recital, art showcase, and horse show they could. They loved Jo with everything they had.

Grace had Neal after several years of trying. After that, they continued to struggle with infertility. After enduring an ectopic pregnancy, they stopped trying. I knew of all this because Grace supported me through our own struggles before Josephine was born. I had Jo when I was thirty-six years old, and the pregnancy was considered high risk due to my 'advanced age.'

About a year into trying, we'd seen a specialist who found that Neal had some motility issues with sperm, making our chances lower but not unattainable, as the doctor put it at the time. We tried for nearly three more years and almost gave up any hope of having our own child. I was looking into adoption agencies when I found out I was pregnant with Jo.

I remember Grace crying and hugging me so tightly I thought she might break me when we told her that I was finally pregnant. It was through that shared struggle, and then the shared love of our respective children, that we eventually bonded and became close. Grace and my mom, however, never really found much common ground.

My mom came from a wealthy, prestigious French family and enjoyed comfort for the entirety of her life. She grew up on an estate in the south of France surrounded by lavender fields and olive groves.

Grace was the daughter of first-generation Italian immigrants and spent the first few years of her life packed into a tiny apartment in New York with multiple aunts and cousins. She put herself through nursing school in Maryland by working two jobs while going to school. Neal's father was the assistant facilities manager at a private boy's school nearby. They met there when she rotated through the school during her nurse's training. They were both honest, hardworking people, and I knew they saw my mom as flighty, arrogant, and self-indulgent. Jo was the one thing they could agree on.

● ● ●

27

I managed to connect myself to her and found her in the barn, taking after Neal and busying her body to cope. Her knuckles were red and raw. She'd punched something. I wanted to help her wash her hands and carefully apply ointment to them. She used those injured hands to caress Callie's neck as she groomed her and spoke softly to her. I knew that comfort.

I wanted so badly to rub the soft, velvety patch of hair right behind a gently flaring nostril. Mahalo squealed and kicked the wall of his stall when I tried to touch him. The chilly March air hung in wisps of steam around their faces as they ate, and I longed for the simple pleasure of sliding my cold, stiff hands under their blankets to warm them up. When I looked at my hands now, they were less detailed, like I was gazing at them through a greased camera lens. I wondered about this process, this fading, and thought of my encounter with my father. Would I end up like that? Just light and memory? Even now, I couldn't feel the chilly air, or the warmth of the horses, or the softness of their coats. Anger flooded me as I realized the gravity of this loss. I could watch the world around me, but I was unable to interact with it at all.

Car tires crunched on the gravel drive as Grace and Sam pulled into the driveway. Jo moved away from Callie and saw them.

"Well, I guess it's time to go back to the real world now, huh, girl?" She then began to put away her brushes and unhooked Callie from the cross ties to lead her out of the barn. She opened the other stall doors and let the rest of the horses follow. Briony, her old pony, stopped next to me and wouldn't move, snorting. Her dapple grey coat was unruly and thick, and she swished her luxurious tail at me. I stepped out of the way, and she immediately bolted towards the field with a squeal.

Jo shook her head, then closed the gates and walked slowly back up to the house. She seemed to want to linger in the barn as much as I did. Nonetheless, I felt myself pulled along behind her—floating, yet tethered to her presence as she made her way up the hill to the back of the house.

Inside the kitchen, Sam was poking at a slightly loose window pane.

● ● ●

28

"Neal, when was the last time we re-glazed this window? You've got a loose pane here."

"I'm not sure, Dad. I suppose when we first bought the place. I felt a draft last night, and I bet that's where it came from. I'm glad you found it." Neal poked at the window frame with Sam. They both seemed happy to have something tangible to fix.

• • •

Neal

G roaning, I sat on the couch. I hadn't really slept in over twenty-four hours now. The bed still smelled of Nora's lotion, lavender and roses. Each night, I'd set my head down on my pillow only to have the scent fill my mind with thoughts of her. How she'd smiled and squeezed my hand on our wedding day as we said our vows. Her wickedly inappropriate sense of humor. Her cackle and snort when she found something *really* funny. I lay down on my side, face pressed against the soft fabric of the couch Nora had picked out years ago. I had no trouble making hard choices at work but always froze when it came to picking out anything for the house. Nora had no trouble with these decisions, which worked out perfectly. Deciding flowers, casket types, fabric types for liners, and food choices for guests was not in my comfort zone on the best day, and when deciding all of this for Nora's funeral, it was torture. I didn't care about what color the liner was. I didn't care what kind of chairs we set up, or which flowers we displayed, or what food we served.

None of it changed the fact that Nora was gone.

She wouldn't see any of this. All of this was for us. This ceremony. It was supposed to bring 'closure,' but I knew there would never be any closure. There would only be moments when we weren't so acutely aware of her absence from our lives.

● ● ●

Right now, grief consumed everything and filled the void left by Nora with pain. There was no space left for anything else.

Thankfully, Celestine handled most of the planning because, to her, ceremony mattered. She wrote an announcement for the paper and contacted everyone we could think of for the funeral. Most of the attendees were relatively local, with the exception of Flora, Nora's older sister, who was flying in from New York.

Hobbit came in and curled in the crook of my legs, purring more loudly than it seemed possible for such a tiny body. I stroked her soft fur and tried to make my mind become still. I was just drifting off when I heard a car on the gravel drive. I rubbed my eyes and pulled myself together, then displaced Hobbit from my knees. Mrs. Norris was wagging eagerly at the door and whining. Most likely the car I'd heard was my parents'. Mrs. Norris *loved* my parents.

I went out the front door and onto the porch to greet them. The evening sun was already starting to touch the hazy mountains in the distance. Stepping out alone, I habitually looked behind me for Nora. The empty doorway was like a punch to the gut. I swallowed bile down and descended the steps.

"Hi, Mom. Hi, Dad. Can I help you with your bags?" Mrs. Norris, of course, had run out ahead of me and was already rolling onto her back for mom to scratch her belly. She bent down and tucked her silver hair behind her ear to talk to Mrs Norris as she patted the writhing, wiggling body. Her ear sported an old cloisonné earring and a hearing aid.

"No thanks, son, we've just got the one bag," Dad called out to me as he lifted it from the trunk. His flannel shirt was tucked into his khaki pants and came undone a bit as he twisted and lifted. He'd had spinal surgery a few months ago and really shouldn't be lifting that much, but I knew better than to argue. He set the case down and rolled it toward the house, giving me a pat on the shoulder as he passed me. His blue eyes turned to mine, and he nodded solemnly as he passed me toward the house. Mom and I reached each other, and she gave me a sad smile.

"Oh, Neal, I'm so sorry about Nora. How are you holding up?" She gave me a long hug and then held me at arm's length to look at me. Little did it matter that I was now a good eight inches taller than her, let alone a middle-aged man. Her appraising, dark-eyed gaze cut right through me and made me feel like a small child.

"I'm holding up. I don't think I've really let it hit me yet, though. I've been busy preparing everything for the funeral. I'm not sure I've really had much time to think about how I feel."

"Oh, honey, just let us know what you need and we'll do it. Anything that helps."

"I will."

Tears pooled at the corners of her eyes and she pulled me in and held me again, tighter this time. I relaxed into her familiarity and comfort. She smelled as she had my entire life, a mixture of basil, garlic, and line-dried clothing.

We headed inside and I carried their bag up to their room as they settled in. I paused in the hallway. To my right was Jo's suite of rooms and to the left the two guest rooms. Light poured in from a large west facing window at the far end of the hallway. At the right time of day, light from that window would find its way down the staircase and fill the entry hall with diffuse golden light, at the moment it was cloaked in shadow.

I turned left into the guest room and set Mom and Dad's bag down, then put towels out in the bathroom. The Jack and Jill bathrooms that connected the four upstairs bedrooms had been added in the 1920s, as the house originally did not have plumbing. During the renovation, we hadn't had to change much more than scrub away grime. They both still had the original white and black tiles, heavy enameled cast iron tubs and sinks. Nora and I always dreamed of turning the house into a bed and breakfast as a retirement plan. Now I wondered what I would do with all this space once Jo headed off on her own. That picture had always involved Nora.

I walked back downstairs to find Dad rummaging through the fridge as Mom poured herself some iced tea.

The front door slammed and Celestine's voice came from the front hallway. The mood in the room shifted. My mother sighed and looked over at Dad, her eyes cutting over to him under raised eyebrows.

"Hellooo. Neal? I saw a strange car in the drive when I pulled up just now. I wasn't sure whose it was." Celestine's heels tapped on the floor as she strode through the front hall.

"I just came from the florist, and I think we should be set for flowers." Celestine abruptly stopped in the doorway to the kitchen.

"Oh! Hello, Grace. Sam, how are you?" She stiffly set down a vase with huge pink peonies overflowing the edges. Nora loved peonies. She would have loved the arrangement. Mom turned toward Celestine and placed a hand on her shoulder.

"Hello, Celestine...I'm so sorry for your loss. I can't imagine what you are going through." Mom offered her a rigid hug. It may have been the first one I had ever seen pass between them. Celestine let herself fall into the hug and sighed as she pulled away.

"Thank you, Grace. It doesn't really seem fair. She shouldn't be gone while I'm still here." Celestine's eyes fell to her shoes, and she brushed her eyes lightly with her hand.

"Nora was amazing, she really was," Mom said as she placed a hand on Celestine's shoulder.

"Thanks. She was..." Tears were freely flowing down Celestine's face now, and she gave up on brushing them away as she looked up at my mom.

Jo came in and the moment dissipated. Celestine drew herself together, straightening up and turning to greet Jo.

"Hi Grandma, Grandpa, Memere," Jo greeted them as she came in, nodding to everyone in turn. They descended on her like three honey bees to clover, and for a moment I felt I ought to save her. Instead, I started a kettle for more iced tea. Jo made it through the swarm and to the kitchen island where she sat on one of the bar stools. She was filthy from the barn again, hay in her hair and smelling of horse.

"How are you? Are you hungry? I think there's some of Mom's veggie soup left in the freezer." I set out the teapot and put a bag of tea into it to steep.

"I'm not really hungry. I know I should be, but I just don't seem to want to eat." She crossed her arms on the counter and laid her head down on them. She looked small and fragile.

"I can also pull out a frozen pizza. That would feed everyone," I said, nodding toward the living room where the respective grandparents had gathered.

"That'd be fine." She paused. "Dad?"

* * *

"Kiddo," I responded, unsure whether I was prepared to face what was coming.

"I want to save Mom's soup. I don't want to eat it now. I want to wait until we can enjoy it. It's the last soup she made, and we won't get another one." Tears were now welling up in her eyes. I didn't have any words to comfort her. She was right. I could make the same soup, following Nora's recipe to the letter, but it wouldn't be her soup no matter what I did. She always added a little more or less of each thing until it was just right. Dad came in a moment later and helped the situation unknowingly.

"Your mom made some baked ziti, and she has instructed me to turn on the oven." Mom drifted in a moment later carrying a casserole dish covered in foil.

"I brought your favorite. It should be enough for everyone," she said, sliding the covered dish onto the counter as the oven preheated. "I also brought some salad mix and a loaf of bread from that bakery in Catonsville you love."

"Thanks, Mom," I said, genuinely grateful to have her there. I looked over at Jo with a pang of guilt. It wasn't fair that I should still have my mom around to comfort me when she didn't. Celestine came in and gently squeezed Jo's shoulders, leaning down to kiss the top of her head as she did. Her nose wrinkled and she stood, her eyes brimming with tears.

"Oh you smell just like Nor—" The words caught in her throat. "—just like Nora always did. She was always out at the barn, always…" She turned and rushed past me out of the room. I heard her steps as she went up the back staircase to her room.

Josephine

I went up to my room after dinner and took another shower, then sat down on my bed, stomach full of Grandma's ziti. I felt sleepy and warm from it. It was always one of Dad's favorites, and we had it lots of times when we'd go visit them in Maryland. Grandma would emerge from their small, spotlessly clean kitchen and proudly place it down in the center of their dining table. She had this apron she always wore that looked like she'd murdered someone with all the tomato sauce on it. I had so many happy memories around that ziti, but tonight was a somber dinner, with quiet, careful conversation. Everyone avoided the overwhelming sadness that threatened to engulf us all.

I checked my phone. There were a few messages and texts from friends at school. More than I expected. Vague expressions of condolences, the required niceties that meant nothing. But nothing from my supposed best friend. There was still no answer when I called Cece's phone, and no messages from her. I felt a flush of rage and threw my phone down on the bed. It bounced quietly on the covers, a crappy representation of what I was feeling. She should be here. They both should be.

I called Cece's house number. The phone rang several times, and then the machine picked up with the familiar voice of Cece's mom. I tried to keep the anger out of my voice but could hear it shaking as I left my message.

• • •

"Hello, Mrs. Ayers, this is Jo. I have been trying to call Cece but haven't been able to get her. It is important that I talk to her. It's about my mom. Can you please let her know that I need her to call me back? Thank you, bye." I hung up. I was irritated and feeling lonely without Cece to talk to. Why wasn't she answering? It wasn't unusual for her to lose phone privileges, but she usually sent me a message with a heads up if that happened. I wanted my friend. I wanted my mom. I wanted a hug.

I curled under my covers and lay there until Mrs. Norris came barreling in and leaped onto the bed, disrupting my sadness with licks and wags. She rooted her nose up to my face and kissed me happily, then grunted as she curled up beside me, clearly settling in for the evening. Normally, this very muddy, stinky specimen of a dog would not be allowed in my bed, but tonight it was nice to have the company. I curled up around her and finally fell asleep.

When I awoke in the morning, Mrs. Norris was snoring away at the foot of my bed and Grimalkin was back in his spot on my chest, breathing stinky cat breath in my face. I petted him, wishing I could just lie there in this cocoon of sleepiness all day. I didn't want today to be real. I wanted today to be just a regular Saturday. Normally, I would have a riding lesson in the morning on Callie. Then I'd clean up and meet with Cece, or paint, or if I had any pet sitting jobs I would go to one of those. Instead I had my mother's funeral to attend. It didn't seem fair.

An unfamiliar black skirt and blouse were hanging on the back of my door, most likely put there by Memere. They were steamed, de-wrinkled, and ready for the day, even if I wasn't. I could hear Grandma and Grandpa's voices across the hallway. Their door opened and shut and I heard the familiar creak of the stairs as they headed down. The clock in the front hallway chimed eight times. It was late and I needed to get the horses fed. I kicked Mrs. Norris off the bed and sent her downstairs. I heard her nails on the steps and then the slam of the back door as someone let her out. I walked over to my dresser and considered myself in the mirror.

Dad said I had the same coloring Grandpa did when he was young. When I was little, kids teased me about being adopted. I had my Grandpa's blue eyes, which were currently red and puffy, and strawberry blonde hair, which was tangled and messy at the moment. Both Mom and Dad had dark hair. Mom had pale, freckled skin like Memere and the same green eyes, whereas Dad had Grandma's dark coloring throughout. I looked like some kind of washed out, borrowed child between them.

Memere said that my grandfather, Charles, had blue eyes and lighter hair as well, but I never met him. He'd died of a heart attack before I was born.

I wondered now, if there was a heaven, would they be together? My mom and her dad? Or was there just nothing—just life, and then not life. I knew that's what Dad believed. He told me once that, after seeing so many people die in the ER, he didn't really have faith in Heaven or Hell, only in living as best you can in the days you have here on Earth. But I hoped there was something more. I wanted to believe that Mom was still here somehow, or that she was in a better place.

I brushed through the tangles of my hair and dressed in barn clothes I found on the floor among other assorted clothing.

I knew I couldn't hide in the barn like yesterday, but at least I could go be with them for a bit before I had to face a room full of people—and Mom's dead body. Ugh, the thought just kind of creeped me out. It also scared me. I'd never seen a dead body. Occasionally a squirrel, or maybe a mouse or bird that one of the cats killed, but never a person. Not even an animal I cared about. Years ago, my parents had put down their old dog, and one of our old cats a few years later. But that had been when I was really little and not fully aware of what death meant. They'd just gone to the vet and hadn't come back. In the years that followed, we never had anything die or need to be put down. I guess we were lucky.

A knock came at the door and I heard Dad's voice. "Jo, are you up?"

"I'm up. I was going to go do the horses, then get changed for breakfast," I said as I opened the door. He was wearing a black suit, dark grey shirt, and black tie. It was odd seeing him in anything but jeans and a comfy shirt.

"Oh, Memere and I already managed to get the horses done. Go ahead and get dressed, and come down for breakfast. Grandma made pancakes and we saved you some."

"Gee, thanks," I said, regretting sleeping in. "I'll be down in a bit then."

"Okay. Love you," he said, looking at me with eyes that were puffy like mine. "I know today is going to be hard for both of us. If you get overwhelmed, it's okay if you want to come upstairs. I mean, if you need time alone, no one will think you are being rude. This isn't a party. No one should expect you to talk to them too much, okay?"

"Thanks, Dad. I love you too." I turned back to my room to get ready. It was going to be a day full of talking to relatives I barely knew, which I hated under normal circumstances. Today it was likely to be even worse. I tried to call Cece again. I was missing her but also feeling incredibly angry. My best friend was nowhere to be found when I really needed her. Again her phone went straight to voicemail, and again no answer at home. I left yet another message, this one slightly more desperate, then dressed and went down to face the day on my own. When I came downstairs, I could smell pancakes but still didn't feel particularly hungry. I grabbed a plate anyway and sat down at the counter.

"Morning, Jo. Are you doing okay?" Grandma sat down next to me on one of the stools while I speared a bite of pancake and pushed it through some syrup. The dining and living room were cleared out, and Dad and Grandpa were currently putting rental chairs into place from a cart.

"I guess," I said, but the truth was I was not doing okay.

"Thanks, honey." She rubbed my back and I leaned against her. "You'll need your strength today. You know, I lost my mom when I was only a bit older than you. She was sick for a while, though, so it wasn't as sudden. If you get to a point where you want to talk, please do. I know it can be really lonely without your mom. I had my brothers, but I know I had times when I needed another woman to talk to. So, if there are things you don't want to talk to your dad about, I hope you will feel comfortable coming to me. You know, some things are private, and men don't understand them," she said, looking at me with her eyebrows raised ever so slightly. "You can always talk to me about things he might not understand so well." She nodded her head conspiratorially toward me and then kissed my forehead.

● ● ●

"Thanks, Grandma," I said. To be honest, I had never really thought about talking to Grandma about "private things," as she called them. She was much more conservative than Memere, yet always supportive of me. I hadn't known her mom died when she was young. It made me realize how little I actually knew about her. She was always just Grandma, baker of things and maker of food. It never occurred to me that she was someone else before she bore that title.

From that point on, the day went by in a blur. The house was ready and the funeral home set up the casket in the dining room, right in front of the bay window my mom loved. I hadn't gone up to it yet. I didn't want to see it. Instead, I stayed in the living room and was greeted in turn by multiple people who seemed to know all about me. I knew very little about any of them.

Mom's sister had come from New York, and on any other day, she would have been really interesting. I think I'd met her once when I was small, but I only vaguely remembered her. She was wearing a dark grey draped dress and a huge black wide-brimmed hat with a shock of bright-red lipstick. She was taller than Mom and animated in every gesture she made. She was talking with just about everyone except Memere, whom she avoided other than a cursory hello and greeting. I was contemplating talking to her when Dad tapped me on the shoulder to let me know it was time to go in. We filed into the dining room, and silence fell as we sat down. Wooden chairs were set out in rows. My dad had me sit in the front row with him. People filed in behind us to fill in chairs that were still vacant. From my seat, the casket sat directly in front of me, its image a blow to my chest. I couldn't breathe for a moment and just sat, staring at what had once been my mother.

People say the dead look like they are sleeping, but Mom didn't. Her face was different, hollow and sunken without the tension and grace of life. Her face was painted heavily with makeup so that I couldn't see any of the freckles over her cheeks and nose. She never wore makeup in life, and the difference was startling. The room spun around me.

I turned away. I didn't want this image in my mind. This was not my mother. This was a body, just an empty body. I

● ● ●

wanted to remember her laughing so hard she snorted, the way she smoothed my hair back and put her hands on my cheeks when I was scared. I wanted her to save me from this and she couldn't. Just as I started to cry, the casket lid groaned and fell closed with a loud slam. The sound was shockingly loud in the mostly silent room. The stand wobbled, and for a horrible moment the whole thing threatened to tip over. My panic was replaced with surprise. I have to admit, it was preferable to the horror that was my mother's corpse. A collective gasp sounded from behind me. I glanced over at my dad as he rose from his seat. He looked confused—or was that embarrassment? Grandpa went up with surprising speed to try to lift the casket lid, but he couldn't. People were murmuring behind me. There were maybe fifty people behind me, but it sounded like hundreds.

"I don't understand. The latch is open—it should just lift up," Grandpa whispered to Dad in a voice that was close to a growl.

"Just leave it closed. Anyone who wanted to see her already has." There was an edge in Dad's voice as he sent Grandpa to sit down next to Grandma. Memere grasped my hand, and I leaned my head against her shoulder. She kissed my forehead, brushing my hair away from my face as Mom used to do.

Dad, already standing, turned to the room and cleared his throat. He had a sheet of paper in front of him, and it vibrated in his grasp as his hands shook. Mom's perfume wafted over me, strong and distinctive hues of rose and lavender, reassuring me that at least part of her was here, even if it wasn't the part in the casket.

Eleanor

It is a curious feeling to watch your own funeral. Caterers brought food and florists brought flowers. Chairs were arranged just like they were for our wedding: two sections of rows with an aisle between. The set up was so similar to that previous, more joyful event, but when the funeral home arrived and displayed the casket, the distinction became crystal clear.

I always thought I would die as an old woman. I'd imagined it multiple times over the years. Jo would be all grown up, and there would be grandchildren. I would be old enough that no one was really sad. "It was her time" or "She led a full life," people would say. Then they'd eat food and talk about how great I was. People would tell stories about me and laugh about good times we all had together. It would not have been this dreary, sad gathering with my family drifting through the process, trying to do what was required by society but clearly wanting to retreat into their grief.

The casket was propped up in the bay window of the dining room, my favorite spot in the house. Ironically, the exact spot where I first experienced consciousness without a body now held my body without a consciousness. Many evenings had been spent in that nook, reading by lamplight with the house quiet around me as I waited for Neal to come home late from his shift. I could see most of the downstairs from this spot in the window. It had a view of the adjoining kitchen and living room through a column-flanked opening in the wall. The bay

• • •

window had absolutely the best view in the house. At the moment, scattered clouds clustered along the horizon, promising a spectacular sunset in just a few hours. I had a feeling no one would notice the show nature would be putting on, at least not in this house, not this evening. The casket sat in this space, but I refused to look down at myself, not yet.

I watched as people started to file in. One benefit to dying young was a bigger turnout for your funeral, even with short notice. Most of the people that knew me were still alive. They all mingled, everyone cordial and polite with the restraint in the pleasure of seeing each other always found at funerals. Neal led Jo into the room, and they sat in the row set aside for family. My mom sat beside her, and then my older sister, Flora, sat down, with Neal's parents on her other side.

I hadn't seen Flora in a good ten years. She lived in New York and taught acting at a small liberal arts college. She was a failed actress but never really saw herself that way. She always said people just didn't appreciate her true talents. It was probably killing her that this event was all about me. Growing up, we'd had a strained relationship. She always wanted—and usually got—all of the attention from everyone around us. She was stunning to look at, even at her current age of sixty.

Flora was tall and slender with very striking coloring. She naturally had the same dark hair as Mom and me, but she'd inherited Dad's icy blue eyes. She was pale like me but somehow didn't have any freckles. Her skin had always been flawless, even when we were teenagers. When she'd started drama school, she began dyeing her hair blonde; currently, it was cut into a modern sleek bob, and silver now. She wore a rather dramatic hat. She was probably blocking the view of half the room.

I turned my attention to Jo. She was looking at me...well, my body, anyway. I saw her expression change as she stared at my made-up face, the unfamiliar mannequin in the coffin. She was upset, and I could tell that the open casket was making this harder for her.

Neal and I had once talked about this, and I thought I had made it clear that I didn't want a viewing. Sometimes he forgot certain details of conversations. Though, in his defense, it's not like we thought of this as an event that was anywhere in our near future. It had been an abstract concept, not a plan. We'd

● ● ●

spoken of it the same way we'd spoken of what we would do with our lottery winnings. Abstract ideas that would never solidify. Abstract until faced with the physical reality of it. That was *my* body in that box.

All of these people, just gawking at the corpse they associated with me. But here I was, unseen and powerless to stop any of it. I felt exposed and horribly vulnerable. To top it all off, this was clearly torturing my little girl. I could feel her revulsion and fear as she stared up at a corpse I couldn't even bring myself to look at. Slowly, I stared down at my dead body. It really didn't look like me. They'd plastered makeup all over my face, making me look like some sort of store mannequin, but someone, probably my mother, had at least chosen a nice dress.

It was a pale green silk chiffon with a high, gathered neckline that I'd always found flattering. The color highlighted my eyes, which at the moment were glued shut. I had good square shoulders and strong, well-muscled arms, which I generally thought were my best features. This dress highlighted them when I wore it in life, but a matching shawl was draped over my once-strong arms, and my limp hair covered my shoulders. Whoever had done this had done it with care, but this wasn't me. I didn't want Jo to have this as her last memory of me. Angry, I slammed myself against the lid of the casket with all the force I could muster, and to my stupendous surprise, it slammed down with a thunderous crack, rocking back and forth.

The onlookers sat stunned, their faces staring open-mouthed at my casket as it swayed on the stand. Mom wrapped her arm around Jo and kissed her head. Grace was crossing herself and muttering. Sam mumbled something about faulty hinges and rushed up to try to fix things. *No, I don't want this thing open.* I gathered all of my weight, all of my energy and power, and pressed down on the lid. He and Neal tried in vain to lift it, grunting and muttering to each other, but they gave up quickly. Sam returned to his seat, and Neal moved over to the podium where an ashen-faced funeral home employee stood speechless.

Jo seemed better, less upset, even if she was a little shocked. Good. I had done my job as a mom and discovered in the process that I could, in fact, move things if I really tried. My funeral was turning out to be more useful than I thought it might be.

● ● ●

Neal

My whole body hurt as we sat down at Nora's funeral. Well-wishers had repeatedly placed hands on my shoulders and given me looks of mixed pity and fear. Pity that this loss should have happened to me, and fear that it would happen to them. Jo sat beside me, staring at Nora's coffin and the body within. I wasn't sure about the open casket, especially now that I saw my daughter's reaction to it. My parents convinced me that it would provide closure. I was having doubts about that decision, but I couldn't really do much about it now.

Someone from the funeral home began the service at the podium. He was only a minute or so into his introduction when the casket lid slammed shut with a loud bang, shaking the stand and stunning everyone into silence. Relief swept over me, followed by the scent of Nora's perfume.

The funeral home attendant began to move toward the casket, but I waved him off. My dad was already at the casket, trying to lift the lid. I halfheartedly went up to help but quickly told him to stop. This was better. Jo seemed less upset now, and I couldn't help but feel like anyone who wanted to see Nora like that was something of a voyeur. I ran my hand down the smooth wood of the casket and turned to see everyone's face staring up at me. I had their attention now whether I wanted it or not, so I decided to go ahead and start the eulogy. My whole body wavered, and I was afraid people would hear it in my voice.

• • •

45

Earlier in the morning, I'd carried my laptop into Nora's office to print out the sheet of paper that now shook in my hands. It was the first time I'd entered her room since. Her chair was pushed under the desk, one of her sweaters draped over it. She always got cold. Her computer monitors were set up, ready for the next work day with a little basket of lip balm, lotion, and tissues to the side. The shelves above the desk held multiple textbooks, but also pictures: Jo and Nora at Jo's first horse show, Nora and me on our wedding day, a few of just Jo, and a few of holiday gatherings with ragtag groups posed together. These photos highlighted things she deeply cared about. Had I captured her in this eulogy? How could I?

As well as I knew Nora, I knew there were always depths to a person that were never revealed. We have our vision of the people around us, but, like those photos, our lives are made from snapshots of memories. Eventually, the person behind those snapshots disappears and the images are all that are left. As I set the paper on the podium, a warmth spread over my shoulders where Nora used to lay her hands when she was alive. I steadied myself and began to read:

"Eleanor Marie Turenne was a daughter who grew into a powerful woman, a loving wife, a brilliant doctor, and a devoted mother. Nora could make people laugh when laughing was the last thing they thought they could do. I think we could all use her right now, because she would have known just what to say to lighten the mood of this moment. Nora was taken from us swiftly, much too soon. I know that there was more to come for her, so much that the world will now never see from her. I don't know what her future would have held, but I know what her story was with me.

"Nora gave me the best years of my life. When I met her twenty-seven years ago, I had no idea that this petite person would completely change my life in such an enormous way.

Nora and I met when we were both freshman in college. We were both in the pre-med program at UVA and started orientation at the same time. I remember sitting in class and watching this vibrant, beautiful girl come in on the very first day. I was immediately smitten, as were most of the other guys in class. I never worked up the nerve to speak to her until a party one night during our sophomore year. Nora was talking with some other girls when a male classmate came up to her and started laying it on

● ● ●

thick. Saying things I dare not repeat. Nora made a Nora face at him—you all know what I'm talking about—that said she was really not interested. Then he put his hands on her and began to get rude, trying to pull her upstairs. I don't really remember what happened next, but he ended up on the floor, and I ended up face to face with Nora. She said it was heroic. I said it was a complete loss of temper, but whatever it was, it led to Nora dating and then marrying me. I like to think of it as the best punch I've ever thrown. It might also be the only punch I've ever thrown. Whatever the case, it landed me the best partner I could have ever had.

"One of Nora's most amazing attributes was her presence. She was always much bigger than her five-foot three-inch height implied. When Nora entered a room full of people, they would turn and look at her no matter what. She hated that, and constantly asked if she had something on her face. She almost never did.

"She was one of those people who made you feel better than you are just by being next to you. She made people feel at ease whether they had known her for five minutes or five years. I don't think Nora was aware of this power she had. One of my regrets is that I never fully expressed this to her. Nora always worried that she might have said the wrong thing, or laughed at the wrong moment. What she didn't know was that she somehow tapped into what everyone else was feeling and expressed it without even trying. To everyone who knew her, Nora was a safe place. To me, Nora was so much more. She was my home, and she made every place we lived feel like home because she was there. She gave me the greatest gift a person could ever receive: she gave me love; she gave me a family; she gave me Josephine. She showed herself to be a mother who was loving, patient, and fiercely devoted. I would never have had a life this beautiful or this complete without Nora. She built people up, and never tore them down. Her default was kindness; her thought was that if you show people kindness, they will return it. She was right, and I'd like to share a story that proves her point.

"Nora and I bought this house not long after we finished medical school, and it was a bit of a wreck. Nora and I were doing most of the work ourselves, but we hired a man named Mr. Charles to come in and do plaster work for us. It was summer, and very hot. The house had no air conditioning, no working kitchen—it was truly awful. Nora would make iced tea at our apartment and bring a huge pitcher out for Mr. Charles every day, complete with ice cubes and cups, everything. He would leave her an empty pitcher every evening. She also made him sandwiches, and made sure we had a fan going in each room. This went on for a few weeks until the project was complete. When the work was done, he delivered our final invoice,

• • •

and there was a five-percent discount. I asked what it was for. I was definitely not complaining. Just curious.

"He turned to Nora and said, 'No one has ever cared for me while I was working like you have. You made me feel at home, so just call it the iced tea discount.'

"Nora told him, 'Thank you. I didn't do it to get a discount though, so you really didn't have to do that.'

"And he replied, 'Neither did you—but you did anyway.'

"That was Nora. She would always do nice things for people that she didn't have to do, but she still did them whether the kindness was returned or not. Most of the time, it came back to us many times over. Nora was my best friend, and I miss her, but I am saddened even more that the world has lost her. I am saddened that she will no longer be here to see it. I wish I could talk to her, I wish I could hold her hand, I wish that she could still be here to see all of you. I wish that she could see how loved she was, and how greatly she will be missed.

"Selfishly, I miss Nora because I was a better me with her. I don't really know who I am without her, and I am afraid I might not be as good as she made me believe I could be. She and I were preparing for a life that would soon look very different. Our house would be a bit empty with Jo away at school, back to just the two of us. She envisioned a life of joy for us that I hope Josephine and I can still have.

"Nora often spoke to me of her hopes for the future. Love for Josephine, and maybe one day grandchildren. One of her greatest wishes was to one day hold her grandchild in her arms and see our daughter become a mother. We also planned to travel to places we had never seen, meeting people we'd never met. Rediscovering each other as a couple and not just as parents. Our plans were not grand, but I grieve the loss of them just the same.

"We may never get to know what Nora would go on to do, but we know all the great things she did. It is now up to us to keep her alive in our memories, to keep the light of her life lit, even though she is no longer here to shine."

I looked up at the faces in front of me, many dabbing eyes with tissues.

The funeral home attendant came back to the front, placed a hand on my shoulder, and addressed the group. "If anyone else has anything they would like to share, they may do so at this time."

• • •

All the energy drained from me and I slipped back to my seat next to Jo. She was teary-eyed and rested her head on my shoulder, sniffling into a tissue.

"Good job, Dad. You got her right."

I kissed her head, breathed in the scent of her shampoo and tried to hold myself together.

• • •

Josephine

I walked along the stream in the bottom of the south pasture until I got to our spot, an old iron bench in a small level clearing. Mom and I came here together most Sunday mornings after bringing the horses in to feed. Somehow talking to her always seemed easier here. I hadn't slept much at all last night and had already fed the horses in the dark before the sun came up. Now, I sat in silence as the sky came alive around me, changing slowly from a deep navy blue to pale lilac, then exploding with color in tones of apricot, crimson, and gold. The light of it shone through the frost on blades of grass, turning them into blades of shimmering colored glass. My breath misted around me, and I closed my eyes to listen to the water as it ran over the smooth quartz stones.

Impatient whinnies came from the direction of the barn. The horses obviously didn't care about solitude. I made my way back up the hill, let the horses out, and then trudged back to the house.

My bedroom door stood open as I came up the stairs. An oddity that made me wonder if Mom *might* still be around. I'd closed it when I left to go to the barn, and here it sat, open again. Dad said it was just the fiddly latch, but it had never done this on its own before Mom died.

• • •

Once inside my room, I plucked my phone off the charger and checked my messages. Finally, there was one from Cece, *Call me, we need to talk.* Cece never texted in full sentences. Maybe she had finally realized how terrible of a friend she was being.

It was six in the morning. She'd sent the text last night at eleven o'clock while my phone was on do not disturb.

I decided I would go ahead and call her back, mostly because I was still angry with her, and I savored the idea of waking her up. Petty, I know.

The phone rang several times until she finally picked up. "Hello," came a groggy voice I barely recognized.

"Cece, it's me, Jo. Where the hell have you been?" I couldn't keep the hysteria out of my voice, even though I was trying not to lay into her right away.

"Jo, I've been in the hospital. I was in a car accident on the way to meet you. I had head trauma and they kept me for observation, but my mom said no phones while I was recovering. They discharged me last night, and I went straight to my phone to get in touch with you."

"Cece, my mom is dead—" My voice cracked as I said the words. "—and I needed you. I'm glad you are okay, but I'm upset and disappointed that I couldn't talk to you over the past two days. Cece, this has just been so hard." I was sobbing now, the release of talking to my best friend unhinging me.

"I know. I'm so sorry." There was a long, heavy silence. Then she continued, "Jo, umm, I think I need to tell you something." Her voice sounded afraid.

"Anything, Cece, just tell me."

"I, umm, I was the other driver."

"What do you mean you were the other driver?"

"I was driving, and I looked down for a moment, and then there was a bang. I don't remember anything after that, and I woke up in the hospital the next day."

The realization of what she was saying poured over me.

"I just hit send on a text to you, that's all. It was like two seconds, then bam!"

"Cece, do you mean—" Dread started to drown out everything else I was feeling.

● ● ●

51

"Jo, I—the other driver involved in my accident died." Her voice started to crack and break. "I didn't want to know a name, but then when I heard about your mom, I asked, and well…" I dropped the phone on the bed.

A loud hum filled my ears. I walked out of my room and down the stairs. I knocked on Dad's bedroom door and waited.

"Come on in, Jo," Dad called from within.

I went in and curled up beside him. I sobbed until the pillow—Mom's pillow—was soaked with my tears. Dad held me and stroked my hair like he'd done when I was little. He kissed the back of my head and just let me be. For once he didn't try to ask what was wrong, or how he could fix it. He just let me be broken for a while.

"Dad, Cecilia killed Mom. It was her. She was driving the other car. How do I do this?" I blurted out, my face still buried in the pillow.

"Jo, we don't know for sure yet," he said, but I could hear the doubt in his voice.

"It was her! I just talked to her! She was sending me a text. I had a part in it! This is my fault too!" I could hear the hysteria in my voice. Then utter panic that I had somehow caused my own mother's death hit me, dimming my vision. Dad's voice drifted to me as I lay curled next to him.

"Oh, Jo, you didn't do this, I promise you that. Even if it was Cece who hit your Mom, you didn't know she was driving when she sent you that message. You didn't force her to be irresponsible. You weren't even in the car. You can't control her actions."

"But Dad, what if I hadn't been so impatient? I was so worried about being late for dinner. Dinner with Mom." My body felt heavy and my stomach lurched and pitched. "What if Cece hadn't felt the need to send me that message? Mom might be alive right now."

"Jo, you can spend your entire life worrying about '*what ifs.*' I promise you, I've done it plenty of times as a doctor. It's not good for you. What happened happened. It was not your fault. It was just a tragic accident." He was right, of course, but the fact that her death involved my best friend made things so much worse. Now I felt like I was losing them both. I went back to my room, closing the door behind me. Rage and loss flooded through me and I held my pillow to my face and screamed into it. I lowered the pillow and attempted to get my breathing under control, failing miserably as I took shallow, rapid breaths. The door latch clicked and the door slowly opened. I turned toward it expecting Dad, but no one was there. Cool air from the hallway drifted over me. It smelled like Mom. I breathed deeply and finally started to calm down, the familiar scent wafting around me heavily.

"Mom?" I said, a crazy person talking to an empty room. Only the room didn't feel empty at all.

● ● ●

Neal

S omeone lay down in the bed next to me. The mattress sagged under the weight and I turned over expecting to see Jo. There was nothing there. I reached over to smooth the covers and the sunken form faded as the mattress sprang back again. I called out to Jo. My bedroom door was ajar, and if she was just outside in the hallway she would hear. I got no response. I felt the hairs raise on my arms as I sat up and glanced around at the empty room. I knew from studying the process of grief that things like this often happened. On the verge of waking, people in the midst of grieving have vivid dreams. Perhaps I was experiencing this manifestation of grief. It had been a month since Nora passed, and weeks since anyone but myself was in the room, let alone in my bed.

The last time was when Jo came to me about Cece the morning after the funeral. I confirmed that Cece had in fact been the other driver involved in the accident. I remembered her bruised and bloodied face, clenched in a brace on the backboard, and the feeling of something familiar then. I just couldn't fathom that this was the same child Jo had grown up with. Granted, with my schedule, I hadn't seen Cece in at least a year, but still. I'd been so focused on my job, I hadn't seen what was right in front of me.

Cecilia traveled with us on vacations, slept over more times than I could count, and was Jo's closest friend from kindergarten on. One text, one stupid text that could have—

● ● ●

should have—never been sent from a moving car. I was so angry with her, and the fact that she was not some anonymous idiot somehow made things both better and worse. It forced me to try to let go of my anger, but it doubled the loss for Jo.

She was never someone with a large group of friends, and I worried as I watched her isolate herself more and more. I enrolled us both in grief counseling. I tried to reach out to Jo however I could, but she seemed like she was still slipping away.

After I showered, shaved, and dressed, the eerie feeling of the depression in the mattress seemed far away. I was sure I must have been dreaming when it happened. I held no belief in ghosts. Sure, I smelled Nora's perfume from time to time, but she had lived in the house for years. I was sure it permeated everything by now.

Celestine and Jo were now pressing for us to see a medium. Celestine had planted the idea in Jo's head, since she saw a medium after Charles, Nora's father, had died. Jo latched onto it immediately, citing her bedroom door as evidence that Nora was still with us. I thought it was ridiculous. Jo was convinced that every night Nora would close her bedroom door just like she had when she was alive. It was the perfect time of year to sleep with the windows open, and I was pretty sure drafts were responsible, not my undead wife.

Still, I spoke to my therapist about going to a medium, and he told me that unless they were obviously manipulating her for money, it may help bring some closure for Jo. I decided I would go along with it, but held a very low opinion of mediums in general. Most appeared to be skilled at reading people and deciphering clues from things around them, but thus far I had seen no real evidence that they were anything more than con artists. But, as long as this person didn't take advantage of Jo and try to get money out of us, I had to agree that it seemed like a relatively harmless idea. Celestine arranged for a reading this weekend, assuring me that the medium was the "real deal." I planned to be there to challenge them as much as possible.

I made myself coffee and a bagel to eat in the car on the way into the hospital. I'd started taking shifts again two weeks ago. Work distracted my mind from Nora for a bit, which gave me both relief and guilt. The clinical side of my brain understood that it was healthy to move forward with life, but the other part of me wanted to cling to the grief as a way of holding on to Nora. It was as if letting go of this sadness would somehow make me lose her completely. I had to try to hold on to the fact that there was more than sadness left. There were memories, of course Jo, the house, and all the things in it. Nearly everything here was hand selected by Nora. All I needed to do was walk through the living room and I could remember craft fairs, estate sales, art projects, and family heirlooms. These collected memories made me feel more connected to her, but at the same time they made me miss her more because I knew there would be no new ones.

I reached for my keys on the hook by the front door, and they weren't there. Damn it, this was happening all the time now. Forgetfulness is a very common and inconvenient sign of grief. I'd always teased Nora about how often she lost her keys, but I now was the one losing them. Finally, I found them on the table by the sofa in the living room. I patted Mrs. Norris, who had settled on the sofa for a busy day of napping, and headed out for the day.

Right now, heart attacks, stabbings, and strokes were more comforting than the oppressive emptiness of this house.

Eleanor

With the funeral behind us, I began to accustom myself to existence as a person who no longer had a body. I still had a hard time referring to myself as a ghost. Ghosts were the things in horror movies that frightened people and threw plates. Since I saw no purpose in breaking my plates, and even less in terrifying my family, I mostly puttered around the house, oscillating between consciousness and unconsciousness.

In life, Neal always taunted me about my forgetfulness and how often I lost my keys. Now that I had discovered I could move things, I decided Neal's keys would be the perfect test subjects. At first it was quite hard to move them. The collective energy of the attendants and my rage at the funeral allowed me to pull off the casket lid trick, but without those things to help me, I found I had to focus hard just to grasp the keys.

At first I would only move them a bit, but with practice I could pick them up and carry them to other places in the house. It provided me with entertainment to watch Neal grab for his keys, only to find them a few feet from where he left them or in an entirely different room. Of course, he appeared to blame it on the forgetfulness that often accompanies the grieving process, which made me wonder how many other recently deceased people had played this game. Enough to make it a symptom of grieving, no doubt.

● ● ●

When I wasn't poking fun at him by moving his keys, I would sometimes lie beside him in bed, just to be close to him. He rarely woke up, but one morning he did seem to notice me there. Neal never believed in ghosts, or an afterlife. Making the leap to cuddling with your ghost wife wasn't one he would make easily. It saddened me to know he needed me, and I was here, but due to his adherence to evidence-based belief, he and I couldn't connect.

As for Jo, I tried to comfort her as much as I could. She seemed to sense my presence more than Neal, or maybe she just allowed herself to be aware of me. I dared not touch her or do anything that might frighten her, but I tried to be near her. I found I could send feelings of comfort to her, and she seemed to receive them. I could see and feel her relax in response.

In life, I was always the last one in her room at night, and I would pull her door closed behind me after saying goodnight. Now that I was gone, she would often forget to close her door. After she was asleep, I would quietly close it if she hadn't. I heard her comment about this multiple times to Neal, but he brushed it off, saying she must have closed it and forgotten. The forgetfulness of grief certainly was a handy deflective device.

When left on my own, things became murkier and less familiar. This other world was one of images and sensations, detached from the physical form. My father always arrived first as his familiar scent of cognac and cigars. We communicated mostly via shared memory, with one in particular that changed everything.

My father lay in bed, eyes closed, room dark. His memories up to this point were from his perspective, just as he'd experienced them. This was markedly different, the tactile nature of his prior memories completely missing. He lay in my parent's large bedroom, the walls covered in the familiar blue and white toile wallpaper. I thought of how I used to trace the shapes with my fingers as a child, trees, horses, streams, the slightly rough fabric trailing under my fingertips. Next to the bed stood Dad's ancient side table, intricately carved out of mahogany and likely older than the house itself. On it sat an empty pill vial with its

* * *

lid cast to the carpeted floor below. The pill vial lid was accompanied by an empty cognac bottle. I looked at the label. It was the bottle Dad always claimed to be saving for a special occasion. That specific bottle sat in a place of reverence in the liquor cabinet for close to a decade, dusted but otherwise never touched. Mom burst into the room, the door smacking against the wall with a thump, and went to his side of the bed, kicking the cognac bottle aside.

"Charles. Charles, wake up! Please don't do this again. Not now." Her voice was irritated and stern. She pushed on his shoulder, then stood, her face now ashen. She pressed her ear to his chest, which I now realized was still, and her scream filled the room.

"Goddamn it, Charles, no! Please. Please." She clawed at the phone beside the bed and dialed 911 before collapsing onto the floor, sobbing as she screamed, "My husband, he's not breathing! I think he's dead!" into the receiver before curling up on the floor. A blink, and EMTs arrived in the room.

Mom stood up, backing away from the bedside. "He's gone already. I know that now, but I didn't know what else to do." Her voice was flat, and she stood folded over and small, completely unlike her normally statuesque, perfect posture. Her face was pale and mascara stained her cheeks. Her eyes remained cast down to the floor.

The paramedic leaned over and checked for a pulse, then listened to Dad's chest with a stethoscope and sighed.

"Yes, ma'am, he is gone, likely for a good while. We will contact the coroner and police who will then take his body to determine cause of death."

"Can't you see? You can see what he did." She held up the pill vial and Cognac bottle then deflated, arms hanging loosely at her sides, tears streaming silently down her face.

The images faded, and I was left with them replaying over and over.

Why? Why did he do it? Why had she lied? She'd always insisted he died of a heart attack. I'd had cardiac screening done when I turned fifty because I'd thought I had a history of heart

• • •

disease, but it turns out that was a lie. I was angry but saddened as well. Obviously my father struggled more than we knew.

I began to reflect back on his withdrawn nature. I always attributed this to the fact that he was very old fashioned and expected my mother to do the whole business of child rearing while he brought in the money. Clearly, there was more to it than that. I knew my father drank (that ever-present cognac), but most of the people we were around as children drank. It was just what upper-class people did after dinner. I'd never really thought about it as a potential problem. It had most certainly been a problem.

I thought back to Mom's lack of shock in finding her unconscious husband in bed. How many times had this almost happened? He was obviously deeply depressed when he took his own life, but how long had he struggled with mental illness? Even in the medical field, it is something that isn't discussed the way it should be, and polite society would *never* discuss it. So many people still thought of depression as weakness, so it was hidden, untreated, and ignored until it was undeniable. Evidently, according to my mother, it could be denied even when it cost a life. There was this entire alternate reality unfolding hidden from me in life, only made apparent to me now that I was dead and could do nothing about it. Well, I was going to do *something* about it. I just had no clue as to what yet.

Josephine

I took a deep breath, savoring the heady mixture of garlic-laden Mediterranean food and roasting coffee. I was sitting alone at a cute cafe Cece and I had vowed to try when we still talked about things. I sipped my iced tea and nibbled on crispy pita dipped in hummus. I was so nervous I could barely taste it. Cece walked in, fifteen minutes late as always, wearing a pair of high-waisted jeans with heels and a cropped t-shirt. She sat down across from me and sighed, tossing her long hair over her shoulder. She'd had her nails done and they looked like fuschia talons as she launched directly into an apology.

"Jo, I feel terrible. I know you're mad at me. Just tell me what I can do to make things right between us."

Just looking at her enraged me, so I took a deep breath. "Cece, I don't think there is anything you can say or do that will make it better. My mom is dead. I will never talk to her again, I'll never see her again, and all because of a stupid text message."

"A text message to *you*, Jo. You were the one who was all upset that I was a little late. I felt pressured into texting you."

"Excuse me?" My voice rose, and people started to look in our direction. My palms were sweating so much I had trouble holding the edge of the table to settle myself.

"I didn't tell you to text me from a moving vehicle! You could have just texted from *Dumbass's* house and *then* drove my way." I nearly knocked my coffee over as my hand swept across the table.

● ● ●

"Of course it wasn't your fault. That isn't what I meant at all. But he has a name, Jo. Please don't call Micah a dumbass."

"Oh my god, are you fucking serious right now? You honestly think I care about your goddamned cattle-driving boyfriend? My mother is DEAD, Cecilia. Dead! I don't give a fuck who you spread your legs for. I'm talking about things that actually matter here!" People were definitely staring now. Chairs screeched against the cement floor as the couple next to us moved out of their seats to get away from us.

"Jo, I love him, and it hurts that you don't like him. I know that doesn't really matter at the moment. I just...I am really sorry. I feel terrible. You're my best friend, and I feel like you hate me." She started crying, obscenely loud. I wondered if it was even genuine.

"Cece, I don't hate you. I just don't know how to do this." So many emotions coursed through me, I felt completely overwhelmed. I wanted to leave.

"Neither do I, Jo."

Cece reached for my hand. I withdrew mine from the table.

"Look, I thought maybe seeing you in person would help, but I just feel even more confused. I wanted you to be there for me. I wanted you to help me through this, and you weren't there. You haven't been there for a long time though."

"I'm sorry, Jo. I haven't been a good friend lately. Falling in love does that. Maybe one day you will understand that."

"Maybe I will, maybe I won't. I just know that I needed my friend." I could feel myself tearing up, conflicting emotions of anger and sadness spilling over. I stood. "This was a bad idea Cece. I'm not ready for any of this."

"Okay. If that's the way you feel, then I guess call me when you are." Cece's voice was cold and hurt.

I left money on the table for my coffee and pita, then walked out, still drowning in more emotion than I could handle, wishing my mind would go blank.

• • •

At home, I changed clothes and tacked Callie up for a ride. Thirty minutes later, everything finally fell away as we cantered on a twenty-meter circle. I could feel Callie soften and her back lift under me. Through the reins, I could feel her mouth gently contacting the bit. She always had trouble with her right lead, but today she was free and light underneath me. I relaxed further and let her stretch down before asking her for a downward transition. She tensed, lifting her head briefly, but then transitioned into a balanced trot for a stride or two before slowing to a walk. I let her have her head and patted her neck, then slipped my feet out of the stirrups to let her know she was done for the day.

Dad had mentioned something about the horses and how much they cost, that they should be enjoyed by someone. I'd been afraid he might sell Mahalo or Georgia until I listened through the door after my therapy session one afternoon. I could hear Katrina, my therapist, tell Dad that selling Mom's horses so soon after her death should be avoided unless it was financially necessary. Thank goodness for that.

Since I took care of them, I didn't know why he even cared if they stayed. I had already decided to go to UVA for school instead of Corcoran in DC. Last year I'd told Mom I didn't want to stay local, but she'd said I should apply just in case I didn't feel ready to leave home. At that point, I wanted nothing more than to leave home. Now it was the only place I wanted to be. I could literally feel Mom in the house, and horses were better company than people. They didn't feel sorry for me or tiptoe around me like I might explode at any minute. They let me just be in the moment.

Friends from school called and tried to drag me out of my bubble. Everyone else was enjoying their last semester of high school before heading off to college. When I did manage to drag myself to a party, it seemed so pointless. Everyone got drunk or high, then made out with someone or puked in the yard. I couldn't find any enjoyment in it. Drinking made me end up thinking bitter thoughts about how other people still had parents. I couldn't stand being in a room listening to people bitch about how awful their moms were for giving them a curfew.

Once, someone gave me some weed so strong I ended up lying on the floor and crying, replaying my imagined idea of Mom's body in the car over and over in my mind. After that, the party invites pretty much stopped. I hadn't told Dad yet, but I wasn't planning on going to graduation. It would just be another

• • •

reminder that Mom wasn't there when she should have been. At least, her body wasn't there. I comforted myself with increasing conviction that some part of Mom was still around.

Dad was such a non-believer, he was ignoring the evidence right in front of his face: my bedroom door, his keys moving, Mom's perfume. I found comfort in these little things. Memere and I had *finally* convinced him to go with us to a medium. Memere worked with her when my Granddad died and said she would give us a free reading with her medium in training. He finally relented. Especially when Memere told him the reading was free.

Neal

We decided to meet this 'medium' at her office. Initially it was suggested we have this woman and her apprentice come to the house, but I shut that down immediately. Surely they would be able to gather information from photos, paintings, pictures, and the house in general. Any halfway-observant person would be able to give details about us just from looking at our house. Nope, that would have given them way too much of an advantage. We were instructed to bring an item for anyone we wanted to communicate with, and there was much discussion over what item to take. I told Celestine and Jo that it had to be gender neutral and not give too much away, so they finally chose her tea mug. It was an old, handmade ceramic mug, and she'd carried it with her almost all the time when home. It was stained inside from the constant presence of Earl Grey, and had a small chip on the handle from having been dropped once on the kitchen floor.

They both agreed it would be a good choice, since evidently objects that the person had a strong connection to in life were more likely to bring them in contact after death. It still all sounded like phooey, but hopefully harmless phooey.

We all packed into the car and headed over on a Saturday morning.

"It should be just up here on the left," Celestine said as we passed a nice old barn with arched doorways. She was navigating after revealing that she had been to see this woman

• • •

many times since Charles' death. Odd the things you discover about someone you thought you knew. Celestine didn't seem the type to go to a medium, but then I suppose everyone has secrets they keep.

"Okay, yes, right here, there it is. Joan is very good, you know. I think you will be impressed by her, Neal," Celestine chirped.

I grunted.

"Well, we will see what she is all about, won't we?" I pulled up to a small converted outbuilding with a home a few feet away. Both buildings were painted a buttery yellow and looked very old but neatly kept and well maintained. A painted wooden sign hanging in front of the office read *Joan Meeks, Communication Services* in a hunter green script. It sounded like a telephone company, not a medium.

Celestine knocked on the door, and the woman who opened it was not what I expected. She was dressed in a crisp button down shirt and pressed slacks. Her hair was in a pixie cut and was a uniform silver color. She had reading glasses on a beaded holder hanging around her neck and wore only a wedding set as jewelry.

She led us into the front room of the little building and had us sit down. "Hi, Joan, it is so nice to see you again," Celestine spoke as she settled onto the couch.

The woman nodded. "It is always nice to see you, Celestine. I am so sorry for your new loss. Would you like any water or snacks while you wait? It will be about ten minutes until we bring you all back." We'd arrived fifteen minutes early, so she was right on time.

"No, thank you, none for me," Celestine replied. "Anyone else?" Both Jo and I declined and sat down on the sofa.

"Okay, I will be back in a bit." She exited through a door toward the second room, and we were left alone in what I assumed was her waiting room. It was a brightly lit room with large picture windows on opposite walls, through which you could see Joan's immaculately maintained garden. It was now late April, and her daffodils and a few late tulips were blooming everywhere. I had to admit it was a pleasant space, but a thought started to weasel in, shoving aside the pleasing imagery.

● ● ●

"Celestine, how did she know you had a new loss? Did you tell her anything about Nora?"

"No, I haven't told her anything, Neal. She always specifically says to not give her any expectations of who you want to come through."

"I expect she read it in the paper. Nora had an obituary that you wrote. She may have read it."

"Neal, she knows because *she knows*. That's why," Celestine replied, lifting her eyebrow in that always-irritating way she did when she felt she knew something you didn't.

A couple came out of the doorway that Joan had exited through minutes before, their eyes reddened and tissues clutched in their hands. They nodded to us and left. A moment later, a young man in his early twenties came out and introduced himself.

"Hello, I'm Luke. If you would please come in and sit. Joan will be ready for us in a moment." He was tall, tanned, and surprisingly muscular for a medium's apprentice. I noticed to my dismay that Jo definitely noticed him as well. She stared at him, cheeks flushed, with her mouth open until I nudged her, and we entered the office space. He nodded at her with a little smile and she nodded back. I wondered if they knew each other.

"Joan is just clearing her mind in the garden before your session. She gave most of the last session, with myself finishing it up, but I will be working with you today until the end where she may come in to close. I have been training with her for a year now, and hopefully soon will be working as her partner."

We sat down in a surprisingly sparse room: pale blue walls and bright yellow curtains, a sofa covered in a soft grey fabric with a plain sisal rug on the floor. Across a wooden coffee table from the sofa were two wing back chairs in the same grey fabric, and behind those stood a large built in bookcase. On one central shelf there was a platter, and on it sat a bundle of herbs that were smoking. It smelled vaguely of the herbs in the room, but not enough to be offensive. I hated incense and was relieved to not see any. In fact, there were no crystals, or candles, or dark draperies.

Luke must have noticed me looking around. "It helps to have a space that is relatively neutral when working with people outside of their home. It helps us to focus, and it doesn't

● ● ●

offend anyone we want to come over. This should be a safe, neutral space for everyone involved, for communication to happen most easily."

Joan quietly entered the room and sat on the chair to the left of Luke.

"Shall we begin?" She nodded to Luke and to each of us in turn. "Luke will be communicating for you today. He is naturally talented and has been honing his skills both with myself and other communicators for the past year. He is almost ready to be on his own, but at his request he asked that I remain present for his sessions for now. You are in very good hands, and often at his sessions you get some extra insight because I will not withhold anything I receive as well. Right then, off you go." She gestured to Luke, who leaned forward in his chair.

"Have you brought anything with you to help with our session today? If so, I will hold it as I start to open up." Jo passed him the mug.

"If you don't mind, just remain silent for a bit while I try to focus my energy and concentrate." He closed his eyes while holding the mug, and every so often would tilt his head as if trying to hear a far-off sound. He had the performance down, I'll give him that. Joan picked up a notepad and began to write something. After what felt like forever, Luke finally began to speak. "Josephine. Your mother loves you very much." He spoke without looking up. Celestine must have given them our names for the appointment, and it's not a stretch to say a mother loves you. "She is repeatedly telling me 'no pain, no pain.' Was this an accident? I get the impression of a sudden impact, and confusion, but no pain." He started to wave his hand in the air and nod. "I am not sure why she is telling me this, but she also said to make sure you know this is not your fault." Tears streamed down Jo's cheeks. "Eleanor…yes, Eleanor. Was that your mother's name?"

"Yes, that was her." Celestine nodded and put her arm around Jo to hold her closer. Surely they could have gotten all of this from the obituary. He may not be psychic, but he had done his research.

"Okay, this is strange—she is showing me a bedroom door and some keys. Does that make any sense to any of you?"

This was more specific. How would he know this? Doubt crept in, but I pushed it aside. Most people have doors and keys.

"Dad! It's her, you know it!" Jo excitedly turned to me, her cheeks flushed, tears rolling down them. She looked hopeful for the first time in ages.

"Well, I don't know, that is a strange thing for him to say, but..." I trailed off. I didn't really know what to say.

"Okay, Neal." He looked over at me. "She is showing me horses and telling me 'home, home.' Does that make any sense?"

"Well, yes, we do have horses at home." I couldn't really explain that one either.

"No, she is reinforcing this idea, holding, keeping? I'm not sure. She is a bit fuzzier now." I was a little shaken. I'd discussed selling Nora's horses with the therapist briefly but decided it was best to keep them for Jo's sake.

"I am getting something else now. Oh, Celestine, she is drawing me over to you. This is difficult...hmm, secret, okay. Umm, no, not her, someone else committed suicide?" Celestine's face went white.

"No! No, you are way off there." She leaned away from Jo and stared at him, arms crossed.

"Okay, I just, she is very insistent. I suppose it could be a family member you are unaware of. She is giving me the sense of a secret. You may not have known about this." After several minutes, he spoke again. "I'm now just getting a few images: bricks, an iron railing, animals, a dog, cats, a chair by a window, mountains. Everything is more scattered now. Maybe I am getting a little tired, or she is." He set the mug down on the coffee table. "I'm sorry. After that last detail, I only got bits and pieces."

Joan spoke up from her chair. "Sometimes we can receive images we don't understand or we don't want to see, and they can be confusing without the context of life. Generally, the messages we get are not wrong, but they can be hard to interpret. Especially when multiple people are in the room." She pursed her lips and gazed with narrowed eyes at Celestine, almost as if she were chastising her. I had never seen anyone dare to give her that look.

● ● ●

"If you are willing, we could set up another session sometime with a more one-on-one set up." There it was—the ask. They had Jo hooked. I could tell by the way she was nodding.

Joan turned to me. "Neal, I know you don't believe in any of this, but just because you don't believe it doesn't mean it isn't real." She handed me the piece of paper she had been scribbling on, folding it over as she did so. "I do hope you will consider setting up another session. I think there is a large amount of healing that needs to go on. Light can be cast on many shadows through this work. Just think it over, and if you would like to set up another session with either myself or Luke, please let us know. I do hope we have been able to give you some comfort. I think the overarching message we should take away from this is that Nora is peaceful, she is not suffering, and she is with you. Even playfully, I might add." She smiled, but her expression was still thoughtful.

"You don't have to look at it now. Just please do look at it. She loves you very much."

Later that evening I sat on the end of my bed and pulled out the folded sheet, carefully unfolding it until I could see what was written on it.

Neal it's Nora, Keys, Not forgetful, not forgetful, Love, the bed, it was me, not a dream, it was me beside you, it was me, let her talk to me, I'm here, never left. Below that was a perfect drawing of Nora's engagement ring.

There was no way Joan would have been able to know it in such detail. It was custom-made nearly one-hundred years ago, and I had never seen one quite like it. It was made of interwoven vines of white and rose gold with tiny diamonds for leaves and two rose blossom-shaped settings holding solitaire diamonds inside each as the centerpiece. Celestine had given it to me when I'd told her of my intention to propose. Of all Nora's possessions, it was the one she was the most connected to. We'd had a wedding band made that fit against it and she'd worn the set every day, only taking them off to clean them or ride.

The rings sat on my dresser, still in the plastic bag from the funeral home. I opened the bag and held them with my right hand, touching the smooth surface of the metal with my thumb. I absently turned my own wedding band on my finger. Tears began streaming down my cheeks, and I gripped the rings tightly as I sunk to the floor. I lay there curled around Nora's rings and let myself go for the first time since her death. I held them to my lips and wept until I physically couldn't anymore. I smelled her perfume all around me and let myself think for just a moment that maybe she was there with me.

• • •

Eleanor

I was pulled into the physical world by an unfamiliar tug. I followed along until I felt more familiar energies as well as the source of the pull: Jo, Neal and my mother were all pulling me along, joined by two strangers. I emerged in a bright, sun-filled room that smelled slightly of sage. I heard a male voice and found myself face to face with a handsome young man of about twenty. I turned and saw Mom, Jo, and Neal seated on a long sofa, and an unfamiliar woman sitting next to my new friend.

"Hello," he said, not speaking out loud but directing his thoughts to me.

"Hello, Eleanor here," I said hesitantly.

"I am here to help you speak to your family. They love you very much and miss you. Is there anything you want to say to them?"

It was so refreshing and lovely to have someone speak with me in actual words.

"Oh my. Well, I want Jo—Josephine, that is, my daughter there in the middle—I want her to know that I love her very much." I looked over at Jo's face, full of sadness, hope, and guilt. Always the guilt. It hung over her like a cloud, blocking the sun from her face.

"Anything else?" His face was a study in concentration. I thought of the final few moments I had been able to decipher, the impact, then the nothing that followed until I emerged in my

● ● ●

home only to find out from overheard conversations that my life had ended in a freak car accident that I barely remembered. One which Jo seemed to feel guilt for.

"I want her to know that I didn't feel any pain, and that none of this was her fault. I am not sure why she is blaming herself, but she shouldn't."

I could hear and see him passing my messages along and felt elated. Here was a way to speak to my family. A way to still be in their lives. I could feel Neal's suspicion. He would never let them come back if I couldn't prove to him I was really here, communicating with them. He was a born skeptic. I needed to convince him most of all.

I thought hard, then showed this young man my bedroom door and keys. I tried to show him as much detail as I could. I also directed thoughts at the woman beside him. She possessed a very different energy, much calmer and very reassuring. The young man was excited and friendly but came more in fits and starts. Her energy was like a beam of light, steady and warm, guiding me toward her without any words.

I introduced myself and told her about hiding Neal's keys. I told her about lying in bed with Neal. I tried to impress on her that I wanted to see Jo again, that he should let her come back, and then I showed her my wedding ring in detail. I knew it was something he would recognize, something that was specific and meant a great deal to both of us. I hoped it would be enough to convince him that these people held the truth.

Then I turned to my mother and started to deliver my message for her. I showed him my father, the bottle of pills, the cognac. Depression. Suicide.

"She knows, but she won't tell anyone," I said to him. I heard him ask my mother about it, then watched her turn pale and close down completely, denying any knowledge. Wow. Really, Mom?

"Please, I don't want these secrets to be buried," I snapped, watching her continue to lie. My father clearly suffered from a major depressive disorder. What if he'd passed this on to Jo and my death somehow triggered it? We needed to know her history, and clearly no living member of the family seemed to know it. This was my daughter we were talking about, and my mother was still worried about making sure the family looked perfect. Perfection was a lie, and it could be dangerous. My anger built until it started to affect my ability to stay present. I wanted to go home to my house with its gracious porch, and my animals—I wanted to sit in my chair and look at the mountains. I wanted to leave, so I did. Amazing how even in death, my mother could still make me go running to my room in anger, even if the animals were the only ones there to hear me slam the door.

Neal

I pulled into the drive and stopped for a moment. It was a Friday afternoon in late May and the air felt warm with impending summer. The leaves on the trees were still new, the fields a brilliant green. Behind the house, the mountains stood, a hazy blue against the bright cloud-scattered sky. Birds sang to one another from trees, and the croaking of frogs reached up the hill from their revelry in the stream. The towering magnolia in front of the house smelled earthy and damp after rain showers earlier in the day. I unlocked the heavy wooden front door and stepped into the pleasantly cool foyer.

"Jo, I'm home!" I called as I entered, bending to pet Mrs. Norris, who whined and wagged as she greeted me.

"Back here, Dad, in the pantry," Jo called back, her voice muffled by the thick plaster walls.

I walked through the front hall, into the kitchen and back to the butler's pantry. I saw Jo on the footstool reaching for a box of cereal high on the top shelf of one of the old maple cabinets.

"Hey, Dad. What are you doing home so early?" She carefully pulled the box down and set it on the worn copper counter.

"Well, I asked for a short shift a while back when I thought you were still going to graduation, and just never changed it. The least we can do is go out to dinner to celebrate."

● ● ●

While I understood her reasons for not attending her graduation ceremony, I selfishly felt robbed of one of the crowning achievements of parenting. I could see how it would be hard for her though. All those teary-eyed mothers with flowers, taking pictures and hugging their kids. It would all be a reminder of the distinct absence of Nora, who most definitely would have loved every minute of a graduation ceremony. I would have needed tissues at the ready, because she surely would have cried multiple times.

"Is Memere still coming up this weekend?" Jo carried the cereal into the kitchen to pour herself a bowl.

"As far as I know. She's looking forward to seeing you, and unless she gets sick for the first time in thirty years, she'll be here." Celestine was just about the healthiest person I'd ever met. Grimly, I thought of how Nora and I often joked about her outliving us.

"Oh good. I think she's planning on us all visiting a new gallery opening in Charlottesville before we go to dinner." Jo munched on her cereal while taking sips of soda between bites.

"Well, I think she was planning on taking us to Gruyere, so get your stomach prepared for that." It was Celestine's favorite place. Classic French fine dining, delicious food…but it always gave Jo and me heartburn for days. Evidently Jo had inherited my pauper's stomach.

"Oh man, we'll have to take some antacids with us, huh?" Jo laughed. It was nice to see her happier.

After the psychic session, Jo had started going regularly to see Luke. It was clear the visits helped her feel better about the loss of her mother, so, while I still had reservations, I gave my blessing. Overall, it seemed to be a positive influence on her. It brought her around in a way I hadn't been able to, which I was grateful for.

"Definitely, but where do you want to go tonight? Just the two of us, wherever you want to go." I watched her contemplate the possibilities and wondered how she really felt about missing the graduation ceremony.

"Let's go to Maria's," she said, looking up at me, and for a moment, with her big grin and a piece of cereal stuck to her chin, she was five years old again. I swallowed the lump in my throat. It seemed unreal that she was going to college in a few short months. It seemed like only yesterday when we'd nervously taken her to kindergarten orientation.

I thought back to that evening. She'd been so nervous that she'd started crying before we met her teacher. I'll never forget her teacher bending down and asking if she was nervous for the first day, then confiding that she was nervous for the first day too. Jo had immediately calmed down, and thus began a love of learning that I hoped would last her through college as well.

Maria's was a small Italian restaurant about twenty minutes north. We drove up and settled into the familiar vinyl booths.

I picked up my menu and looked at it absently. Nick, the owner's son, came over and set down two cups with iced tea.

"So, the usual?" He looked between us expectantly.

"Yes for me," I answered.

"Me too," Jo said.

"Okay, one baked spaghetti for you, Jo, and linguine with red clam sauce for you, coming right up!"

"Dad, I think this dinner will be better than dinner tomorrow, but don't tell Memere, okay?" Jo smiled over the table at me.

"I won't, I promise," I said. "Jo, I am so proud that you are my daughter."

"Dad, no graduation talk, remember?"

"Oh, no, not that. Well, yes that, but no. I'm proud that you like spaghetti, and vinyl booths, and plastic drinking cups over fancy food and cloth napkins."

"Oh, okay." Then she crinkled her eyebrows at me in that way she did when she thought I was clearly out of my mind. We talked and laughed, and while the absence of Nora was always present, somehow in those vinyl booths the space around us was full.

"Dad, are you sure you don't want to come with me some time to talk to Mom?"

"Honey, I'm glad your sessions with Luke are helpful, but I just don't think it's the thing for me. Plus, I'm not swayed by a handsome boy. I'll talk to Nora in my own way."

● ● ●

"Dad!" Jo huffed at me. "I'm not going to him because he's cute!" Her face flushed bright red.

"He is, though, right? I mean he's not my thing, but I could see how someone might find him appealing."

"Jesus, Dad. Gross. I'm not thinking about making out with some boy while talking to my dead Mom." She had stopped eating her spaghetti and was looking at me with the same offended look Nora used to give me when I said something asinine.

"Okay, okay." I held up my hands in placation. "I'm glad it's helping. We'll leave it at that, okay?"

"Okay." Jo reached up and we toasted our plastic cups together in agreement.

Josephine

I felt the familiar coolness wash over me like a breeze. Sometimes it was stronger, chilling me, but today it was gentle, cool, and reassuring. I relaxed my mind and breathed deeply, trying to let myself slip away from the tangible world and toward the energy surrounding me. I breathed in, and there she was: Mom, as she had always been. I couldn't see her yet. The best I managed was a shift in the air, like looking down a highway on a hot day and watching it shimmer in wavy lines. I could feel her, though, the strong scent of her perfume wafting over me. I tried to open myself up and let her speak to me.

We had been working for a while, and Luke had already invited Mom to join us. He assured me she was there, and all I had to do was relax and let her in, which was harder than it sounded.

I had a flash of Dad and me at the gallery opening on graduation weekend. We were walking down a hallway, looking at the art on display. Then I heard my mother say, "One day, it will be your work on those walls." I felt a tear run down my cheek and had to take a moment.

"I'm getting there, I think. Unless I'm just telling myself what I want to hear," I said, dabbing my cheeks with a tissue.

"It's so hard to tell if it is real, or just all in my head, just wishful thinking," I complained, but Luke nodded in agreement.

"I know, I felt the same way when I started to get things from people. I thought I was going crazy, and didn't tell anyone for a long time. Eventually, though, I saw and spoke to my great-grandfather and delivered a message to my mom because he insisted. My mom didn't doubt me after that. It was so specific to her and to him that she had no other explanation. Because you are mostly focusing on your mother, it will be hard for you to know because she is already so close to you."

"Well, whether I am actually talking to her or not, it helps me to feel better about this. So I'm just going to keep doing it, I suppose." I was scared that I wanted to believe so badly I was fooling myself. It was one thing for a trained medium to deliver messages from my dead mother, but another thing entirely for me to get them directly from the source.

Initially, Luke spoke to Mom without focusing on me as a communicator. Once he found out that I smelled her perfume and felt her presence, he asked if I'd like to work on being able to communicate on my own. The idea was both enticing and scary. We worked over the whole summer, but with college starting in just two weeks, this was likely to be my last session for a while.

"I feel her more strongly at home, but here it's less of a physical presence and more of an impression." Luke smiled as I spoke and nodded again.

"That makes sense. At home, Nora has all of her items and energy from those items to draw on. She left her energy in those things over a lifetime of caring for them. That energy well can then be used to make stronger contact with you."

"I'm nervous about starting school, and whether I'll be able to do this on my own." I couldn't meet his eyes.

"You'll be fine. Honestly, it takes most people years to get as far as you have. While most people have the ability to connect with the energy around us, most people also suppress that ability their entire lives. You've chosen to let go of that suppression, but it takes a long time to fully connect. It can be scary and overwhelming. Plus, let's be honest, being open to energy means you are more affected by the people around you, and lots of people have energy that can be toxic to others. Closing yourself off is sometimes a protective measure."

When I looked up, Luke was smiling his crooked smile, and his warmth made me feel better immediately. I certainly still felt an attraction to Luke. Dad wasn't entirely wrong about that.

* * *

But I suppressed those feelings in order to connect to my mom. Crushes and connecting to your dead mom just didn't seem to go together. I stood to leave.

"Thanks. I'm not sure how things will be with school starting, but I'm going to try to come as often as I can."

"I hope you will, and you can always call if you just want to chat, even if it's about art. I'm going to miss our sessions, and talking with you. You definitely have the ability to become a medium if you choose that path, but if you don't, then I am always here to help, even just as a friend."

"Thanks, Luke. You've helped me so much. I will definitely keep in touch." I hugged him, feeling his comforting presence wrap around me like a soft blanket.

"Alright, and make sure you invite me to your first gallery showing!" He walked me out into the waiting area.

On the drive home, I thought about starting at UVA. This summer was one of insulated safety. I'd retreated to the safety of Luke's sessions, painting, and riding. I hadn't really talked to any of my high school friends. After giving up texting, I felt relieved instead of cut off. Most of the texts I got weren't important, and anything that was could be left in a voicemail. In fact, I still had the last voicemail from my mom stored in my phone, and I'd also recorded it onto a file on my computer. It was from the morning the day she died. When I got home, I sat in the driveway and listened to it again, savoring her chipper, unknowing voice.

"Jo, it's Mom. Don't forget dinner with Memere tonight. Think about where you want to go. I've got to run out this afternoon and get a few things for Memere's visit, but should be back in time to feed the animals so you don't have to. I love you, bye."

I sat in the car for a moment after listening. Sometimes the longing for Mom was stronger, and sometimes it was just a dull ache in the background. Only occasionally, like when I was with Luke and already speaking to her, or riding and focused on that instead, did that longing go away completely.

I felt a wave of grief wash over me. I wanted her advice on starting college. I wanted to hug her. I knew I would never feel her touch again. Mom had always been a touchy-feely mom. It definitely could be embarrassing, but deep down I'd always loved it. When I was little, sometimes she would pepper my face

● ● ●

with kisses until I started to laugh. She hadn't done it since I was maybe ten or eleven. I suppose she felt I wouldn't have liked her rapid fire kisses anymore. Here I sat, at seventeen, wishing my mom could pepper my face with kisses until I was spit-covered and laughing. Instead, I was sobbing into my steering wheel, afraid and alone, nowhere near ready to face college, and whatever came after that.

Eleanor

S ummer was always my favorite season. Everything was green and lush, and the air hummed with the calls of birds and insects. The steady drone of cicadas in the evening was always a familiar and welcome sound. People around me always complained about the heat, the humidity, the rain, the lack of rain. I never did. Summer always brought out dreamy memories of summertime as a child. Going to the coast, swimming in the ocean. Sailing on the bay. My father never owned a boat, but he had plenty of friends who did. The smell of the wood and canvas, and the sound of the water rushing beneath the bow. I loved it as a child, and now I could slip away into memories as vivid as real life any time I wanted. Memory and reality were startlingly close now in my consciousness, the stark difference between them in life made hazy in death.

One such memory was of sailing with my parents on July 4th weekend when I was fourteen, about to start high school that fall. We were out with some of Dad's international connections. I honestly had very dim memories of them, but I had vivid memories of the day.

It was warm. I could feel the sun prickling my skin and turning it slightly pink. I pressed on my arm and could see the pale imprint of my finger, promising a bit of a tan later, or more likely just freckles. I held onto the lines at the edge of the boat

● ● ●

as we turned, spray flying up from the bow of the ship and misting me with salty water. I looked over the bay and watched a pelican dive after a fish. I was always amazed at how cumbersome they appeared on land, contrasted with how, in the air, they could fold their bodies and plummet into the water with lightning speed, surfacing with a prize in their gullet, or flying off to the next target.

As I watched the pelicans that day, a judge Dad knew came over and stood beside me. He placed one of his hands over mine and leaned into me. I could smell his stale coffee breath over the salty air.

"You certainly have grown up, haven't you, Eleanor?" His leering smile revealed tobacco-stained teeth.

"I...yes." I froze and found I could barely form words. I desperately wanted to remove my hand from his sweaty grip but couldn't move. His other hand brushed my hair from my face, and he leaned forward as my father's voice cut through, breaking through my panicked mind.

"Paul, come up here with the adults. No need to hang out with teenage girls, is there?" I turned to look at my Dad. His tone was jovial, but his face was menacing in its intensity.

"Of course, Charles! No reason at all." His eyes moved over my body before leaving for the bow of the ship. I felt nauseated and wanted to disappear. I looked out across the water at the pelicans again, longing to be able to change my shape that easily. To be able to fold myself up and disappear under the waves. Even without the attention of men older than your father, there is an awkwardness that only girls during puberty feel. I often wished my body didn't exist, that I could just shed it and exist without it. Turns out I could, I just had to die first.

In life, I tried to hide my body to no avail. The more I hid, the more men seemed to notice it. I was petite but not necessarily slender. I wore baggy t-shirts and sweatshirts, but it was no use. Once I began to curve in certain places, men stopped noticing my face and started staring at me and nodding when I spoke, eyes never lifting to mine. Sometimes I would test them and say something absurd to see if they were actually listening. They never were.

Neal was different from the start. On our first date, he looked at nothing but my eyes, and when I said my absurd statement as a test, he caught it right away. We were talking about flying. He had never been in an airplane, while I had traveled to Europe every year since I could remember. I told him I wanted to be a professional skydiver, and I remember his eyebrows furrowing before he responded.

"So, what's the point of flying in a plane if you're just going to jump out?" He didn't seem to care about the flash of my cleavage, and didn't agree with everything I said just to sleep with me. He honestly wanted to know how my mind worked. I laughed and lifted my glass to his.

"Cheers to that! I see no point in jumping out of a plane either. I just wanted to see if you were paying attention." I smiled at him, and although he looked thoroughly puzzled, he clinked my glass with his and smiled back.

I watched Jo go through that change, but in a different way. She was built like her father: slight, but strong. She was not what you would call curvy, but Jo was definitely feminine, with fine bones and features. She always fretted that she looked too boyish. When Cece began to develop into a head-turning kind of girl, the fractures in their friendship started.

It's hard as a mother. You can't pick your child's best friend. You can't tell them, "Oh no, this one is going to hurt you. Don't pick her." I saw it in middle school, when Cece grew up fast. Her body changed, and she embraced the attention. It was likely the most attention she'd ever received other than when she was at our house. Her family was barely functional.

Her father was a disabled veteran and dealt with his PTSD by drinking and hunting. Her mother worked full time and tried her best to give herself to her children, but with five kids, her love was spread pretty thin. There was always a part of Cece that was jealous of Jo, understandably. We were very comfortable and had only Jo to spend our love and money on. Cece spent most of her time with us during the summers. We tried our best to make her feel part of our family, but she knew eventually she would have to go home.

Once puberty came along, Cece was suddenly the center of attention, and she had something Jo didn't have. Breasts are an amazing anomaly. How a glorified pair of udders became the focus of so much attention was always beyond me. Whatever the case, Cece had them, and Jo didn't. Unfortunately

• • •

for Jo, that never changed. Funny how a simple fluke of anatomy can start to chip away at a friendship without anyone really knowing it.

I saw Jo distance herself from everyone after my death, including Cece. I understood, but worried. When Jo found Luke and began communicating with me, it brought me joy but also concern. I didn't want her to hold on to me and end up holding herself back. I wanted her to live her life, which I suppose wasn't really so different from any parent watching their child prepare for college.

Parenting is always a balance. The goal is to create a functional adult, but in doing that, you find they slip away from you, taking pieces of you with them. In letting them go, you have to push down urges and desires of your own. The urge to kiss them in front of their friends; the desire to shelter them from everything. Then there is the terrible knowledge that they will at some point experience pain you can't prevent. It's an awful thing, the evolution of your role as a parent. In the beginning, it is so simple: give love and protect them. At some point, you have to face the terrible knowledge that in order to let them grow, you can't protect them. You can't always keep them safe from harm, and sometimes you are the one to cause the pain. These thoughts washed over me as I watched Jo weeping in her car listening to my last voicemail, unable to comfort her.

● ● ●

Neal

Jo moved into her dorm room on what had to be the hottest day of the year so far. By the time we brought everything in, I was sweating in places I didn't know could sweat. Luckily, she was placed in a dorm with AC, which we cranked as high as we could.

I once thought the moment we brought her home from the hospital was the single most terrifying moment in parenthood. I was wrong. That moment—the most terrifying, heart-stopping moment of a parent's life—is the moment you leave your only daughter alone at college.

It helped slightly knowing she was going to be within five miles of me while I was on campus. This turned out to be a major benefit to working at UVA's hospital. I also fiddled with my schedule to ensure that I was doing more classroom work and less work on the ER floor this year. I loved the floor, but classroom hours meant I would be there when Jo was up and about, and we might be able to meet for lunch.

A knock sounded on the door frame, and a tall girl with dark brown skin and waist-length braids cautiously stood in the doorway. Jo beamed. "You must be Mikayla! I'm Jo." Mikayla smiled, revealing dimples and perfectly straight teeth.

"Hi, Jo. It's nice to actually meet you instead of just talking through email!" The girls chattered until a male voice from the hallway grunted.

● ● ●

"Mikayla! I'd rather not hold this box for the entirety of your college experience, so could you please move from the doorway?"

Mikayla's Dad rounded the corner and set down an admittedly giant box which sounded as it landed on the floor like it might be filled with stones.

"Books. I got the books. Go figure." He held out a hand for me to shake. "I'm Lucian, nice to meet you." A woman came up behind carrying an equally large box that appeared from her effort to be much lighter than Lucian's. She carefully placed it on top of the book box with a smile that was the mirror image of Mikayla's.

"I'm Jacklyn, and it appears our daughters are roommates!" The girls were chatting excitedly in the hallway.

"I'm Neal. It's so nice to meet both of you."

After our introduction, we turned to conversation, and it was revealed that by the craziest of chances Lucian and I had grown up in the same small town of Catonsville, Maryland a few years apart. We continued chatting until I realized how hungry I was.

After much discussion, we eventually decided to go together to a Mexican place nearby for dinner. It was walking distance, so we filed out toward the restaurant, Mikayla and her parents in front, Jo and I walking together just behind.

"So, honey, are you nervous?" I asked as we walked.

"No, mostly just sweaty." She puffed out a breath, smiling as she pushed me with her elbow. "I am, a little," she admitted, "but Mikayla seems nice, and you'll be close by."

"Mikayla does seem nice, and with a dad from Catonsville, you can never go wrong!" Jo rolled her eyes. "I will be close, and anytime you want to use me for a free lunch, go ahead. Just don't bring your laundry."

"Haha. Don't worry, I'll just bring that home with me on weekends," she quipped back, giving me a grin. I thought about my college experience as we walked the rest of the way and hoped Jo was more prepared for this environment than I was.

I went to a private boy's school, but only because my father was their maintenance supervisor, which allowed for a steeply discounted tuition. I always felt like a bit of a fish out of

● ● ●

water around the kids I went to school with. I went home to a small two bedroom bungalow in Catonsville, while they went home to luxurious homes in and around DC, or boarded in the dorms. Many of them were senator's kids who lived on a different wavelength than I did. The feeling of not quite belonging didn't change much when I went to UVA. I felt like an impostor for a long time. Like someone would pick me out of a crowd and notice that I didn't belong there. Nora helped me get over that. She came from that world, but looked at it with enough perspective to see how much of a closed society it was.

She always told me I belonged more than the others because I'd earned it, while they just happened to be lucky enough to be born into the right family. I think her difficult relationship with her father made her resent the super wealthy and their self-absorbed tendencies. Nora was always my biggest cheerleader. I hoped Jo would find someone like that. I hoped college wouldn't grind her down and make her conform to what society told her to be.

We arrived at the already packed restaurant and by some miracle only waited a few minutes for a table.

"I called ahead," Jacklyn explained.

"Good thinking. Nora always did that too," I replied.

"I am sorry about your loss. Mikayla told me," she said, placing a hand on my shoulder, her perfectly manicured hand gently draped there for a moment. "The girls talked a lot over email and she mentioned it to me. I hope it's okay."

"Of course. I'd rather it be in the open, and I think Jo is through the worst of it."

"My mom passed this year and my dad has been a wreck without her. I think after sixty years together, he was just unprepared for how to live on his own. He ended up moving in with us, because he just wasn't taking care of himself well enough."

"I'm so sorry for your loss as well. It's true, I never realized how many little things she did in everyday life that I never even noticed."

We settled into a booth and looked over the menus. I heard bubbly laughter between Jo and Mikayla and looked up to see them sitting next to each other, heads together as they watched a cat video on Mikayla's phone.

• • •

"I'm glad Jo is rooming with Mikayla. College can be hard, so I'm glad she is with someone like her, someone with parents as kind as you two." I was not normally this forthcoming and heartfelt. Jo looked up at me with eyebrows raised.

"Thanks, Neal. I think we can agree that we feel the same way," Lucian replied.

"UVA wasn't really our first choice for her. You know, demographically speaking, it will be harder for her here than at some other colleges, but she was determined to come here, to prove herself, I suppose."

I hadn't really considered it that way. While I'd felt like I didn't belong, on the surface I could hide it because I looked like most of the people on campus. People wouldn't assume I didn't belong just by looking at me. Mikayla, with her dark skin and braids, would immediately appear different. She couldn't hide any feeling of not belonging under the surface. I hoped the girls would be able to support each other and navigate the minefield of college successfully.

We ate our meal, and Lucian and I reminisced about our shared neighborhood back home and how it was growing up back then, which bored both Jo and Mikayla terribly. There was plenty of eye rolling and sighing going on from their side of the table. It made me happy to see her look so normal after so long.

I pulled up to my empty home later that evening. Mrs Norris barked and wagged over to the car and back to me as I stood on the porch waiting for her to do her business. She seemed confused, and I realized she must be looking for Jo. Once I brought her in, the house was quiet, though I heard the characteristic thump of a cat jumping off the bed that portended complaining for dinner. I filled their bowls and sat in my chair across from Nora's.

The sun had fallen behind the mountains but hadn't completely set, and the sky was a pale purple color. To the southwest, a storm cloud hung over the ridge, flashing and ominous. I thought of my journey as a parent up until this point. All the fear and joy mixed into every major moment in Jo's life, from her first teetering steps to the first time she drove off by herself. This was the goal, right? To make a functional adult who leaves home.

● ● ●

We are told this imaginary endpoint of the next eighteen years, but that's a lie. I was going to be a worried parent until I died. Potentially even after if Jo and her medium were to be believed. I told myself I should trust her to handle this, as she had handled everything else in her life up to now. However, as I sat there alone, all I wanted to do was get in the car, drive back, scoop her up, and bring her home. Instead, I showered and went to bed.

I lay there sleepless for a long time, more worried than I had ever been in my life as a father. The anxiety of knowing she was so far from me made it impossible to go to sleep. When she was little, and even when she was older and in high school, this kind of blind anxiety would sometimes take me over. It was easy to remedy then, because I could just go upstairs and peek into her room. Seeing the breathing lump under the covers, draped in other sleeping furry lumps, would immediately ease my anxiety and allow me to go back downstairs and drift peacefully off to sleep.

I saw so many things at work in the ER. So many people's children, hurting and scared. It made me fear more for my own. I saw on a daily basis what could happen in an instant to anyone, regardless of how hard someone tried to protect them. If I was truly honest with myself, that was another reason I'd opted to take more classroom hours. The thought of Jo coming into my ER made me shake and feel nauseous.

I resisted the urge to call Jo and looked at the clock. It was one in the morning, and the world at large was asleep. I glanced around the bed. Animals surrounded me, dozing happily, oblivious to the increasingly terrible scenarios I was making up in my head. I got up, which caused a groan and sigh from Mrs Norris, followed by a stretch that included taking over my pillow. I walked to the kitchen and made myself some chamomile tea. It was as I turned to go back to bed that I saw Nora, sitting in her chair, looking out the window. As I squinted into the darkened room, I could swear I saw Grimalkin in her lap. I nearly dropped my mug, but when I looked back again she was gone. It must have been the moonlight coming in through the windows, making odd shadows. It was impossible, because Grimalkin was asleep in my bed, and Nora was most definitely not sitting there.

● ● ●

I shakily carried the unspilled portion of chamomile back to the bedroom with the intent of lulling myself to sleep with a few thrilling journal articles. As I settled into bed, I reached over to pet Grimalkin and realized that he wasn't moving. When I turned on the light, it became clear that he was not breathing. I grabbed my stethoscope from the hook on the door and confirmed. He was dead. Curled up, by all appearances peaceful, but most definitely dead.

Eleanor

I felt him first. I could feel the weight of his body as he hopped in my lap and nestled in, purring. The animals had largely ignored me since I couldn't fulfill my major roles as a human, which were petting and feeding them. It was strange to experience touch after months of nothing. I looked down at the form in my lap and reached a tentative hand down to pet him. I could feel his soft tabby fur as clearly as anything. He lifted his head and rubbed his chin against my hand, his characteristic loud rumbling purr vibrating against my legs. The sensation after months of nothing was intense. Either I was coming back to life (unlikely), or Grimalkin had passed into my plane of existence.

I sat for a long time basking in the joy of touching something. My exchanges with my father were so abstract and ethereal, they were still hard for me to fully understand. This confirmed my suspicion that we must lose more and more of our earthly form the longer we are unattached to our bodies. My father was all images and flashes of light. I couldn't really make out his human form at all, other than in the memories he shared, which played like movies around me. I could feel him, but not in a solid, direct way. I suppose it must be the way a spider feels when an insect is trapped in its web. It may not see it immediately but instead feels a tug, a pull, drawing its attention toward the movement. Grimalkin felt solid and real. He was very

• • •

93

much there with me. I relished the contact and sat for a long time just touching him and listening to his rumble.

I was so absorbed in this new companion, I almost missed Neal wandering around the kitchen making tea. Neal often had trouble sleeping when he was under stress. I'd watched them earlier that day as they packed several boxes into the car to move Jo into her dorm. Sweating and grumbling, they'd driven away into the sweltering heat of the August day. Of course he was worried. Maybe we would have lain awake together talking. Perhaps with an empty house we would have made love to try to release that anxious energy. I pondered this and thought that, aside from the love-making, not being tied to a physical form was a benefit when it came to anxiety about our daughter. I could drift towards her at will.

Her work with the medium, Luke, allowed for a much easier time connecting to her. Whether that was all Jo got out of it or not, I wasn't so sure. Luke was undeniably attractive, and her feelings for him were suppressed but still there. Nevertheless, thanks to him, I could focus on the web of energy around me and tug on her line with my mind. I would feel myself drawn steadily towards her, floating along on the cord of her intention. I did this now as I kicked the ghost form of Grimalkin off my lap and discovered that even ghost cats are annoyed when you do this before they are ready to leave.

With steady concentration, I found her sleeping in her dorm room with a person whom I guessed was her roommate asleep in the bunk above her. I watched over Jo's dreaming form and wished I could tell Neal that she was just fine, thus allowing him to drift off and sleep as peacefully as she was at the moment.

Neal was always a more anxious parent than I was. He was more suspicious of people and their intentions toward our one and only daughter. I don't know if it was from working in ER for so long, or his less privileged upbringing.

While I enjoyed the benefit of the copious safety net afforded me by class and wealth, Neal had lived his life without that safety net, and therefore had much more fear of falling than I ever did. He also saw horrific things happen to people all the time in his work. The black and white images of broken bones, gunshots and other atrocities that I looked at all day were separated enough from the blood and gore of those injuries to

• • •

provide a decent buffer. For Neal, they were much more tangible and real.

As Jo was growing up, I would often feel him tossing and turning beside me, only to then hear him rise out of bed and creep up the stairs to Jo's room. He would only stay up there for a minute or so. Then he would creep back down and settle into bed, snoring within minutes of returning. How I longed to be able to give him that peace of mind now and let him know that she was okay, that he could rest.

Instead, as I returned to the house, Neal was wrapping Grimalkin's cold body in a soft blanket. Grimalkin had come with the property, so we had no idea of his exact age, but he'd been an adult when we took over his care, and we'd lived here for nearly sixteen years, so by all accounts he was quite elderly. As I watched Neal carry his small body out into the moonlight, I wondered how he would muster the strength to tell Jo. Grimalkin had always been more her cat than ours. Maybe his old body was only holding on until she left. He carefully lowered Grimalkin's body into our garage chest freezer. A grim job indeed, but one that Neal did with care. Most likely he'd call a cremation service in the morning and eventually Grimalkin's ashes would rest next to mine on the mantle.

After he finished, Neal sat in a chair on the porch in his pajamas, listening to the night around him. His head turned as a fox vixen began to call for a mate that failed to return her mournful cries. Neal wept alone on the porch, head in his hands, body curled onto his knees. Through his sobs, he kept repeating my name, and like the fox in the woods, his cries went unanswered, but not unheard.

● ● ●

Josephine

Meeting Mikayla that first day helped clear away my fears about starting school. She was one of very few people I'd ever met who made me feel instantly comfortable. Knowing I would come back to our little dorm room made meeting new people and the anxiety that came with it much easier to deal with. Orientation ended, and with the first day of school came an introduction that would change everything.

Colin McCleary walked in ten minutes late the first day of Drawing I, and he chose the seat next to me. He had dark hair, pale grey eyes, and a body that was muscular without being too bulky.

"Hey there, I'm Colin, and what is your name?" He smiled over at me, tilting his head to the side in the most unnerving way. I felt fluttery and shaky but attempted a human response.

"Hey there. I'm Josephine, but most people just call me Jo." I noticed my voice was a good bit higher than normal. *Breathe, Jo, damn. He's just some boy in a class. Just breathe,* I told myself.

"Hmm, Jo. You're too pretty to call Jo. I'm going to stick with Josephine," he replied. "Is that okay?" He leaned towards me slightly, and I could smell a mixture of soap, cigarettes, and a slightly masculine scent that made my face feel warm.

"Umm, okay, that's okay I guess." *Wow, so far, super smooth,* I chided myself. Why did this guy make me so nervous? I could handle and direct a twelve hundred pound animal over a course of three-foot tall solid wooden fences at a gallop.

Our professor began to speak, and we got our tools out for the charcoal project she wanted us to start. It was a basic exercise, one I could do without much thinking, which left my thoughts available to wander over to Colin. His hands were clean and uncalloused, nails trimmed neatly. I tried to hide the shaking of my own hands as I worked, noting their various scars, untidy nails and calloused from riding and barn work.

The next few weeks of school went by in a blur. I met so many people and forgot so many names that I felt completely overwhelmed. My classes were amazing, and I finally started to feel like myself again after so many months of grieving. I was enrolled in a mix of studio and art history courses. The art history courses were a little boring after life with a grandmother who ran galleries and discussed artist history with me from the time I could speak. My studio classes were obviously my favorite. The art teacher at my high school was wonderful, but this was different. It all seemed so much more official. Plus, the other students were so good it made me both nervous and excited to be working alongside them. Colin, as I learned, was a psychology major. This studio class was an elective for him. Despite this, he was irritatingly talented, and I found myself looking forward to seeing him in class twice a week.

He complimented my work and often leaned close enough to touch me without needing to. The way he smiled and spoke to me made me think he might be flirting, but I was unsure of myself. I noticed how other girls responded to him, opening their shoulders, lifting their breasts and smiling at him. I wasn't sure he would want someone like me. Most of the other girls in our class had unique style and cool haircuts. They seemed much more sophisticated than me. However, Colin consistently chose to work next to me.

One Thursday after class, he walked with me to lunch. Colin sat down next to me on a bench, and we ate our sandwiches while we talked. Somehow, we ended up on the subject of my mom, and I told him everything, with the exception of Luke and communicating with her. I didn't want him to think I was a crazy person and bringing up Luke around Colin felt wrong.

● ● ●

"Wow, you are so strong to get through that." He reached over and held my hand. His hands were surprisingly strong. When he touched my skin, it felt like I had grabbed an electric fence. My whole body went rigid, and my heart raced.

"Thanks. I guess I didn't really have a choice. I can't just lay down and quit, can I?"

"You know, you aren't really like most girls. I like that. Most girls are so caught up in themselves, all they think about is what they are going to wear and how to fool people with makeup. You are just you. You're real. I find that sexy." That last word made something happen to my body that I couldn't put into words if I tried.

"Um—uh, thank you," I said, tucking a stray hair that may or may not have been loose behind my ear.

"Would you want to go out this weekend? There is a great restaurant I'd like to take you to." Colin looked over at me, his eyes focused on mine. He cocked his head again, waiting for my reply.

"Sure, that would be nice. I was planning on heading home for the weekend, but I could wait and leave Saturday morning. Does tomorrow work?"

"Does seven o'clock sound good?" He pulled out his phone and glanced at me.

"Yeah, that works." I gave him my cell number, then got up and walked to my next class. I could feel his eyes on me as I left. It made me feel good—maybe even sexy for the first time in my life.

When I told Mikayla about it, she went full girlfriend on me, and we spent the evening picking out my outfit. I had limited options because most of my wardrobe was jeans and t-shirts. Mikayla had amazing fashion sense and amazing clothes, but she was nearly a foot taller than me, and none of her clothes had any chance of fitting my tiny body.

"Okay, I know what we need to do." Mikayla grinned. "You are so nice and petite, I know just the store. They have tons of cute things, but none of it ever looks right on my giant frame." Mikayla was 5'10" and gorgeous, with balanced curves and a muscular frame.

"What are you talking about? You look like a freaking model!"

● ● ●
98

"Well, models aren't shaped like me at all. But you, you're perfect for this! We've got to get you out of jeans and t-shirts and into a skirt!"

"Okay. Okay. I give in." I laughed as she dragged me out into the sunshine for a shopping spree. Three hours later, we stood in the changing room of a boutique and I studied myself in the mirror, unconvinced. I wore a flowy floral skirt that stopped mid-thigh, paired with a black crossover tank top. I did indeed look different. Mikayla gushed.

"You are so tiny and cute! You look incredible, and he won't be able to resist you!" I had to admit I felt good in it. I looked like a proper girl. *If only Cece could see me now*, I thought bitterly. She had tried and tried to get me to wear more feminine things, but I'd never really given in. When Cece tried to dress me up, it somehow always made me feel like there was something wrong with me that she wanted to fix. With Mikayla, it felt like she was encouraging me to embrace a part of myself I didn't know was there. Growing up, Cece and I were both self-avowed tomboys, preferring jeans with holes and ratty shirts to dresses.

Then, seemingly overnight in middle school, Cece got boobs. After that, she wanted to wear tighter and tighter clothes. Once we hit high school, she either wore tight jeans or a skirt, and her necklines were as low as school would allow. Guys always saw her. They always looked at her and right past me.

Admittedly, the guys in my high school were not what I wanted anyway. They were mostly farm boys with thick legs and chewing tobacco in their back pockets. They certainly weren't going to discuss how the light hit a tree at sunrise, or how shadows fell across someone's face. The remaining boys were just as unlikely to talk to someone they felt attracted to as I was, leaving us in a stalemate of mutual fear. Then came Luke, for whom my feelings were still complex and so intermixed with Mom that I didn't even know what to think about him. Plus, he had never indicated any interest other than friendly professionalism.

Colin was different. He was confident and sensitive. He saw beauty in things. I could tell by the way he drew, from his use of line and shadow, and the way he really looked at things when deciding how to draw them. Now he was looking at me, and he saw beauty in me. It made me feel special, and noticed, for the first time I could remember.

I tossed and turned in bed that night, thinking of Colin and the way his hand had curved around mine. It was a strange relief to be kept awake by possibility and anticipation, instead of regrets and memory.

• • •

Neal

I came home from lecturing and set my keys down on the kitchen counter along with my bag. I had an exciting weekend of grading ahead of me, and was going to start by putting it off until tomorrow morning. It was my first Friday night alone in a long time. Jo had called this morning and told me she was going to come up tomorrow instead of tonight. She had plans to go out with some friends. I was happy she was opening up socially, but worried all the same. With the exception of Mikayla, I was unlikely to meet most of her college friends until they were well established in her life. Yet another sign of my waning influence on her and her transition into adulthood.

It appeared that Jo was adapting well to school. She was socializing more in the past three weeks than she had in the past three months here at home. I suppose the change in scenery helped her let go of some of her grief, allowing a welcome escape. I must admit, there were days when I wanted to get in the car and drive away, letting new scenery and new people fill the empty space left behind by Nora's death. I knew I couldn't, and deep down I knew it wouldn't fill that void, but the idea was tempting just the same. Still, a distraction like the one Jo had right now would have been welcome. As it was, I soothed myself with routine instead.

The quiet house stirred as the animals awoke to greet me, and I heard the distinctive thumps of a dog and a cat jumping down from my bed, then the *tip tap* of nails on the hardwood floor. Mrs. Norris whined until I let her out, and I watched her romp happily off in search of the perfect spot to pee. Hobbit hopped up onto the counter (where she was forbidden, of course) and wound around my bag, knocking it to the ground.

Three weeks had passed since Grimalkin's death, and I still hadn't told Jo. She'd come home last weekend to do laundry, work in her studio upstairs, feed horses, and ride Callie. She was so busy I wasn't sure she noticed. Grimalkin was somewhat aloof in life, and he did have a habit of wandering off and not coming in at night, preferring to spend his evenings in the barn hunting mice. I felt guilty. Initially, I hesitated because I didn't want to upend Jo's first few weeks at school. I was afraid the loss of Grimalkin might reopen the grief from Nora's passing. Now I hesitated because I knew she would be angry that I hadn't told her sooner. It was a trap I was unlikely to escape from easily.

A blue sedan pulled into the driveway and parked by the barn. A figure got out and entered the barn. I watched as the horses drifted over from the pasture in anticipation of their evening meal. Jo had lined up a high school acquaintance of hers to come and feed the horses twice daily on weekdays. She'd also agreed to meet the farrier at the barn once every six weeks for their feet to get done, and the vet for any visits. The girl was dependable but never seemed to talk to me more than was required. In exchange for her work, she had access to Briony and Georgia as much as she wanted for riding and shows. It was essentially a free work lease on two excellent horses, and a good deal for everyone involved, so I was told.

To me, it meant they got exercise and I didn't have to do much other than occasionally feed them on weekends if Jo couldn't. Horses were nice to look at, but they were always Nora and Jo's thing. They made me nervous up close. They were too big to be such nervous creatures themselves.

Other than the distant presence of the girl in the barn, whose name I should have learned by now, I was alone as usual. The house was completely silent aside from the purring and crunching of kitty kibble coming from the pantry, and I heard my stomach rumble. I pondered dinner and wandered through the kitchen, trying to decide what to make for myself. I finally decided to cook a grilled cheese and bowl of tomato soup. There

● ● ●

was no one around to chide me. Nora would have insisted I was eating lunch food and it was not adequate for dinner. With a small pang of guilt for how much I enjoyed not being admonished for my food choices, I relished my simple meal in the living room while watching TV.

As an only child, being alone was something I was comfortable with. If I couldn't find anyone outside to play with when I was growing up, I would play alone in my room, making up extensive fantasies often involving my Star Wars or GI Joe figures. As I got older, I would listen to the radio and make mix tapes. I'd listen for hours, trying to catch a certain song and hit record right as it came on. Now anyone could call up any song they wanted from the internet at any time, with no problem.

After finishing my dinner, I put my dishes in the sink and looked over at the dining room window. It had been three weeks since I saw Nora sitting there with Grimalkin in her lap. I still wasn't sure whether the thought of it was reassuring or frightening, but her chair sat empty tonight, filling me with the much more familiar feeling of loss that her absence always brought.

There was a howling and scratching at the door. I let Mrs. Norris in and washed my dishes after feeding her and freshening her water. She always dripped drool and debris that was caught in her jowls into her bowl every time she drank. I patted her as she happily crunched away at her meal. With everyone fed, I decided to head to bed early, relishing a hot shower and settling in with a book. Mrs. Norris relaxed in her new spot with her head on Nora's pillow, and Hobbit lay down on my legs purring. I read until my eyelids were heavy, then turned out the light before nestling into my pillow.

After what felt like only a few seconds, I was jarred awake by my phone ringing. I glanced at the clock and saw it was just after eleven. I was still groggy as I picked up my phone to answer, but when I heard the voice on the other end of the line, I was wide awake within seconds.

Josephine

The day leading up to my date with Colin dragged by, with seemingly endless hours on the clock. He wasn't in any of my classes on Fridays, so we only communicated by phone. He accepted my habit of not texting and called to confirm where and when we would meet up. Finally, after classes finished, I headed to my dorm to meet up with Mikayla and get ready.

"Oooh, you look perfect!" she exclaimed after we finished. I even allowed her to guide me in putting on some eyeshadow and mascara.

"The nude lip with your eye make-up really highlights your blue eyes. I just wish I had more stuff in shades that would suit you, but this works." Mikayla looked at me thoughtfully after completing her work.

"Thanks, Mikayla. I've never really known how to do make-up at all. You're amazing!" She was. Mikayla was rapidly becoming a good friend to me, and I only hoped I was a good friend to her. She was strong and confident, and always looked perfect without seeming like she even tried. She turned heads on campus and guys took notice of her, but it was different from when I was friends with Cece. With Cece, as soon as a guy paid attention to her, I disappeared and was left to my own devices. And if a guy happened to pay attention to me, she fell all over herself to attract more attention from him. Mikayla never did that. In fact, she didn't even acknowledge most guys even if they were obviously flirting.

"So, are you ready? You should head out soon if you want to be there at seven. Unless you plan on playing hard to get and want to make him wait." Mikayla said with a grin.

"Yeah, you know I'm not nearly that smooth. I'm ready. Also, I'm planning on coming back here, and I'm most definitely not planning on sleeping with him on the first date, so don't avoid the room, okay?"

"Okay." She laughed. "You're not going to hang a sock on the door and bump the headboard all night?" She was cackling now.

"No!" I said, laughing until my sides started to hurt. "God no! This is my first date ever. I'm not going all in right away!"

"I know, I know, I just had to give you shit before you left, get you to relax a little. Call me if he is super boring and you need me to come rescue you, okay?"

"I don't think I'll need rescuing. He is so not boring, but it's good to know just in case." I hugged her and headed out into the evening air. It was still warm on my skin at the moment, one of those perfect days in early September before the chill of autumn really set in.

As I approached the restaurant, Colin walked in ahead of me, not realizing I was there yet. He said something to the hostess, and I watched her laugh and lean into him. I felt a flash of anger but quickly calmed down, reminding myself that he was going out with me, not her. Colin turned as I approached and opened the door for me.

"I got us a good table. I know the hostess here, and she is getting it ready for us now." He smiled and put his arm around my waist, pulling me against him. "You look beautiful," he said, considering me.

We settled into the table—which I had to admit was good—near a window, a two seater set slightly apart from the other tables. It turned out to be Moroccan food, something I'd never had, and judging by the smell wafting through the place, and looking at the food on other people's plates, it promised to

• • •

be delicious. I picked over the menu and tried to decide what I wanted. It all looked tasty. Finally, I decided what I wanted just as the waitress came up to the table. I handed the menu back and abruptly realized I now had no excuse not to talk.

"So, you're a Virginia native, right?" Colin looked unruffled and cool across the table.

"Born and raised. How about you? Are you from Virginia?"

"No, my dad moved us all over for years, but now he works in DC. I hate northern Virginia, but my parents didn't want me to be more than two hours away from them, so this was the compromise. My older brother is here at the medical school, so they figured he could keep an eye on me."

"Why does he need to keep an eye on you?" I dropped my eyes as I asked, maybe not wanting the answer.

"Oh, well, I haven't exactly been an angel, if you know what I mean," he replied with a grin. "But enough about me. Tell me about you. Everything about you. I want to know all of it."

We ate as the food came, and it was every bit as delicious as it had smelled. I attempted to eat without spilling all over myself, which meant conversation was doubly hard.

"My cat died, but my dad hasn't told me yet." I blurted out between bites.

"So your dad isn't all that attentive?" He leaned in, and his intensity made me freeze for a moment.

"I wouldn't say that. No. I think he just doesn't want to because he doesn't want to hurt me."

"Of course. Nobody would want to hurt you." His tone went flat for a moment, and he set money down for the bill.

"I can walk you to your dorm if you'd like. It's dark out now, and I would feel safer if I knew you were not out there alone," he said, holding my hand outside the restaurant.

"I'd like that, thank you." He held my waist as we walked, and I nestled against him.

"Do you mind if I have a cigarette?" he asked as we were walking. I hated cigarettes but figured we were outside and agreed. The acrid smoke was luckily carried away by the breeze, and his warmth next to me felt wonderful as we walked. The night air had turned chilly, and I appreciated his arm around my

• • •

bare shoulders. We reached my dorm building in what seemed like no time at all. Colin put out his cigarette on the wall of the building, dropping the butt in the grass. It irritated me, but I said nothing.

"So, are you going to invite me in?" He grinned and leaned against the wall.

"Oh, sure, I suppose you can walk me inside." Once inside the confines of the dorm hallway, the smell of cigarettes was stronger on him, but as he put his arm around me, I realized I didn't mind as much as I should.

We reached my room, and he watched intently as I unlocked my door. It was just after ten o'clock, but Mikayla was still out, evidently not paying attention to my request and giving me extra time with the room.

"Would you like to look at my sketchbook?" I tried not to sound nervous.

"I'd love that," he said, stepping through the door as I swung it open.

We sat on the bed and I pulled out my book. He glanced at it before leaning over to kiss me. First just on the lips, then pushing through them with his tongue to kiss me fully. His mouth pressed hard against mine, and the taste of cigarettes was overwhelming. I pushed him away and tried to catch my breath.

"Don't act like this isn't what you want," he said, pulling me in again.

"It…I don't know, it's just too much," I said as he leaned closer.

"Too much? No, this isn't too much—you are too much, with your skirt, and legs, and lips. I need you." He panted as he pushed me down against the bed. I couldn't move. I could feel his weight pressing me down, and his hands, those hands I had admired, one of them now holding my wrists together above my head and the other pushing my skirt up. I couldn't breathe, my chest painfully crushed under his weight. I struggled and managed to get one hand free and hit him in the face as hard as I could.

"Cunt." He grunted, then laughed as he pushed my hand back down, gripping my wrists painfully hard. His pupils made his pale eyes turn black as he stared me in the face and spit on me.

I tried desperately to push him off, but I wasn't strong enough. I heard him unzip his pants. Complete and blinding panic set in.

"NO, no please stop!" I screamed. There was no one there to help me. The thick walls between dorms only allowed the low thump of music to pass through. No one was coming. I thrashed and tried desperately to get myself out from under him, but no matter how hard I tried, I couldn't get him off of me. Tears streamed down my face as I struggled under his weight.

"Mom! Help me, MOM!" I screamed.

"Your mom can't help you, you stupid bitch. She's dead," he whispered in my ear as he forced my thighs apart with his knee.

Eleanor

Jo's panic pulled me toward her as if on a ripcord. She was on her bed crying and screaming, struggling with someone on top of her. It was immediately clear to me what was happening. I just hoped I wasn't too late. I felt rage and hatred pour into my being, and I pulled him off of her as hard as I could. I heard a high-pitched scream, and then he was on the ground. He was lying where he landed, apparently unconscious for the moment. Jo was on the bed, her skirt pushed up, her torn underwear lying on the floor. She curled into a ball, pulling the blanket up around her, and started to heave with racking sobs, mascara darkening her pale, freckled cheeks. I sat on the bed next to her, desperate to be able to hold her. After a few minutes, I could tell the asshole on the ground was waking up and moving around. He was still a threat. I couldn't let him hurt her. I pushed at him again, but my energy just went right through him. I used all of it pushing him off of her and was now doomed to helplessly watch what came next.

With immense relief, I heard the doorknob jiggling and realized that her roommate must be coming into the room.

"Oh, fuck no," she said, then dialed her phone and began speaking to campus police as she blocked the doorway, her glare directed at the thing on the floor. He got up and tried to leave, but she pinned him against the door frame.

"You piece of shit. You stay where you can take some responsibility for this." Her voice was dead calm, but I could feel

• • •

the rage boiling off of her. I knew right then and there that Jo was in good hands. I turned to see Jo staring at Mikayla with her eyes wide and her entire body shaking. Damage had been done. Physical or not, something in her was breaking.

I thought of the time I caught Grimalkin with a bluebird in his mouth and plucked it from his jaws. It appeared unharmed and I set it in the bushes by the barn in a protected spot. Later, when I went to feed the horses, I found it drowned in the water trough, dead despite my efforts. That was how I felt now. I'd rescued Jo from the immediate danger, but what fallout was occurring in her mind, under the surface?

Jo never really felt comfortable with boys. She told me about all of her crushes, including the older boy at the coffee shop she and Cece always went to, whom I now knew as Luke, the medium who'd helped her reach me. I had faith that she would tell me when she became physical with someone. I even took her to the OB-Gyn to discuss birth control and safe practices. We talked about it after, and she said she really didn't feel ready for sex, then promised she would tell me when she did. I trusted my daughter, and she had never come to me.

If this was her first experience, what was that going to do to her? I could feel myself faltering, her concentration obviously shaky, and most of my energy spent defending her. I was starting to fade in and out when campus police entered the room. I could hear her start to unsteadily answer questions. I heard her say he had not completed what he wanted to do, thank goodness. She would at least be safe now, and I could fade back into oblivion. I felt mixed emotions—I wanted to be able to hold her, to physically comfort her, but I knew if I had still been alive, I would have been at home asleep, blissfully unaware. He could have gotten much further than he had. The thought made my non-existent stomach churn.

Josephine

Campus police came, accompanied shortly after by Charlottesville police—I'm not sure what Mikayla told them, but the response was swift. One officer took Colin outside while the other turned to me and brought me into the hallway. After getting my basic info and contacting Dad, he began asking questions that were hard to answer.

"Do you know the gentleman outside?" he asked quietly. *Gentleman* is not the word I would have used to describe Colin at the moment, but I answered yes anyway.

"Can you take me through your account of what happened?" He pulled out a notebook to take notes.

"I was on a date with him, and he came into the room." The officer nodded and wrote in his notebook.

"Did he push into the room, or did you invite him in?"

"Umm, well, I asked him if he wanted to come in and look at my sketchbook." His eyebrows lifted, and he scribbled again.

"I see. So you invited him in." He studied my face closely. I tried to pull my skirt down further over my legs and felt aware of the curious eyes now peering from various rooms down the hallway.

"Does she really have to do this now? Can we wait until her father is here? She is still a minor, and he legally should be here for any official questioning, which would be more appropriately done at a station, not a hallway."

• • •

"Okay. Miss....?" His face clouded, and it was apparent that he didn't like being challenged.

"Bates, Mikayla Bates. Officer....?" Mikayla's voice was stony and cold. The officer turned to me.

"Officer Staten. You don't have to answer any questions right now, but it is in your best interest to do so. It's best to get an account while memories are still fresh, so I would do it as soon as possible."

I wasn't sure how this memory was ever going to be any less horrifically clear. It was currently replaying in a tortuous loop.

"You can come into the station and make an official statement when your father arrives."

Mikayla stood beside me and gave my hand a soft squeeze. Her steady yet gentle grip made me feel stronger and less afraid. A sharp contrast to the last hand that had touched me.

Officer Staten continued, "If you want to press charges, you should have a medical exam performed as soon as possible and make a statement while your memory is still clear. Your statement *can* happen tomorrow, but your exam needs to happen tonight."

"Can I change first? I don't want to be in these clothes anymore." Tears welled in my eyes and I hastily brushed them away. His eyes left my face and passed over my legs, making me want to crawl into myself and never come out.

"We generally don't advise that." He shook his head. "If you do, you'll need to place them in a paper bag and take them with you for your medical exam. Try not to touch anything in your room."

I grabbed some sweatpants and a sweatshirt from my drawer and went into the bathroom down the hall to change. The face in the mirror was not my own. Makeup streaked over my cheeks, and my hair was tangled and sticking to my neck. I brushed it away with my hands and took off the clothes Mikayla and I had so joyfully picked out earlier. I then placed them in a large paper bag. My inner thighs were already showing the blooming of bruises, and my wrists had deep gouges from Colin's nails. My own nails, so carefully painted earlier today, were broken and frayed. I gingerly put on pants and a thick

● ● ●

sweatshirt. Their thick, soft comfort made me feel marginally better.

When I left the bathroom, Dad was standing in the hallway speaking with Mikayla and the police. He must have absolutely flown here. His face was ashen. When he turned to me, tears welled in his eyes.

"I'm okay, Dad. I'll be okay." He wrapped his arms around me and held me, kissing the top of my head.

"I'm so sorry, honey," he whispered as he held me. He pulled away and lifted my chin with his hand. "I'm here. No matter what. Are you okay to go over to the hospital with me?"

"Yeah." All I wanted to do was go home and shower for days to wash this all away.

"I spoke with the police. We can make an official statement in the morning, but the medical exam should happen now. Okay?" Nothing felt okay.

"Yeah, okay." Mikayla gave me a hug and waved as Dad and I walked down the long hallway amid the stares of strangers.

Neal

When Jo came out of her room, cloaked in baggy sweats holding a paper bag, she looked small and afraid. All the police told me on the phone was that she'd had an altercation with another student, and I needed to come down. Now that I saw her holding the tell tale paper bag, I felt a lurching realization of what my little girl had just gone through.

"I don't care what happened. I am on your side, no matter what," I told her, then hugged her close. I glanced over her shoulder at Mikayla, who looked frightened but mostly angry.

"Thanks, Dad." Jo's voice was as small as she looked.

"Do you want to fill me in while we head over to the ER?" *Did* I want to know? I felt my stomach churn and my head swim. *Get it together*, I told myself. I had to make sure I was strong for her. Though by the look on Mikayla's face, she had another fighter in her corner.

"Thank you for being here," I said to Mikayla.

"Don't worry, Mister—sorry, Dr. Brooks."

"Mikayla, please call me Neal. I think we can do away with the doctor. Especially now. After this."

"Okay, I think I got here before…umm, but, well, I wish I could have done more."

"You did all you could. Thank you, Mikayla. Thank you." I looked into her eyes and hoped she knew just how grateful I was. Mikayla nodded.

● ● ●

Jo was silent as I got her into the car and started the drive to the ER. When we parked in the deck, I turned to her.

"Jo, you don't have to tell me anything if you don't want to. Just know I will do everything I can to help you. I love you so much."

"I know, Dad. Mom stopped him before he could do anything more than he did." Confusion flooded me before I realized what she was implying.

"What? Mom? Honey, you know that isn't possible." Although, thinking back to the past few months, I wasn't so sure that was true.

"She did, Dad. She saved me. She's the only reason it wasn't worse. It almost was." She swallowed and looked toward me. "It was her, Dad. I know it. I called out for her, and she came. She protected me. She pulled him off of me." Jo turned away, her face was still streaked with mascara and tears.

"Okay, I'm sure she did, honey. I'm just glad the worst didn't happen." A few minutes later, we walked into the bright lobby. The front desk admissions nurse recognized me as we came in.

"Dr. Brooks!" Her smile faded as she looked over at Jo. "Oh." She swallowed and put her hand to her chest.

"Are there any open rooms?" My voice sounded strange to my ears, its normal authority in this space absent.

She nodded. "Yes, I'll get you all straight back." A female officer showed up a few minutes later to oversee the exam, which took over an hour. I knew what was happening in that room, swabs, photos, questions, all because of some asshole who decided my daughter was his for the taking. Eventually, a long time friend, Dr. Nichelmann, came up to me.

"I'm so sorry, Neal. I'm sorry she's going through this. From the looks of it, he didn't achieve penetration, but she's pretty bruised up, and she's scared." She patted my shoulder, then disappeared down the hall. Didn't achieve penetration. I felt sick again. My hand hurt, and I realized I was clenching my fist so hard, my nails were digging into my palms. I had the urge to kill someone I had never even laid eyes on.

"Do you want to go to the police station now or tomorrow?" It was well after midnight now and Jo looked exhausted.

● ● ●

"Can we do it in the morning? I just want to go home."

"Of course, honey, of course," I replied, knowing she still had a hard road ahead of her. Working emergency medicine meant I had testified in sexual assault cases as a professional witness. They were notoriously difficult to prosecute, especially in cases of 'date rape' or 'spousal rape.' As if rape couldn't just be called rape. It didn't seem to matter that I had treated assault victims for horrendous injuries perpetrated by strangers, or people who claimed to love them. The defense always seemed to twist the facts and turn everything around on the victim. They'd focus on what they'd been wearing or how much they'd had to drink. As if any of that changed the fact that someone had hurt them in a violent and deeply personal way. It had always been my worst fear for my daughter. Now it was reality.

I drove Jo home, where I heard her in the shower for much longer than usual. When the house was finally quiet, I peeked into her room. She was sleeping curled around Hobbit's tiny, purring body. I quietly closed her door and got into bed myself. I was exhausted, but my mind wouldn't turn off. Had Nora really saved Jo? It could be that Jo had found strength in panic and was able to get him off of her. I didn't know which I preferred, the idea that Nora was watching over her, or that she had been able to defend herself against this attack. I suppose both proved how strong the women in my life were.

I was sleeping in bed while this happened to my daughter. Wasn't I her father? Wasn't I the one who was supposed to protect her from this kind of thing? I felt helpless and inept. What could I possibly do to help her now? I lay awake for so long, the light in the room started to change, and I realized the sun was coming up.

I got up and took a hot shower long enough for the water to end up tepid at the end. As I stepped out onto the tiled bathroom floor, I looked in the mirror, and my feet slid out from under me as I scrambled in surprise. *"Just love her,"* was written on the fogged mirror in Nora's scrawled handwriting. Nora always had a way of holding us together. I suppose death wasn't going to change that.

● ● ●

Eleanor

Jo slept fitfully, but thankfully she was able to escape the awfulness of the world for now. Neal tossed and turned in bed for hours. The turmoil wasn't over for anyone in this family. This trauma would eat away at Neal. He would want to fix this for her, and he couldn't. He was accustomed to being the one to solve problems no one else could solve, both at work and at home. He was the one people went to when the shit hit the fan and they needed a cool head and steady hands. He was good at solving problems.

One particularly memorable incident happened when we first moved into the house. It was the first winter we were here, and we were roughing it. The kitchen wasn't completed yet, so we had a microwave and fridge in the dining room. Plastic sheeting covered the opening between the two rooms to keep dust in the kitchen from invading the rest of the house. While it worked well for dust, it did not work well against a skunk.

It was February, also known as skunk mating season. We had started the kitchen renovation a few weeks prior, and it turned into more work than we expected, as renovation projects are wont to do. We ended up having to cut holes into the floor due to rotted wood we found under the linoleum, so what was supposed to take three weeks became six. It was during the few days between hole cutting and hole patching that a skunk decided to explore our nice warm basement by pulling open an access door, and then found the hole leading into an even warmer kitchen.

I was sitting down in the dining room feeding Jo breakfast when I looked over to see a large black and white shape move toward the plastic sheeting we had taped up. I was about to yell, thinking it was a dog or cat, when it poked its very skunk-shaped head under the plastic. I panicked. I didn't want to yell and scare it, so instead I stage-whispered to Neal, who was in the living room.

"Skunk! There is a skunk in the kitchen. What do I dooo?" I looked at him in desperation, and he calmly came in with his finger over his mouth in the universal "be quiet" signal.

Luckily he was folding laundry and had an old beach towel we used to wipe muddy dog feet. He held it in front of him and moved slowly toward the skunk. On his way, he grabbed some of the cereal from Jo's plate and threw some to the animal. As it turns out, skunks love cereal. The creature happily ate, so Neal tossed some more behind it, causing it to turn around. It was in this slow, cereal-tossing manner that he "led" the skunk out the back door and away from the house without it spraying everything and everyone inside.

I would never have had the presence of mind to cajole a wild skunk out of our house with cereal. Neal was very good at direct threats, like stinky skunks that were a clear and present danger to the olfactory sanctity of our house. But tonight's incident was not a clear and present danger. This threat was insidious and murky. I was better with these kinds of situations. I was better at grey scale.

In both my personal and private life, I was always better at finding the subtle differences in shades of grey, the small shadows that most people didn't notice. Something that might look like a slightly brighter shadow on a lung could be so significant it meant the difference between life and death, cancer and no cancer. My job was predicated on the importance of seeing what other people didn't see in front of them. It was what I was good at. I could read shadows and light. On an MRI, radiograph, ultrasound, or the faces of the people I loved.

Sometimes it wasn't the bullet fragments but the mass I saw 'incidentally' in an image that ended up not so incidentally killing someone. This was where we were now. Whatever was

• • •

going on in Jo's mind had the potential to break her. We as her parents couldn't change what had happened, nor could we do much to change what it did to her. This couldn't be fixed easily, and it was eating away at Neal. I knew what I would have done, if I had still been around. I would do what I always did, and what always helped.

With the help of steam, I figured out a way to convey this to Neal. He just needed to love her. It was all any of us could do now.

After a long draining evening, I slipped away and found solace with my fellow non-corporeal companions, staying close by in case I felt Jo's familiar tug on the energetic line that connected us. I rubbed Grimalkin in the spot he always loved to be rubbed, under his chin and along his chest. Then I let myself dissolve into my father's consciousness. Sharing in his memories and images of his admittedly beautiful life. I couldn't help but worry, though. His memories were largely of beautiful places and sunny days, but I knew there was something darker under the bright surface that he wasn't sharing. Something painful enough that it led him to end his own life, rather than go on living. I had to figure out why, because underneath the surface, my daughter now had a darkness I could feel. I didn't want it to eat away at her and lead her to follow in her grandfather's footsteps. Depression was genetic, as was alcoholism. If she was facing these issues, I needed to know and somehow help her to avoid repeating a dark and hidden family history she had no idea existed.

Josephine

After an entire morning in the police station, answering question after question about what I was wearing, whether I said no, whether this was a misunderstanding…even with my dad's lawyer friend at my side, I was done. Just done. Nobody seemed to believe my account of the events. I talked to Mikayla on the phone, and she went into the station to give her account as well. She told me they grilled her about why she pushed him enough that her dad, who was also a lawyer, told her to stop answering any more questions. Colin was threatening her with an assault charge according to the police, and anything she said could end up being used against her in that case.

How was this turning around like this? How was it that Mikayla was now the bad guy? My mind was reeling when we finally got home. I just wanted it all to go away. I didn't want to have to keep reliving it. I ran to the barn as soon as I could and decided to go for a trail ride.

I tacked Callie up and got on. I could feel a tight soreness in my thighs from the night before and winced as I settled into the saddle. Callie turned her head and nuzzled my foot in the stirrup. I leaned down and hugged her neck, inhaling her scent as deeply as I could, then nudged her forward. We rode at a walk across the field and into the woods behind the house. All around me, the trees were still mostly green, true autumn still a month or so away. I was surrounded by the sound of Callie's hooves on the path, a few straggling cicadas, and the soft rustling of the trees. As we rode along the trail, my mind cleared, allowing only this moment into my consciousness. We came to my favorite spot on the trail, a wide creek crossing with a small clearing. Often I would come upon deer in this spot, and once we surprised a black bear. The clearing was empty now, so I let Callie have her head to drink from the creek. She sipped from the cool stream, ears softly moving back and forth with each swallow, once finished, she lifted her head and gazed up the trail, water dripping from her chin. The sunlight bounced off the water and formed a halo around her profile. Eventually, I turned her and we made our way back up to the barn.

When we emerged from the trail, I saw that cars filled the driveway. They were here for my birthday. Dad had asked this morning if I wanted to cancel. Part of me did, but I also knew it would draw attention to the fact that something had happened. I didn't want to worry anyone, and the distraction was probably good for me.

Dad was giving Jacklyn, Lucian, and Mikayla a tour of the property as I rode toward the barn to untack Callie. They were walking along the fence, Dad gesturing out toward the tree line that marked a rough boundary between our property and the neighbor's. Mikayla saw me and waved, a smile lighting up her face. She walked over to me and into the barn.

"Are you okay?" she asked, her face clouded with concern.

"Yeah, I don't want to think about it though." Mikayla nodded with understanding and followed me as I led Callie to the cross ties and took her bridle off.

"You know, I took lessons when I was young. I rode for about three years, even showed a few times. " she said, helping unhook the girth.

"We should go riding some time then! Georgia is super sweet. We could do some trail riding together." She smiled and patted Callie's neck.

"I really liked riding, but at the time, Dad was doing public defender work and we couldn't really afford to keep going with lessons. I'd like to hop on one again."

"It's a plan then." I smiled at this new friend of mine, thinking I would never be able to repay her for everything she

• • •

brought to my life. I finished untacking Callie, sponged her off, and put her back out in the pasture with the others. She pawed the ground and rolled, then took off as fast as she could, farting and bucking her way across the field. We then walked up to the house, where I was expected to be jovial and happy.

"Let's do this," Mikayla said, turning to me and giving me a 'chin up' kind of look that bolstered my resolve.

"Alright. Hopefully Grandma made tiramisu. It's almost good enough to make me forget last night."

"There she is!" Grandma exclaimed as we entered the living room a few minutes later.

"Here I am," I replied. Grandma got up and gave me a hug and kissed my cheek.

"I made your favorite. Tiramisu." She held me back to look at me, and a faint cloud crossed over her face. I wondered if she knew about last night.

"Yes, and I am going to take us all out to dinner at Sapporo!" Memere responded, jumping up to hug me as well, nearly shoving Grandma out of the way. Grandma shot her a look that would have turned a lesser person to stone.

"That sounds really nice, everyone. I am glad you all came up," I replied, knowing the grandmas would be sparring for my attention tonight. Maybe I could manage to sit between Mikayla and Dad.

"Well, we wouldn't have missed our only granddaughter turning eighteen, now would we?" Memere chirped.

"And I never miss a chance to make something from scratch for my most beloved of people!" Grandma cut in, getting a dig in at Memere, who couldn't cook a microwave meal without assistance.

"Is it okay if I take Mikayla up and show her my room? I've got to change from my riding clothes anyway." I gestured at my ratty old breeches and muddy boots.

"Of course, honey. Take your time. We are on your timeline, birthday girl." Dad planted a kiss on my head.

"So, how *are* you holding up?" Mikayla asked as we got upstairs.

"Honestly, I'm mostly angry. I can't believe he is threatening to press charges against you. It's bullshit. You were just protecting me, and now I've gotten you all mixed up in this. I'm sorry."

"No, don't apologize to me. I'm all in, no matter what. This entitled dickbag is exactly why I want to go into law."

"Entitled? I don't know. I mean he's definitely a dickbag, but he said his family was military and moved around a lot."

Mikayla's eyebrows raised in surprise as she turned toward me. "You mean you haven't googled him?"

"Nope, I probably should have. Why?"

"Oh boy." She sat down on my bed with a sigh. "Well, turns out, Colin is the son of Douglas Mcleary, who happens to be a United States Congressman. They are most definitely not going to want this to stain their family record."

"You're shitting me. So you mean we're fucked. They're going to have the biggest, best law team ever." I felt despair replace all my rage.

"No, we are not fucked. You know what my dad does, don't you?"

"No. I mean I know he's a lawyer, but you said he doesn't do criminal law."

"My dad is a civil rights attorney. He's handled some of the biggest cases to go before the courts. He has argued Supreme Court cases. We got this."

"You mean he would represent us? Wouldn't that be a conflict of interest?"

"Yes, it would. He most likely would not represent either of us since this is criminal, but he has lots of friends in high places. The Mcleary's aren't the only ones with connections. He'll make sure you get a good prosecutor. This asshole picked the wrong people, Jo. I promise, he is not going to get away with any of this." She looked at me intently. I genuinely wanted to believe her, but I had significant doubts about how things would turn out.

"Okay, well, for now, can we have dinner, and tiramisu, and just ignore this giant looming problem for tonight?"

"Of course, Jo. So, fill me in on the weirdness between your grandmas."

"Oh, only the longest stretch of good old passive aggressive warfare I've ever seen. If you hear either of them say 'bless your heart,' you know we are in for it."

"Oh damn. Why don't they like each other?"

"I don't really know. I mean they are super different. Memere is originally from France. From a prominent family filled with diplomats and judges. And Grandma is second-generation Italian from cleaning ladies, cooks, and hairdressers. I think they just came from different worlds. Plus, Memere is pretty progressive, and Grandma is a conservative Catholic. I mean, she's not one of *those* conservatives, but still, they have different views on how the world should work."

"I get that. Well, it should make for some interesting conversation."

"Oh it usually does. At least we can sit back and watch." I fiddled with my outfit, feeling uncomfortable in my own skin. I wished vehemently that I could just stay here in this room and hang out in my PJ's with Mikayla all night.

To my surprise, the showy distraction of hibachi flames and good company let me almost forget last night. I pulled my sleeves down, covering the marks left there by someone I thought I could trust. Dad saw and bumped me softly with his shoulder.

"I love you, kiddo."

"I love you too, Dad." I rested my head on his shoulder for a moment, and he put his arm around me, giving me a little squeeze.

The smell of his clean shirt wafted over me like a protective blanket. It was the same thing he'd done since I was little. I thought about the fact that this birthday meant I was now an adult.

If only I could have gone back to the days when Mom was alive, and my main worry on my birthday was what was in the perfectly wrapped box.

Later that evening, Dad was in the kitchen cleaning up dessert plates and mugs after assorted grandparents had gone to bed. I began to help him, and he stopped me.

● ● ●

"Jo, there's something I need to tell you, and I hate to tell you after all of this, but I have to tell you before you find out the hard way. Grimalkin passed away," he finished, looking at me with guilt and sadness.

"I know, Dad. I figured he was gone. I didn't say anything to you because this weekend has been so crazy, but I saw the urn in the living room next to Mom."

"Oh. Okay. Well, do you have any questions?"

"Was it peaceful?" That was my only hope for him. After all, he was ancient, at least as old as I was.

"As peaceful as it could be. He was asleep in bed with me. I didn't even know. The only reason I checked him was..." Dad trailed off and hesitated. "Well, I saw him sitting in your mom's lap. By the window, in her chair."

"You did?" It was the first time he'd actually admitted that Mom was still around. I pushed down an ugly pang of jealousy. I hadn't seen or heard her.

"Yeah, I tried to tell myself it was a trick of the light, but then when I got in bed, there he was, dead. Now, after last night, I can't deny anything anymore. Your mom is evidently still here with us, and apparently so is Grimalkin." While I still longed to be the one who saw her, it felt better now that Dad believed me.

"Glad to see you've finally come around to reason. I love you, Dad."

"I love you too. Goodnight." A glimmer of worry crossed his face and he kissed my forehead, sending me off to bed.

I headed up to bed and crawled between the sheets, exhausted but distracted. As I settled in, I heard my door click shut as it did each night. I felt safer here, knowing there were people that loved me all around, both living and dead. It was out there in the world that I wasn't so sure about. I felt afraid of what was to come.

Mikayla seemed prepared for this fight, but I just wanted it to all go away. I wanted my life to go back to normal. I hated the ball of anxiety that had seated itself in my belly, gnawing away all other emotion. Fear was not something I gave into often, but right now, I just wanted to sleep with my door shut and my light on.

• • •

Neal

It had been a month since the assault and Jo was losing resolve. We went forward with pressing charges, but the police were dragging their feet on whether they felt there was enough evidence to go to trial. Lucian pressed them and had managed to get the McCleary's to drop their case against Mikayla, but the police kept saying it was still under review. It was infuriating.

Jo came home on weekends and disappeared on horseback for hours. I could barely get her to talk about the case. I think she just wanted it to all go away. As her father, I wanted him to pay; I wanted revenge. Jo changed her schedule around so she wouldn't have to see him. I think she was hoping it would all disappear if she didn't run into him on campus.

Evidently, Colin had a record as a juvenile, but it was sealed until a prosecutor was involved. The police could see it, but we could not. I felt powerless. It was becoming an unpleasantly common feeling.

I was stewing over my own inadequacy while getting ready for my next lecture one morning when a student came into the auditorium to talk to me. He was lean and tall, and hesitantly approached while looking over his shoulder.

"Dr. Brooks?"

● ● ●

"Yes, can I help you?" I asked, trying to place him. I may have had him in a lecture, but not this term.

"My name is Ian Mcleary." The name hit me like a bowling ball to the gut. This must be Colin's older brother. I braced for what he was about to say, looking around for my phone in case I needed to involve the police.

"I know what my brother did to your daughter. He's done this kind of thing before."

"Well, he didn't learn anything evidently, since he's still abusing women," I snapped back.

"I know. That's why I am giving you this." He handed me a card with a name and phone number on it. "Talk to her. She'll come forward and help. My father has been cleaning up Colin's messes his entire life. First it was hurting animals, then other kids, then his girlfriends. He's working his way up to something terrible and needs to be stopped. All my dad cares about is his reputation, and making sure he gets re-elected. Or maybe he just doesn't want to see it. Whatever the case, my brother is a violent narcissist. He will hurt people, and he won't care about doing it. Anyway, just call that number and explain your situation...or better yet, have your daughter call. Maybe it will give you leverage to get the police to go forward with a trial. Maybe not. But at least your daughter can talk to someone who can relate." He started to turn and walk away, his head down.

"Thank you," I called up to him. "Hey...how did you know?" He turned.

"Oh, that. Well, Colin bragged about it to me." He paused for a long moment, as if reliving the moment in his mind. "Please don't make me testify against him. It would tear my family apart. In fact, make sure you don't tell anyone who gave you this information. I suppose that makes me a coward, but that's the way it is." He turned and slunk away quickly this time.

Students started trickling in for the lecture. Ian wasn't ready to face his family, but I wasn't sure that made him a coward. Conflicted, maybe, but not a coward. I looked down at the card in my hand. Alexis Cameron was the name, with a DC area code phone number. I slipped it into my pocket, feeling a glimmer of something approaching hope for the first time in weeks.

● ● ●

Eleanor

There was a man lying in bed next to me, hips draped in a white sheet, his shoulders and back exposed as I lay there in the orange glow of city lights through the curtains. When he turned over in his sleep, I could see his face clearly. He was handsome, with a square jaw and blonde wavy hair just long enough to brush his cheekbone as he rolled toward me in bed.

"Can't sleep, huh?" He opened his eyes, looking at me with a whisper of a smile on his well-formed lips.

"Not with you in bed with me," my father's voice replied. It sounded husky, with a hint of a smile reflected in its tone. I realized I was in one of my father's memories, and by appearances it was a very intimate one.

"I love you, Charles." The stranger brushed my father's cheek with his fingers.

"I love you, too, but I can't leave them. I love them just as much." I realized with a jolt that I was one of the 'them' he was referring to.

"No, you don't. You know they've always just been a showpiece for you."

"That's not fair. You know it wasn't always like that for us. I did love her once, and the girls...I love my girls. What am I supposed to do, tell her who I really am?"

"Yes, exactly. People do it all the time now."

• • •

"Not this person. I'm the D.C. Attorney General for God's sake. Can you imagine the fallout if I came out? My career would be done, and my family would be destroyed."

"See, that's your problem. You are assuming people won't get over it. Give Celestine a chance. She might let you go, and understand."

"No. She wouldn't. She worries about the family face more than I do. Plus, there are the girls to think about. What would they think if they had a father like me?"

"What does that mean?" He sat up and turned away from my father.

"No, it's not what you're thinking. They think of me one way, and I don't know if they would be able to accept me as someone else. It would make them doubt everything."

"You're just ashamed," he whispered over his shoulder as he stood up and walked out of the room.

My dad was right. Even though I liked to think of myself as inclusive and progressive, I was taken aback by what I'd just witnessed and what it meant. It made me wonder if anything was real between all of us.

I thought back to memories of him, always there in the room but somehow slightly detached, as if he were observing a life that belonged to someone else. I realized now that, for him, he was. My father came of age in the 1950s. A time many look back on as innocent, but only if you fit into the mold. Being gay or, worse yet, bisexual was not an option for anyone who wanted to be part of normal society. My mother developed some close friendships with gay artists over the years, but what would she have done if she'd discovered her own husband was gay? My mother could be infuriatingly obsessed with perfection, or at least the appearance of it.

Family is supposed to be based on unconditional love, but clearly there were conditions, or at least perceived conditions, inside all of us. We all worry that if we aren't the person we are supposed to be, whether that is a capable college student or a heterosexual man, we will somehow be less than we were before. Why are we so afraid to live in our truth? To allow our family of all people to see our soft underbelly and trust them to not hurt us?

• • •

It was painful to realize this stranger knew my father better than I did. He knew the whole truth all along, and I never did. I wondered how many other people knew his secrets... hotel clerks, cab drivers, perhaps even random strangers might know him in a way I never had. I was angry with him for not trusting us enough to tell us, angry that he thought we were too shallow, or too weak to handle it. I was also angry at him for cheating on Mom, the cowardice of that decision based on fearing we would not be able to handle the truth. He underestimated me anyway. While this knowledge was difficult, it was something I know I could have gotten over with time. Maybe he would still be alive even if he hadn't let this secret eat away at him. I might have been able to have an honest relationship with him before he died, but instead, our entire existence together was based on shame and secrecy.

I thought of Jo, largely alone with her burden. I was terrified that somehow history would repeat itself. I had to figure out a way to communicate with her more clearly. I needed her to know she was supported by me, but also that other members of her family had held their struggles too close, and it killed them in the end.

● ● ●

Josephine

My phone rang as I was walking across campus to eat lunch. I hesitated because I didn't recognize the number but finally answered. A girl's voice reached me, soft and slightly hesitant herself.

"Hello, is this Josephine?"

"It is, and who is this?"

"My name is Alexis Cameron. I know Colin McCleary. I spoke with your father, Neal, and he asked me to call you." I almost hung up and would have if she hadn't mentioned Dad.

"Okay." Pinpricks of anxiety moved through my body. I found a bench and sat down to hear what was coming next.

"Colin and I dated in high school. I'm the reason he has a sealed juvenile record. Your father told me in general terms what Colin did to you, and I want to help you make sure he pays for his actions." I felt a pang of betrayal that Dad had shared my experience with her.

"Colin McCleary is a violent predator. He broke my jaw for refusing to give him a blow job when I was fifteen." The words hit me: *broke my jaw.* I thought about how lucky I was.

"Go on. I am definitely listening."

"He lied to the police and said I tried to give him a blow job while he was driving and he had to brake for a deer, making me hit my jaw on the steering wheel. He painted me as a stupid slut, and it worked. The case never went to trial. The worst of it is that his father paid my father to drop the charges. I was still a minor, so it was up to him as to whether we continued with pressing charges. Men are awful, Josephine, but your dad seems to be better than mine, so maybe you have a chance. I assure you, Mr. McCleary has probably already offered money to your dad even if he hasn't told you about it yet."

What she was telling me was tragic but completely believable. Douglas McCleary was an elected senator, and his reputation was invaluable. If his son was in jail for assault of a girlfriend, it would tarnish his record and put his re-election in jeopardy. It saddened me to think her own father would turn against her. My father was ready to pummel Colin into the dirt. I could see it in his eyes whenever the subject came up.

"I'm so sorry for what you went through, but how does this help my case?"

"It establishes a pattern and can be used to press your case forward. Sometimes they don't move forward with a trial if there is not enough evidence that wrongdoing occurred. If you can petition, stating that there is a pattern of behavior, they may be more likely to move forward with court proceedings. I would be happy to give a statement if needed."

She didn't even ask me what had happened with Colin and myself. She just took my side, no questions asked. I wondered if anyone in her life had done that for her. I was now more grateful for my little group of supporters than I had ever been in my life.

"Thank you, Alexis. I'm sorry for what he did to you and that your family didn't help you."

"It's okay. I went to live with my mom after everything and I'm doing fine. He taught me what not to look for in a man. They both did. Just try to get him for something. He needs to have at least *some* consequences for his actions."

"Well, we'll certainly try." We hung up and I just sat there, absorbing everything.

Without the help of Dad, Mikayla, and her family, I knew I wouldn't have the bravery to face this and would have just buried it deep within myself, hoping unrealistically that it would never bubble to the surface. Even with their support, I found myself jumping when a male classmate brushed against me. I crossed the street whenever faced with a man walking toward me. I triple-checked our dorm door to make sure it was

• • •

locked every time I went inside. The biggest challenge was sleeping there, in the same bed where it happened.

Mikayla and I went out and bought new sheets, and she switched bunks with me so I now slept on the top bunk. Still, when I tried to sleep, flashes of that night would interrupt my thoughts and keep me awake. I would often sit up, rubbing my wrists, bruises now healed, and feel his hands holding them again. Beyond the immediate concern of a possible trial, I wondered if I would ever be able to date anyone. If I couldn't be alone with myself, how on earth was I supposed to feel safe alone with a man ever again?

"How am I supposed to date now?" I asked Mikayla one night while we were locked in our room studying.

"Oh, you'll find a way. Do you like girls? Maybe start by dating a woman. You might feel safer there."

"No, I just don't feel that way about women. Sometimes I wish I did. It might make things easier."

"No, it wouldn't. It might feel safer, but I promise it isn't easier." I heard her sigh underneath me in the bunk.

"Wait, you like girls? How did I not know this?" I poked my head over the bunk rail and stared at her.

"I don't exactly advertise it." Mikayla, brash and bold, looked sheepish as she said this.

"So what? It's not a big deal nowadays. Have you dated anyone here?"

"No, I haven't, and it *is* still a big deal to some people. Namely my parents and family."

"What? But your parents are, like, civil rights warriors. They should be super accepting of you, no matter what."

"Well, they may be civil rights warriors as you say, but that doesn't necessarily extend to gay people. They're pretty conservative when it has to do with sexuality. They'd be so disappointed if they knew who I was in that regard." She looked disappointed as she said this, but I wasn't sure if it was with her parents or with herself. I climbed down out of my bunk and got into bed with her to hug her.

"Look. You have two families now, but I'm sure your parents will eventually come around. They love you too much to do anything different."

"I hope you're right. Wouldn't it be nice, though, if we could just swap preferences? You would have an easier time dating women, and I'd have an easier time dating men…but nope, we want the harder option in both cases."

"Yeah. It's not easy, is it?" I sighed and stared at the bottom of the bunk above us.

"No, it isn't, but I guess that's the point, right?" Mikayla said, sighing and picking at her nails. "If it was easy, no one would be any different at the end of it. My dad always says 'adversity builds character.' I just don't know that I want character."

"I suppose that's true. I just hope it gets better. I feel like a totally different person from who I was a year ago, and I'm not sure whether this person is better or not." I felt afraid all the time now. The me that existed a year ago wasn't like this. That previous me had been brave and hopeful, but naive. Now, I did have more 'character,' but was I better? I wasn't so sure.

"Well, for what it's worth, I didn't know the previous Jo, but I like this one very much."

"Thanks, Mikayla. I feel the same about you." I fell asleep, snuggled with Mikayla, feeling safe for the first time in my own bed since that awful night.

● ● ●

Neal

Halloween came without so much as a hint of change in the house. It was the first Halloween without Nora, and I felt her absence. Nora loved Halloween, possibly more than she loved Christmas. When Jo was little, there was a month-long build up spent making the costume, choosing the planned trick or treating route, and sometimes throwing a party for Jo and her friends.

Nora always talked about how the best place to celebrate Halloween was at home in her parents' Washington D.C. townhouse. She regaled us with legends of full-size candy bars and houses decorated lavishly with lighting, vampires, monsters, ghosts, and smoke machines. Therefore, she always made sure we took the short trip into Culpeper for traditional door-to-door trick-or-treating. As Jo got older, she hosted Halloween parties, or dragged us to some haunted woods event where Jo and I would have the wits scared out of us as Nora screamed and laughed her way through masked, chainsaw-wielding people and strobe lights.

Nora would have dragged me out and made me do something terrifying and silly. As it was, the house was empty, and aside from a glut of horror movies on TV, there was nothing to set the day apart.

There was finally progression in the proceedings with regards to Jo's assault. Alexis, Colin's previous victim, had come forward and given a statement to the police that included Colin's

● ● ●

family bribing her father and detailed Colin's violence against her. This led the police to move forward with assigning a prosecutor to the case. Colin was arrested and immediately bailed out by his wealthy father, but at least it was on the books now as an adult arrest. The prosecutor, Elizabeth Graham, brought everyone in individually for further questioning, and decided the case should move forward. I was thankful for that. She told me these cases often don't go to court, but that we had done lots of things right by keeping Colin at the scene until police got there, recruiting Mikayla as a witness, and having the medical exam the night of the incident. This left no doubt as to the nature of the incident and who was involved. Decreasing *some* of the 'he said, she said' doubt cast on most assault cases.

"I wouldn't get your hopes up for a conviction, though," she advised us during a meeting.

"Really? Even with all of that?" Jo's face fell.

"Really. He will have an excellent lawyer, and he will try to imply that it was a consensual incident, making it your word against his. However, due to his father's high profile, they may try to make a deal anyway to keep it out of the papers. A trial, even if he's acquitted, would be very bad press. I would advise you to take any reasonable plea deal they offer."

"What would that be likely to be?" I asked.

"Most likely, they will try to get it down to misdemeanor assault. However, I will try to push for aggravated assault, meaning we will end up with simple assault, thus why they call it plea bargaining. Their main stipulation is likely to avoid it being classified as sexual. They will want to avoid the possibility of him being registered as a sex offender."

"Okay," Jo said, more quickly than I expected.

"I want him registered, so that people know what he is." I wasn't so easily persuaded.

"Dad, if we go to trial and he gets off completely, that's worse. Plus, I'll have to testify if we go to trial. I'm not sure I really want to do that." Jo's voice was soft. I felt rage boiling up, but knew I should respect her wishes. After all, this was her fight.

"I agree with Jo here, Neal. If they come to me with a deal, do I have both of your blessings to negotiate for as much as I can get?"

"You do," I said, looking over at my daughter as she stared intently at the tabletop. I felt defeated as a father, and as a man. Why was the burden of proof so heavily laid on a victim's shoulders? I had never even thought about it before this. I'd never needed to.

Nora tried to explain it to me, the undercurrent of fear and powerlessness that every woman carries with them. She told me about carrying her keys in her fist in parking lots, the habit of parking in brightly lit spots. The worry about whether an outfit was too revealing and the fear of being violated, then not believed.

At the time, when she told me all of this, I nodded my head, agreeing with her that it was a grave injustice, but I never really felt it until now. Now I sat on the couch, watching Micheal Myers chase down Jamie Lee Curtis, and cringed. I always knew the horrors of the world were much worse than any horror movie, but it felt different now that my daughter was involved instead of someone else's. I turned the TV off and headed to bed surrounded by a silent, dark house that highlighted the emptiness of the space around me. Then I heard a jingle as my keys crashed to the ground in the foyer, dislodged from their hook. Nora always knew how to get me out of my own head. It was a small comfort, in a world that felt more and more frightening. To think, as a kid, ghost stories were the ones that scared me. Now I felt more comforted in the presence of a ghost than anyone else.

● ● ●

Eleanor

After he revealed his full self, something between my father and me shifted. He now stayed with me more often, realizing I accepted him as he was. I could feel his relief the moment I let him know that, while I was surprised and hurt that he didn't tell us, I still loved him. It made me feel a profound sadness for my father knowing he couldn't fully realize his own happiness in life. He'd committed suicide in 1988. It was the middle of the AIDS crisis. Being a gay or bisexual male at that time was most definitely not acceptable. Society as a whole disapproved of homosexuality, especially among men, and for my father, this disapproval was reflected at home as well. As evidenced by another pivotal memory he finally entrusted me with.

Sunlight poured in through the tall floor-to-ceiling windows of my parents' home, illuminating the pale blue walls and my parents' faces as they spoke.

"Celestine, I didn't do this to hurt you. I didn't want to be this way, but I am. I'm so sorry I kept it from you, but I don't think I'd even admitted it to myself until I met Thomas." Tears filled his eyes as he held his gaze on my mother. She turned away from him.

"Don't you dare speak his name to me, Charles!" my mother yelled with a shrill panic in her voice I'd never heard

• • •

before. "It's disgusting. How do you know you haven't brought that disease all the gay men have home to me? What if you've killed me without knowing, Charles? Did you ever think about that? Cheating with some man, hiding, running around behind my back, destroying everything we've built, all for what? So you can defile someone? Or, oh god, be defiled yourself?" She wheeled around and faced him. "What if I die because of this?"

"He is the only person I've been with, Celestine, and he is not some club kid I met while out dancing. He's a lawyer, he lives a clean life, he doesn't even go to clubs. Celestine, I love him." My father looked defeated.

"Oh sweet Jesus, Charles, you love him?! Are you kidding me?!" She was in a full on state of frenzy now. "No! I won't allow this. You are not going to destroy our family for some midlife crisis fling. I won't let you do it."

"Celestine, I can't live like this. I can't keep being two people. I can't keep hiding from myself and from you and the girls." I'd never heard either of them speak this way.

"Well, you're going to have to pick, because I'm not going to bring this kind of thing into the girls' lives. If you choose this man, then you lose us." She stood and faced him, arms crossed and face hard.

"Celestine, please don't make me do this. I can't. I love you and the girls. I really do, but I also love Thomas, and I'm being torn apart by this. Divorce me, fine, but don't keep the girls from me. Please. It's too cruel."

"Cruel?! You have been cheating on me for two years, and may have brought a deadly disease into our lives! I can't expose the girls to that."

"They're not children, Celestine. They can decide on their own. You can't keep them from me."

"Oh yes I can. Besides, what do you think this will do to your career? I mean, are people going to want to vote for a gay attorney general? I doubt it. Are you seriously going to give everything up for this? Because if you choose him, that is what you are doing." My father began to cry. The man I had never seen show any emotion now had tears running down his face.

"Celestine, please. Please just think about what you are asking me to choose between. I've tried. I really have. I've tried to push this away, to make myself be normal. I've tried to deny

• • •

this my entire life, but I can't anymore. I'm being torn apart by this."

"I don't care, Charles. You chose to marry me. You chose to have children with me. That is where your duty lies. Don't you think I've ever been tempted? Don't you think I've been attracted to other people? Did I go off and sleep with them? No, no I didn't. You did! That is what is different here. You chose to lie and break our vows. Did you ever love me? Did you ever feel anything for me? Or was that all an act?" She was crying now too, tears flooding her eyes and making her eyeliner drip down in dark lines.

"No, Celestine, of course not. I love you. I did then and I do now. I just…I think not in that way anymore. I think maybe someone can feel that way toward men and women both. I think I am that way maybe. I don't know. All I know is we aren't happy, and we haven't been for a long time. It is me. It's all my fault. I've been selfish in not telling you. I should have at the start, but I was confused by it all, and I was scared."

"Charles, I can't do this. You don't get both. You don't get to have your picture perfect family for photo ops and parties, and your gay lover on the side for fun."

"Celestine, that isn't what I want. I want to be with Thomas. I want to live with him. Tell me if I choose that, I must be able to be in the girls' lives still in some way. Shun me if you like, but you can't keep them from me."

"I can and I will. There isn't any in between here." She turned and walked out, the front door clicking closed softly behind her. My father sunk down in an armchair and held his head in his hands, weeping. The world faded back to black again, and I was left to comprehend what I had just seen. Most likely this led directly to my father's decision to end his life. Trapped between choices that shouldn't have to be made, he chose to leave all of us.

I was angry with my mother. It was a different time, sure, but to make him choose without even consulting us? He was right, we weren't children at that point. We should have been able to have a choice in this matter. My mother drove my father from our lives without even giving compromise a chance. I understood she was hurt and couldn't have foreseen the tragic

● ● ●

choice he would ultimately make, but I had the distinct feeling this moment led to that terrible choice to end his life.

There was so much pain in this world of human connection, people trying to find themselves and connect to those around them. I wondered if Jo could heal from what had happened to her. Her first attempt at intimacy led to violence and fear. Would she be able to find a real, whole love with someone who made her feel greater than herself? I felt immensely lucky to have found that in Neal, and I was so afraid that Jo may not find it in her life. I wanted to hold her in my arms, tell her she was worthy of so much more than this, and she deserved a love that made the fears I could feel in her fade away. Those fears would never disappear. This I knew as a woman who had once resided in reality. The world was frightening for women. In many ways, the potential of violation in this most private of ways was more frightening than death. Being murdered was one thing, but being raped first was terrifying.

When I was alive, I did all of the things. All of the things women do that men don't consider. For me, these fears were useless. I died before any violence was enacted on my body and I felt lucky for this. Of my friends, especially those I had in college, at least half of them were victims of some kind of unwanted sexual encounter. Whether from a boyfriend, or stranger, or someone they thought of as a friend. Now, my daughter had experienced it, without a mom to lean on afterwards. Luckily, Mikayla was as good a friend as any person had a right to dream of, and Neal did his very best. It helped to know Jo had people in her life that she could confide in and lean on. I hoped it was enough.

When Jo was on campus, it was much harder to be near her unless she pulled me toward her, but I could feel her do this in the evenings as she went to bed, her thoughts drawing me in and welcoming me around her. In this way, I could hold her, enveloping her with my energy, trying my best to bring her comfort, never sure if I succeeded.

● ● ●

Neal, for his part, seemed to have accepted that I was often around him in the house. He would occasionally talk to me, but between dealing with court logistics, teaching classes, and occasionally working the ER floor, he was extremely busy. As always, this was his way of coping with a lack of control in his life. He would apply himself to the working cogs of everything, trying to avoid empty time.

As a kid who grew up learning to lean on himself in many ways, he still did this as his first instinct. Neal preferred self-reliance to a support network. His family was loving and reliable, but in a very pragmatic way. Grace always made sure he was clean, fed, clothed, and kissed on his head, but deep emotions were harder for her to take care of. Grace was made of tough stuff, and to her mind, she was raising a man, not a little boy. Neal's father was even worse. If anyone in the house cried, he would disappear into his workshop and not come out until dinner. Therefore, Neal learned to handle his emotions on his own. In many ways, it made him resilient and strong, but it also meant he would push himself further than he should on his own rather than asking for help.

Nevertheless, they were beginning to move on, and here I stayed. I was forever frozen at fifty-three years old, my story arc over as far as the world at large was concerned. This knowledge brought with it a loneliness I had never felt before. One born of being left behind and possibly forgotten. Not by immediate family, but certainly by acquaintances and casual friends. They might one day find themselves talking to someone about me and realize they had forgotten my name. I would be 'that woman who we used to go to yoga class with, you know, the one who died.' And just like that, the rest of me would be forgotten, leaving a moment in my life I didn't even remember to serve as their only memory of me.

● ● ●

Neal

We sat in a white-walled room with a large faux wood table in rolling office chairs. There were no windows. We were on the basement floor of the court building. It was in this drab room that I listened to the creep who attacked my daughter give his rendition of events. It was also the first time I actually laid eyes on him. His face was smug and detached with a near constant sneer crossing his thin lips. I wanted to beat the look off his face.

Jo decided not to come to the plea agreement meeting. Since she was a minor at the time of the incident, I was the one who had to sign all the paperwork, and she took this as a way out of having to deal with this side of things. As I studied the snide look on this bastard's face, I couldn't blame her. Instead of spending her Saturday morning in this drab room, she and Mikayla were taking a trail ride and planning on watching movies all night at our house. Colin was oblivious to the damage he'd caused and seemed devoid of human emotion. His brother's assessment of narcissistic personality disorder was looking pretty accurate.

He whined about his perceived plight and tried to paint my daughter as a confused, slutty girl who didn't know what she did or didn't want, generally portraying himself as the victim. He couldn't look me in the face as he gave his statement during his selfish moaning and dropped his eyes every time mine found his. As it turned out, this was the only shame he would show. He

● ● ●

protested his plea deal, arguing that simple assault was too much, that he should be able to walk free. His attorney had more reasonable ideas of reality and made him be quiet for the majority of our meeting.

"While my client does make a valid point that we cannot devise intention without both parties here, I must say I feel your offer is adequate, Mrs. Graham. My client would like to avoid a trial and the attention it would invite towards his family, and you have met our stipulation that he not be registered as a sex offender." Colin's attorney turned and whispered something in the brat's ear, which elicited an eyeroll and a sneer, followed by a pouty silence.

"Well, then, if all parties are in agreement, Mr. McCleary has agreed to simple assault as a charge, and due to his cooperation will serve no jail time, but incur a $2,500 fine as previously offered." Elizabeth slid papers over to the other side of the table and waited for him to sign them. Colin sighed and reluctantly signed his copies, passing them back to our side of the table. I read over them lightly and then signed. Elizabeth and I had been over them multiple times, so I was familiar enough to know what they said.

"Well, then. We are in agreement. I will present this to the court for finalization. Thank you for your cooperation, Mr. McCleary." Elizabeth shook each of their hands and turned to leave the room. I stared at Colin, then stood and got ready to leave. I imagined my hands around his neck. The look of shock and fear that I longed to see in him. I wanted to make him feel the fear I now saw in my daughter's eyes. I wanted to make him feel powerless and weak. I wanted to crush his windpipe and watch him gasp for air that would never come again. I turned toward him as he passed me and leaned in, whispering, "Know that you got lucky here because of who your father is, but he won't always be around to protect you. I just hope you never treat a woman the way you treated my daughter ever again, because you won't stay lucky forever." He stared at me, and I turned and walked out. I could feel my muscles in my hands release as I closed the door behind me, my palms bloodied from my nails.

"You had to do it, didn't you?" Elizabeth said as we stepped out into the hallway.

"It's not what I really want to do to that kid, but I suppose it will have to be enough." Elizabeth turned and looked at me seriously.

"Neal, that's the problem with vengeance, it's never enough. Go home, help your daughter heal. Help her live a life full of joy and love. Don't let *his* actions dictate *her* future. That will give you much more satisfaction than vengeance, I promise. Good luck, Neal, and I hope Josephine can move forward from here knowing we got him as good as we could get him."

"Thanks, Elizabeth. Thanks for everything."

"You're welcome. I hope I don't have to represent you or your family again, but just call if you need me. I hope both of you live a perfectly boring life from here on out." She smiled with a nod and put her hand on my shoulder.

"Thanks, me too," I said sincerely.

It was only a few days after the plea agreement when we celebrated our first Thanksgiving without Nora. We were spending the day at Celestine's townhouse, and my parents were driving down to join us. As always at her home, Celestine had a first-class, chef-prepared spread, but I missed Nora. More than I had missed her in months.

We ate in Celestine's large and bright dining room, with modern art pieces hung against walls draped in silk damask wallpaper. The chairs brought over from her family home in France were covered in a silk that matched the walls—or was it the walls that matched the chairs? The food was superb, prepared by a chef Celestine had hired for the dinner. It was delicious but not exactly the relaxed affair we had generally enjoyed when Nora was alive.

Nora's Thanksgiving dinners were of the potluck variety, which meant dishes were always different and homemade. We would often take in stragglers with no other place to go on Thanksgiving. More than once, a lonely intern or resident joined us for dinner after Nora prodded me about where my charges were spending their holidays. Some of our

● ● ●

best sides were from international residents who had a prowess with spices we had never even touched. Bruce, the widowed farrier Nora used for the horses, joined us multiple times as well. He made a killer mac and cheese.

Nora loved the holidays for the fact that it forced everyone to stop and eat a meal together without the daily distractions of work or school to interject themselves into the dinner conversation. Her meals were well made, as Nora loved to cook, but not fancy. I often thought Nora was an interesting juxtaposition to her upbringing. The high society life Celestine and Charles led did not lend itself to children. There were many black tie balls and charity luncheons, none of which were kid-friendly. Perhaps her love of casual, hodge-podge simple meals and silly Halloween decorations were her way of rebelling against such a formal upbringing.

With an abruptness I was fully unprepared for, Christmas came that first year and the feeling of missing was even more profound. I hung some lights around the porch and put up a tree, but there was no joy in it without Nora. She loved Christmas almost as much as she loved Halloween. The house, normally tidy and slightly austere with its brick and iron work facade, would transform into a sparkly wonderland of color and light. She decorated both the second story porch, the lower porch, and the shrubs. Even the barn got lit wreaths on the doors. It was a jangly, blinky contrast to Celestine's home with single white candles in each window, or my parents with only a lit plastic nativity scene in the yard. Of all my known Christmases, Nora's were by far the best. She gave the holiday a warm, if slightly irreverent joy that was infectious to everyone who came to our home.

Jo came home for Christmas break, and we had Celestine and my parents over on Christmas day for dinner and gifts. It was quiet without Nora. Everyone seemed to feel her absence, but no one really wanted to mention it. My mom and Celestine agreed to prepare the dinner, which meant Celestine set the table and filled drinks. My mom was an excellent cook, and Celestine was excellent at pouring drinks, so it worked out just fine. Jo helped my mom in the kitchen, peeling potatoes and cutting up stale loaves of bread for stuffing. I heard them talking about horses and dogs as they worked.

We exchanged gifts after dinner, with the highlight a painting that Jo had made for me. It was of Grimalkin, sitting in Nora's window seat and looking out at the sunset. Nora's favorite mug sat on the table with a closed book beside it, a bookmark tassel hanging over the edge. Grimalkin's paw was raised, as if about to bat at the tag. She had captured all the variations and stripes in his tabby-colored coat perfectly. The title was "The next chapter awaits."

"Thank you, Jo, I love it," I said, tears welling in my eyes.

"You're welcome, Dad. I'm glad you like it. I thought you could hang it in your office." She moved on to open her next gift but brushed a hand over her cheek as she did. We both knew it was not a painting of a cat, but a painting of someone who was not seen in the image, someone who was there all the same, felt invisibly all around us.

Josephine

The new year started with bare trees and cold, harsh winds leaving me adrift and with no desire to set aspirational resolutions. Mikayla was supportive but incredibly busy. She'd met a girl she liked and was gone more often. She always invited me out with her group of friends, and I occasionally went, but anxiety seated itself in my gut too deeply for me to go out and really enjoy it. Once, when we were out with a group, a guy at the bar tried to hit on me and touched my hand. I panicked and shoved him away from me, causing him to nearly fall out of his seat. Mikayla intervened and we left shortly afterwards. The incident made it clear I wasn't ready for the unwanted male attention that came with college bars.

I was invited to participate in an open exhibition in Charlottesville, and while I would like to take the credit, owing the accomplishment to my artistic genius, I am positive Memere had her hand in making sure I was allowed to display my work with older, more established artists. Her generous funding of the arts in the area certainly helped to ease my entry into the local arts scene. I only hoped when people saw what I had to offer, they wouldn't brush me off as Celestine's family project. Maybe because of this feeling of unworthiness, or a desire to escape reality, I worked during every moment I could to make sure my work was as good as I could possibly make it. Now that my project was complete and it was time to share it with

• • •

complete strangers, I was faced with yet another situation where I felt exposed and out of my depth.

When the morning of the exhibition came, I walked in feeling every bit the impostor I assumed everyone thought I was. My collection was a set of watercolors, all of them focused on the horses at home.

I suppose the thing that set them apart was that they were more abstracted and intimate than landscapes with horses in them. I chose my favorite features, like the curl of an ear or the feathery hairs on a fetlock, just brushing the heel of a hoof, the way light caught and illuminated Briony's large eye. I then painted in swirls of color, trying to catch the way the light touches the small details only a person close to horses sees. In short, they were what entered my mind when I thought of horses. I loved them but was terrified I would be the only one who did.

To distract myself from dissecting my work, I walked around to look at some of the other artists' creations, trying my best not to compare. I came to a display of metalwork I found beautiful and resonant. It was mostly done in tiny pieces of aluminum cut from soda cans, then welded together to create free form shapes, some almost human, some just wisps of light. The artist painted them in shades of gold, silver, green and bronze so they caught the light in a way that made their shape ephemeral. They were stunning, and as I walked over to read the name on the placard, a familiar voice greeted my ears.

"Hello, there. Fancy meeting you here." I turned to see the welcoming face of Luke behind me. A feeling of warmth filled my whole body, and I hurried over to hug him. He smelled slightly of woodsmoke, and his stubble caught in my hair as I pulled away. He gently smoothed it down with his hands, which I noticed were stained with paint and calloused.

"Do you like them?" he asked, smiling at me. I walked around and looked at all the pieces.

I thought back to those heady days at Royston's, imagining Luke as someone interested in me. I remember him showing me sketches he'd done, but had no idea he made sculptural pieces as well. Trying to communicate with my mom took so much focus, we didn't talk about much else during those visits. I'd spent so much time with Luke, yet realized I knew very little about him. Looking at his works made me wonder what else I didn't know.

"These are yours? I love them. But when did you start with metal work?"

"Last year. This is my first public exhibition of them. I don't think I'd even be here if the director of the gallery hadn't been a friend of Joan who bought a piece." It was nice to know I wasn't the only one feeling a bit undeserving. He smiled, dimples revealed in his cheeks with his slightly crooked teeth showing behind his full lips. I made myself focus again on his work before I got distracted.

"I can see why they'd want to buy one. I've never really seen anything like it. What's your inspiration?"

"This is as close as I can get to what I see when I communicate with someone. They usually appear to me as a collection of points of light. Sometimes they are human-shaped, but sometimes they are more vague, depending on the person." I thought of all those days spent in Joan's sunny office. *Was one of these my mom?*

"They're beautiful. You know, I never really thanked you properly for what you did for me." He held up his hand and waved me off.

"Eh, don't worry about thanking me. I'm just glad it was helpful. Where are your pieces?" I led him over to my section and watched him, chewing my nail as he looked, anxious for his feedback. He observed each one from afar and then closely, studying them carefully. He said nothing for what seemed like forever, agonizingly silent, his expression unreadable.

"They're wonderful," he said, grinning widely, his eyes properly lighting up with this smile. "You really capture the essence of what it is to be close to an animal like that. All the little details most people never even see, let alone study." He turned and cocked his head to the side, a slight furrow in his brow. "How are you?"

"Okay, as far as losing my mom goes. Okay."

"Yeah, she's all around you, but you already know that. How are *you*, though?" The loaded question hung in the air between us.

* * *

"Well, let's just say the dead people in my life are less problematic than the living." To my surprise, he laughed, a full, heartfelt laugh that made people turn and look at us. Such an outburst was unheard of in a quiet, reverential gallery showing.

"You and me both!" He smiled again, then took a deep breath. "Would you want to meet to talk over lunch sometime?"

"I would, very much." Luke felt safe, safer than anyone else I knew, other than my family and Mikayla. I could almost feel something pushing me toward him, urging me forward. Mom most likely. It would make sense for her to be all over this. We exchanged numbers and set up a time to meet the following weekend.

As people started flowing in, I greeted more people than I could count, and explained my works to anyone who asked. I even sold two pieces, which I found astounding. Grandma, Grandpa, Memere, Dad, and Mikayla with her girlfriend on her arm all made their way through, exclaiming about my genius. I felt loved and supported, and it was nice to have everyone around celebrating something good for a change without the looming absence of Mom. I looked over at Luke's display, where several pieces showed tags indicating their purchase. I smiled at him as he waved at me. I looked at the glittering, shifting sculptures again and made my way over to him.

"Back again." He grinned.

"So, is this what my mom looked like to you?" His face grew serious and was silent for a moment. Evidently Luke did not feel the need to fill every moment with chatter. I could appreciate someone who thought before they spoke.

"Well, at first she was more physical. I could see her dark hair and green eyes, and the green shirt and jeans she was wearing. Over time, though, she became more abstract, her color was more coppery and gold." Tears filled my eyes. I knew the shirt. How had I forgotten? How did I not know?

"Sorry. I didn't mean to upset you." Luke pulled a tissue from his pocket and offered it.

"No, it's okay, I asked. I'm just. I don't know. Sometimes I worry I'll forget her and she'll just be gone. You even know what shirt she was wearing. I don't remember that."

"Oh, you may forget the silly stuff like what her clothes looked like, but you'll never forget how much she loved you. That's what really matters."

"Thanks, Luke. I promise at lunch we'll talk art and living things only." I sniffed and wiped my nose with his now soggy tissue.

"Honestly, just talking to you is good, no matter the subject. I'm looking forward to it."

"Me too," I said, and meant it. Looking forward to something was a nice change from looking back with sadness, or looking over my shoulder in fear.

Neal

D ad!" Jo called from the front entryway as she swung the door shut with a creak and slam.

"In here, honey," I called to her from the bar stool in the kitchen, where I was finishing up my cereal. In the past few months, she had been arriving home later and later on weekends. Often slinking in around noon, slipping immediately up to her studio to paint, then out to the barn to ride in the afternoon.

"You're in early," I said with a grin as she walked in carrying a large basket and hamper with laundry.

"Well, I figured I'd get some laundry done, and see if you wanted to go for lunch later?" She gave me a sheepish grin, implying that I, in fact, would be taking her out for lunch.

"I think we might be able to do that. I assume I'll be paying for this little adventure since you are a starving college student?" I grinned back at her.

"Well, since you offered..." she said over her shoulder as she headed to the laundry room with her tremendous load of clothes. I heard the machine start to hum. Then she returned, flopping down on Nora's chair in the bay window.

"Do you believe in fate?" She looked out of the window as she spoke, a small smile on her lips.

"Wow. It's a little early for philosophy." I noticed, with a start, that Jo was bright again. The glow she normally had was slowly returning. It saddened me to think I hadn't really noticed

* * *

its fading until just now. She sighed and flopped her legs over the arm of the chair.

"Well, it's just that... I don't know. Sometimes things don't feel like it could all be chance. Like when you saw Mom, and you punched a guy out the first time you met her, leading to all of this." She gestured to the house and the field outside the window.

"I suppose, but you could also argue that, had I not been at that party to punch that jerk in the face, I would have met someone different, and never known that this didn't exist."

"Hmmm, yeah, but don't you think some things are meant for us?"

"I think we make our own path, and sometimes things come along that can help us on that path, but we have to be smart enough to make those choices. Why all the talk of destiny?"

"I don't know. I've just been thinking about it. Sometimes it seems like coincidences are way too influential to be just coincidences, that they must mean something more than just chance."

"I see. So is it destiny that brought you here to use my washing machine, then have a free lunch?" I couldn't help laughing. Jo's smile spread into a giggling smirk.

"No, Dad, that's just economics! Do you have any bagels?"

"Of course, in the pantry. You want plain or blueberry?"

"Blueberry!"

"Peanut butter?" I asked, knowing it was her favorite combination.

"Yes, please!" Hobbit jumped in her lap and settled in. "I'd do it myself, but I have a cat here."

"Yeah, yeah, blame it on the cat." Despite my teasing, it made me happy to be able to do something so simple for her. I would have made a thousand bagels and run our well dry doing laundry if I knew it would make things better for her. As always, if she was happy, I was happy.

I remembered back to a time when Jo was small, maybe three years old, and I came home from work to find her in a full-on meltdown in the living room. Nora had inadvertently caused this by trying to help Jo put on her left sock, a grave mistake for any parent of a toddler. I walked in to see Nora with her hands on her hips, calmly explaining to the screaming, seemingly possessed child on the floor that sometimes everyone needs help, and that her feet would not be warm without socks. When Jo saw me, she immediately stopped crying and stood up from the floor with her face still blotchy and tear-stained, looking up at me sweetly, sock forgotten immediately.

"You have good day at work, Dada?" She sniffed as she wiped away copious snot and tears from her face.

Nora burst out laughing and kissed me on the cheek.

"My hero. If only everything could be fixed just by having Daddy walk in the door. She is all yours. I'm going to make a cup of tea."

I soon came to realize this positive force in Jo's life was Luke, the medium. They insisted they were just friends, but anyone with eyes could tell there was much more under the surface. Despite my initial reservations about men around my daughter in general, I begrudgingly found myself liking him over the next few months. He was very intuitive, though he insisted he was not the "fortune-telling" kind of psychic. Still, he often knew what people needed before they even knew they needed it. He would have made an amazing ER nurse. Often, when we ate, I would catch him handing Jo a napkin moments before she spilled something on herself. It wasn't hard to see why Jo liked being around him.

As a father, I was torn. Part of me wanted to keep her forever, but the other, more rational part of me knew this was a selfish and unrealistic view to have. I knew it would be better for Jo to eventually fall in love and have her own life and family, but fear sat like a stone in my core. Especially after all she had been through. I just hoped she had suffered her fair share of darkness, and something brighter was in store for her. If that ended up being Luke, I supposed I would be okay with it.

He was, as far as potential suitors go, a decent one. He held two jobs, the medium work and assistant manager at a local coffee shop, with his sculptures as a hobby. I came to find out he had three younger sisters and, despite his apparent maturity, was only a year or so older than Jo. He'd graduated from William Monroe in neighboring Greene County with honors the year

● ● ●

before Jo graduated, but never started college, instead staying home to help take care of his sisters. His mother and father had divorced when he was in high school, and as a single mother of four kids, the youngest only six years old, his mother had needed his help. He was responsible, considerate, and respectful, but I knew that, even with the most perfect person, things just don't always go to plan.

For now, I was happy enough to hold my tongue and give advice only when it was asked for, which was pretty much never. At least I trusted him around my daughter. I got no sense at all that he would ever do anything to harm her in any way, and I suppose that, given the world we appeared to live in today, this was the best thing I could hope for at the moment.

Eleanor

The red clay in front of the barn was punctured by tiny ice crystals bursting through the loose soil. It had rained the morning before, with the temperature dropping below freezing overnight, causing the water trapped in the soil to expand upwards. The effect created miniature crystalline towers of ice surrounded by the clay. Jo's boot stepped down on one cluster, and the ice crackled and dissolved under her step. Jo set Mahalo's grain to soak, steam rising in soft curls from the bucket. His teeth were poor in his old age, leading us to change him to a gruel of hay cubes and senior feed only a month or so before my death. She called the horses up with a whistle and prepared the grain for their morning feeding. The horses came in, their hooves making familiar music on the old bricks of the aisle.

Once they were in their stalls, the horses ate greedily as Jo took their blankets off for the day. It was a typical Virginia March, winter holding on to the world with an icy grasp even as crocuses began to emerge. It figures that I would die at this time of year, my least favorite. It was always a torturous waiting game for spring. Had I died in May or June, my anniversary weather might have been at least a bit more pleasant for all involved.

Later in the day, Jo, Neal, Mom, and Luke made their way down to the creek where a memorial stone had been placed some time after my death. Neal carried the urn with my ashes. He opened the urn and quietly scooped out a handful of my dusty remains to cast them out over the running stream. Jo and

• • •

Mom followed his lead, with Luke hanging back. Some bits of me floated in the breeze. Others settled on the water and glided along its surface. They followed the flow of water and carried the tiny fragments away from those I loved on ripples and eddies of current. They would eventually float far enough to join a small river, flowing silently downstream as the river widened, fed by other narrow streams like this one. That small river would then feed into a larger river, one that grew wider and deeper until finally the water that carried pieces of my body would enter the Chesapeake Bay and flow out to sea. Fresh water mixing with salt to create a unique bastion of life. It always amazed me to think our little unnamed stream connected our land to the Atlantic ocean and everything beyond, but it did. I mapped out the route once using satellite maps online. I must have been avoiding work that day. I praised myself for good use of procrastination. The very same water in that stream carrying my ashes at the moment would eventually form rain and, for millions of years to come, be part of a perpetual cycle of reuse and reformation as ice, water, clouds, and rain. That water now carried bits of myself with it, inconsequential in the grand scheme of things, but nonetheless connecting me to everything that came before and after my brief existence.

Close to home, at our tiny creekside, I felt more strongly connected to both my loved ones and to the Earth around them at this moment than I had since my loss of a body a year ago. Here, there was no coffin or grotesquely painted corpse to leer at. There were only brittle, winter-torn grasses whispering in the cold air and the tinkling sound of the stream. I focused on those gathered here and felt the tug of their emotion pulling me more closely to them. Clouds of their breath hung in the air as they stood in silence at my memorial of stone and water.

Jo was the first one to speak.

"Mom, I know you are near us, and that you can hear me. I love you no less than I loved you when you were alive, but I miss you so much. I miss being able to hug you, I miss you fussing over me, I miss laughing with you, but most of all, I miss you just being there. I am only now starting to find my footing after the past year, and I wish you were around to fully share it

• • •

with me. I want to see your face again, but I know I will have to settle for knowing you are with me in spirit. I feel lucky that I am able to know you are with me without any doubt. Thank you for that. Thank you for not leaving, thank you for making me feel I am still protected and held in your arms, even though you don't have any." She grinned a bit at that last line, and it made me happy to see her sense of humor returning. She continued, reaching out for Luke's hand, which he extended to hers, holding it gently. Her cheeks flushed, and her smile softened, widening across her face to reveal her crooked front tooth and dimpled cheeks. I loved that smile, and it was a joy to see it after so long.

"Anyway, I just want you to know I appreciate you, and I love you."

Neal spoke next, his hands, cold and bare, clasped around my urn. "Nora, I miss you more than I can even express. I still feel a little silly speaking to you this way, but I'll try my best. This past year has been hard without you, but I think we may be through the worst of it. We are trying to move forward, trying to find the balance of keeping your memory with us while going ahead with our lives the best we can. It's a hard balance, and we certainly aren't masters of it yet, but this ceremony today is part of how we're healing. I love you, and I always will." He swallowed hard and nodded toward my mom. I could see tears in his eyes and knew he wouldn't be able to form more words.

When my mother began to speak, I had a hard time focusing on what she was saying. Strong emotions really weren't a thing for dead people, as perspective on what was worth getting upset about tends to shift after one has lost a physical body, but I thought of my father and what he had shown me. The truth remained hidden, and it bothered me to know secrets had led to so much loss and pain. I had to say something, even if it risked ruining the moment. Luke was the only one around who could hear me rather than just sense me, and his presence was like a homing beacon, giving me the opportunity for communication I might not otherwise have.

"Luke, I need you to give my mother a message. Do you hear me?" He lifted his chin, sending me his thoughts. *I hear you. What do you want me to say?*

"Tell my mom I have spoken to Dad, and I know." He sighed. *Are you sure you want to do this now?*

"Yes, this is the only chance I'm likely to have to speak to her directly. She's been avoiding mediums since I confronted her about Dad's death."

He groaned, then spoke. "I have a message from Nora for you, Celestine."

"Oh, for me?" I saw her eyebrows shoot up under her cropped silver bangs.

"Yes. She is insisting I tell you this, so please don't shoot the messenger. She says she has spoken to Dad, and she knows."

"What? What does she claim to know?" Mom said innocently.

"Tell her I know how he really died *and* why he did it. Tell her she needs to stop burying his truth, and she needs to tell them, especially Jo." As Luke conveyed this message, Mom swayed backwards on her feet and brought her hand to her chest. Flora wasn't the only one in this family with a penchant for drama. Jo glanced at Neal, and he shrugged and shook his head, looking at Mom quizzically and then to Luke.

"I am sorry. I don't really have any other details, but she insisted I give that message. She also says she loves all of you very much."

Thankfully, Luke covered my lack of tact very nicely. I did love them, but at the moment I felt an urgency that overwhelmed me. A desperation to correct the vision my family had toward my father, a vision that was skewed and obscured. I wanted Jo to know her grandfather wasn't who she thought he was, that he was more layered than the one-dimensional, detached father I thought him to be, how much he'd struggled. It seemed she didn't share his depressive tendencies, but she needed to know her true family history all the same. She needed to know burying things, and viewing yourself as flawed or undeserving of love, could do real damage. Both my mother and father limited their own happiness to keep up appearances. If Jo was to have any real chance at happiness, she needed to know that even people who appear perfect aren't. Happiness is found through a road of ugliness. The trick is to find someone who accepts you and supports you as you figure out who you are and what really matters. Luke could be that person for Jo. I felt it in my non-existent bones. Maybe if the facade of perfection were lifted, she would allow herself to have real, messy, imperfect love, and a life of joy.

"Luke, tell Jo she has a right to know who her grandfather really was."

As I spoke, I could feel Dad being drawn toward us, washing over me with his scent of cognac and cigars, light dancing in the air. Luke picked up on him immediately.

"I have Charles here. He wants to say something to you, Celestine."

"Oh for the love of God, are we really going to do this now?" she replied.

"He says he forgives you," Luke interjected. Mom's hands started shaking and she covered her face with them, nails immaculate as always. Luke continued, "He says he understands now, and what happened wasn't your fault. He should have been braver, but he wasn't."

Mom was on her knees now, crying with racking sobs that ruined her makeup. Jo and Neal stared at each other, eyes wide, and Neal bent down and helped Mom up.

"Celestine, I think we all might need to go inside and have a long talk." He dusted her slacks off with his hand as he spoke.

"Yes, Neal, I think we do," she replied shakily as they began to head toward the house. Neal held her elbow as they made their way up the hill.

Luke took up the rear, his thoughts hitting me. *You certainly made that interesting.* That I did, Luke, that I did. I was satisfied with myself. At least my memorial would serve a purpose, moving my family forward into the truth, rather than just talking about how much they missed me. It was good to know I could still influence them from the afterlife, and my story wasn't completely finished yet.

Josephine

The screen door slammed shut and Luke perched in the doorway ready to take flight.

"Jo, I think I should go. I've already stirred up trouble, and I don't really think this is any of my business." Luke clearly wanted to escape this extremely awkward family tussle. Selfishly, I wanted him to stay, but I couldn't justify making him.

"Okay, you sure though?"

"Oh yeah, I'm sure," he said with a slight nod to my dad as he backed toward the front hallway. Dad returned his nod, indicating he might have preferred to leave himself. Dad hated drama, and this was exactly that.

"What was that all about?" I blurted out as soon as the door shut behind Luke. "Memere, what was Mom talking about? What do you need to tell us that we don't know, and what did you need forgiveness for?"

"Neal, do you have any wine? I'm going to need it for this." Memere settled herself on the sofa, stiff, legs crossed with the toe of her ballet flat shaking rapidly in the air. Dad gladly left the room and returned with a glass of wine for Memere and a beer for himself. I paced the room, unable to make myself sit still. After a few hefty swigs of wine, Memere took a deep breath and finally spoke.

"Jo, your grandfather didn't die of a heart attack." She paused, looking pale.

● ● ●

"Then how *did* he die?" I asked, leaning forward against the mantle. I could feel my heart pounding away in my chest and felt lightheaded. I sat down in the chair opposite the sofa. Dad remained silent but was pretty much chugging his beer, eyes darting between the two of us. Memere sighed and finally gave in.

"He committed suicide." Her face fell, and her shoulders slumped forward, her normally perfect posture now gone as she curled in around herself.

"He did this because he wanted out of our marriage. He was having an affair and fell in love with someone else. I gave him an ultimatum, his affair or our family. He chose neither. He chose to leave us all. For years I thought it was my fault."

"Is that why you hid it? I don't understand why he killed himself. People get divorced all the time."

"Well, it wasn't the usual affair. It was…well, it was with another man." I heard Dad choke on his beer from the corner, spilling it down the front of his shirt. After a moment, he was able to sputter enough to speak.

"Wait, Charles was gay?" He stared at Memere in shock. "Nora always told me he was withdrawn. Do you think that was why?" Dad had never met my grandfather as he'd passed before they started dating, but Mom sometimes talked about him. All I really knew was they had a distant relationship, and she never really felt as close to him as she would have liked.

"Well, I suppose he was gay." The word came out in a choked whisper. "He said he loved me, but I don't see how that was possible," Memere said, looking at her now empty wine glass as if it held the answers.

"He could have been bisexual, Memere. He could have been in love with both of you, but trapped between you." I'd heard from Mikayla about the history of gay rights and how much harder things were back then, especially for men in my grandfather's social circles. He definitely could have felt trapped, like he had no viable options.

"Bisexual? Charles?" Her brow furrowed. Clearly it was hard for her to consider this as an option.

"Yeah, lots of people are attracted to both sexes, to different degrees. Think of it as a sliding scale. Like, some people are 100% straight and some people are 100% gay, but many people are somewhere in between."

"Hmmph. Well, I don't know about that, but I do know he was cheating on me and it hurt, and I reacted because of that pain. I told him he couldn't be with us and lead a double life. I just couldn't accept it. And besides the cheating, it was this whole identity that he'd hidden, plus there were diseases to worry about back then. I couldn't let that into my house."

"Memere, really? You work with gay artists all the time!" I was honestly shocked. She seemed like one of the most open-minded people I had ever known. To think she was homophobic was crazy.

"Yes, but that doesn't mean I wanted to be married to one."

"Well, it sounds like he didn't want to be married to you either," I shot at her, a fresh wave of anger rushing over me.

"Jo, honey, we don't know everything that happened between them. We don't even know who this other person was," Dad interjected.

"Well, actually we do." Memere huffed. "His name was Thomas Lawrence and he had the nerve to come to Charles' funeral. I asked him who he was, and he told me straight to my face. Told me he was Charles' lover and colleague. I asked him to leave."

"Well, all that aside, Memere, it is highly likely that Charles suffered from depression as well. Generally, when someone takes their own life, it is not just one thing that does it. Usually things build up for years, and they just hit a breaking point. Charles hit his," Dad continued in an irritatingly clinical voice.

"Yeah, and Memere didn't help him! I could have had a grandfather. I could have known him, but I don't! I lost all of that because no one helped him." I could feel myself spinning out of control. "I need some time to myself. I'm going upstairs."

Memere pleaded, "Jo, honey, please. You have to understand, I regret how I reacted. If I could do it all over again, I would do it differently, but I can't. Hindsight is always clear. Had I known what he was going to do, I would have never pushed him like I did. You have to know that." She looked up at me from the sofa, tears in her eyes.

● ● ●

"I know, I just…I think I just need some time to think about all of this." It hurt me to know I was hurting Memere, but I couldn't process all of this with her there, looking at me like a sad puppy. Mrs. Norris, our actual, perpetually sad hound, got up from her favorite chair and followed me upstairs.

The quiet of my room closed around me as I collapsed on my bed. Mrs. Norris jumped up and burrowed under my arm, snuffling my face. I hugged her and tried to make sense of everything. My grandfather was a closeted bisexual with depressive tendencies who committed suicide as a result of his situation. I turned the other man's name over in my mind: Thomas Lawrence. There was this entire alternate history of my family. I had to talk this over with someone. Mikayla picked up on the second ring.

"Well, damn!" she said after I finished explaining everything. "I guess my coming out should go better than that at least. I'm sorry, I shouldn't joke."

"No, it's okay. It helps. It's what my mom would have done. She was the master of the inappropriate joke."

"Okay, but damn, and he cheated on her to boot. I mean, it *was* a big pill to swallow for your grandma."

"That's true. He did hit her with a lot at once. I don't know what to do with all of these feelings and I didn't even know him. I love *you*, though, so I want you to promise that if you come out to your parents and they react badly, you will come to me for support."

"I will Jo, I promise. It won't be long now. The semester will be over soon, and Hannah is talking about taking a trip together this summer. I want to tell them before that. I don't want them to feel like I lied to them." Mikayla sighed through the phone.

"Yeah, clearly hiding it didn't go well for my granddad. I wonder if things would have ended up the same had he told Memere sooner. You know. If he hadn't bottled it up for so long."

"Oh, Jo, don't do the what ifs, they don't help. Just try to move forward with the truth, and make peace with it."

"You're probably right." I sighed, wishing I could sort through all the thoughts swirling around my head.

● ● ●

Mikayla was right. There was no way cycling the past over in my head was going to help. At least I knew the truth now. I knew my actual family history, not the story I was told. Difficult as it may be to process, at least it was real and honest.

• • •

Neal

C elestine sat on the sofa, small and defeated. I sat across from her in the rocking chair, attempting to absorb all this new information. Charles had cheated on Celestine with a man, and then committed suicide when faced with her ultimatum. It was a lot.

"Neal, I don't know what to do. Jo is so angry with me. Rightfully so, but still. If I had known... " She held her face in her hands, her voice muffled as she spoke.

"Celestine, it's okay. There is no way you could have known what he was going to do."

"I know, but I blamed myself for years after his death. Telling me today that he didn't blame me was a relief, but now Jo hates me." Tears were streaming down her cheeks as he lifted her face to look over at me.

"Jo will forgive you. She loves you. One day she will come to understand things. Why did you lie about his suicide, though?"

"I didn't want the girls' image of their father muddied by the truth. I thought it would be too much for them. Like losing him twice. That's how it was for me. I honestly thought I was saving them from pain."

I felt sympathy for Celestine, trying to save her daughters from the pain associated with a parent's adultery and subsequent suicide. I knew what families went through after suicide. I saw the pain of questioning whether they could have

● ● ●

prevented it compound itself on their loss. Suicide created a special combination of grief, guilt and anger that few other deaths left in their wake.

"You carried it all this time on your own?" I asked, moving over to the couch next to her.

"I did…well, I talked with my therapist about it. She tried to make me feel better, telling me depression was not something anyone outside of a depressed person's mind could understand fully, and I shouldn't blame myself for his suicide. He most likely had a chemical imbalance that went untreated. She told me all the things that are supposed to assuage guilt, except nothing she told me helped. The only thing that could have helped me happened today, when he came through and told me himself. That's why I went to the medium, but when he hadn't given me that message, I got discouraged and stopped going. He was still angry, I suppose. I don't know what changed. Maybe having Nora there with him helped somehow."

"Maybe. What I do know for certain is that you reacted irrationally once, and have been paying for it ever since. Let yourself off the hook. You can't control other people's actions. None of us can, and as much as we'd like to think we have control of the world around us, we don't. You lost your temper when faced with a horrible shock. It's not unheard of. Plus, he *was* cheating on you. No matter the gender of the other person, there was still another person. That hurts."

"I know. Thanks, Neal. My head tells me that makes sense. I just hope I can internalize it and truly find some peace now." She sat back and rubbed her face with her hands. "I think I will go up to bed for a bit."

I sat for a while in the living room, sipping my now warm beer and trying to wrap my head around everything that had happened. I looked up at the mantle where Nora's urn sat, back in its usual spot, only slightly emptier than this morning.

"Don't look so pleased with yourself," I told it, scanning the mantle filled with seemingly random items.

Next to the urn was an old lantern we'd found in the basement while renovating the house. I remember clearing out the basement and finding it. It was caked in dust and way in the back corner of the basement under a chair, but it was completely intact. It was from the 1850s and likely predated the house by a

• • •

few years. The glass was wavy and curved in a globe around the base, which was originally designed to work with whale oil. It was made from tin and had done its job well, only to be left forgotten in the corner of the basement for many years until we found it. Nora was bewitched by it immediately. She lovingly cleaned it, and took it to an antique dealer to find out about it. It sat in its place of honor on the mantle ever since. Nora always valued the things other people forgot about, uncovering their mysteries and enchanted by their imperfections that told their stories. I wondered if she would find that feeling for her mother. Sure, Celestine could have reacted better back then, but as she'd said, she was trying to shoulder the burden for her children. I thought about myself and what I might have done if Nora had come to me with what Charles had come to Celestine with. How would I have handled that? How would Nora have reacted had the tables been turned on her?

For Jo's part, she had never been in love, and never been spurned by someone she loved. She couldn't comprehend the anger and hurt that could be unearthed with relative ease between any two people who truly loved each other. Maybe it was because I wasn't related to Charles, and hadn't had him as a father, but I could easily see both sides of the equation. Depression combined with self-hate and rejection had led Charles to make decisions out of pain that only expanded that pain. While, for Celestine, the pain of betrayal and lies had led her to lash out, only to then experience profound guilt. No matter which way you looked at the situation, there was pain leading to poor decisions with long term effects, rippling out for generations, stretching all the way into the afterlife.

• • •

Eleanor

I firmly believe there is no such thing as the 'fun mom.' You know the ones. The ones who sing songs to their kids in that chipper happy tone constantly. The parents who don't seem to care if their children are screaming and running rampant in a restaurant, and instead join in on the fun. I like fun, I really do. I just prefer it in the spaces where it is appropriate, at home or outdoors at a park. In public, I had a hard time letting loose and being spontaneous. I suppose in some way I reflected my own mother in this. I didn't want to be judged for a child with bad manners, bad habits, or dirty clothes. Women carry a burden of responsibility for a family's well-being that men don't quite get saddled with. Women are the ones expected to maintain the perfect family while men are applauded for simply showing up.

Once, when we were having lunch at a local bakery cafe, a five year old Jo was singing too loudly and I told her to shush. People were turning to look at my child as she loudly recited a very off-key version of Jingle Bells in August. Natural artistic talent ran strong in our family, natural musical ability did not.

"Not everyone wants to listen to children while they eat," I told her. Neal was busy ordering our food at the counter. I was alone in my battle for relative silence.

* * *

In the next booth over, a woman was playing thumb wrestling wars with the child seated with her.

"Why can't you be a fun mom?" Jo asked me, pouting but finally quiet after multiple shushings.

"No moms are fun, honey," I replied.

"*That* Mom is," she said, with a sassy head tilt and eyebrow lift that seemed more appropriate on a teenager than my normally sweet five-year-old. I suppressed the hot flash of anger it incited and replied as calmly as I could.

"Well, I'm sorry, honey. I'm just not that kind of mom."

Neal brought our food over and Jo needed to use the bathroom. As we walked by the 'fun mom,' I heard the child say, "Cindy, I hope Daddy marries you one day." *See, she's not a mom. That's why she's still fun.*

I still think this is true. As mothers, we end up saddled with the hardest part of parenting. From the actual physical sacrifice to the increased judgment of the world at large. If fathers take their children out on their own, people praise them even if those children behave like heathens. If a mother takes her children out on her own, and they behave like heathens, she gets dirty looks from all sides.

The judgment never ends. Maybe this is why my mom felt the need to bury secrets. To her mind, if her husband was gay, it meant she had failed as a wife and mother. It would also bring pain and shame into our family. While I'm not sure she picked the right path, I understood it. I didn't want this knowledge to turn Jo against my mom. I just wanted them all to be aware of a family history of depression, and that we were not as perfect as we seemed. I needed that to be known. It needed to be on their radar, and now it was. Job done. Not fun. But necessary.

On this side of the afterlife, things between Dad and me were more open and connected than ever. He brought me to the day of my birth, with Mom holding me in her arms, sweating, pale and tired, but smiling down at my tiny body. She grinned up at him and whispered a quiet 'I love you' as she held me out for him. My father's arms, young and strong, held my tiny body swaddled in a blanket. I felt panic, *his* panic, welling up inside of

● ● ●

him. Love, too, but so much fear that I was overwhelmed by it even in memory.

He showed me nights when he didn't sleep, lying awake in bed beside Mom as she slept, his thoughts a tangle of worries and self-doubt. Agonizing over wrongs he felt he'd perpetrated, some of which occurred many years prior to the night of his memory. I felt more guilt in his memories than anything else, mostly guilt over perceived shortcomings on his part. Many of the things he shared were memories I knew, but seeing them from Dad's eyes made them new again.

Once, Flora fell from her horse and broke her ankle during a show. I remembered being pulled off of my pony Barnaby, and told that we were leaving the show. I was to pack up my things and go home with Dad while Mom took Flora to the hospital. It was my first show, and the last one Dad attended, meaning he never saw me ride in a show at all. I held it against him for years, feeling that he cared more about Flora than me. That *my* shows were somehow less important. Now I saw it had nothing to do with either daughter, and everything to do with my dad.

Once plunged into his version, the day looked very different. It was filled with worry and fear for Flora, and an overwhelming feeling of being unprepared for the task of bringing a wailing six-year-old and two horses home from a show. Loading the horses into the trailer was the easy part. Impartial as always, both horses walked right on and happily munched hay as he set about collecting me. He carried me kicking and screaming from the show grounds in front of complete strangers and acquaintances who seemed to enjoy the spectacle. Instead of helping, most people just watched. He was alone, terrified and inadequate, which meant he closed himself off to avoid further embarrassment from a breakdown in front of everyone there. In my version, he was cold and distant. What I took for lack of care was actually hidden panic and fear masked by neutrality.

As he showed me more memories over time, I began to see that his death was years in the making, with many small cracks in a smooth facade eventually shattering his entire being. Thousands of tiny perceived failures, insults, and frustrations over his entire life.

● ● ●

I had shining memories from our visits to France while I was a child. My memories were filled with lavender-scented fields, rough plaster walls, and sunlight pouring in from every window. They were punctuated by the smooth terra cotta tile kitchen floor that was always cool under my bare feet and the worn wooden table that held our family meals. Windows in the big old house were left open to let the breeze come in from the fields, scenting everything with lavender. My grandparents showered my sister and me with attention, gifts, and adoration. I loved our visits and complained many times that we didn't go often enough.

My father's memories of these trips were very different. There were many memories of his in-laws grilling him on his latest accomplishments. Which never seemed to amount to enough to them.

His own parents were worse. When he graduated from law school, he was immediately reminded that the real accomplishment was passing the bar. Then, once he had done that, it was going on to make partner at a big well-renowned firm. It was made clear to him that becoming a partner at a small firm such as the one he'd started at was mediocre by their standards. His father, a foreign affairs minister, and mother, a diplomat, both climbed quite high in French society. His mother's accomplishment made even more impressive because of the very few women who attained that title then, or since. To them, it was never enough. I saw them make him feel guilty for leaving the country and not returning, for not taking opportunities when they came up, for not being a better father.

"Why are you and your children not achieving at the highest levels?" they constantly asked him.

I saw now that he had been instilled with a feeling of never being good enough early on and successfully broke that cycle by moving abroad and marrying my mother, who, while flawed, never pushed us to be anyone we didn't want to be. My father, for his part, remained distant and limited in his words or affection, but never directly made either my sister or myself feel that we weren't good enough. As my image of my father and his life became clearer, I understood his tragic end was not really my mother's fault, but a sad end to a life filled with unattainable expectations.

• • •

I let my mom off the hook. How many times in life had I lost my temper and said things I later regretted? The only difference was that I always had the chance to apologize and work things out after my initial anger subsided. My father took that chance away for both of them when he took his own life.

Josephine

The door to my room slowly opened wider and wider, allowing a darkened figure behind it to enter the room. I tried to sit up in bed but couldn't. I was completely frozen. My body wouldn't obey my commands to move, and I lay there staring at someone in the dark as they came toward me.

"Josephine, I'm not finished. I need to finish this." Colin's voice crashed over me and I was seized with panic. *How did he get in here? Why can't I move?* I tried to scream but couldn't even open my mouth. The door slammed shut behind him, and I snapped awake to find myself alone in my room with only Mrs. Norris as company. She was blissfully snoring on the end of the bed, unaware of the panic I felt. My heart was racing, tears streaming down my cheeks. I struggled to free myself from my sheets, which were stuck to me with sweat.

I rubbed my eyes and tried to clear my mind. It had been almost a year since the assault, and I was doing better up until a few seconds ago. Initially, I had nightmares often. Almost nightly. But after working with my therapist and several different anti-anxiety medications, I'd gotten through the worst of it. As a kid, I often had dreams that seemed supremely real, but they were rarely this scary. Sometimes I would wake up disoriented, standing up somewhere in the house. The farthest I'd gotten was the top of the stairs when I was eleven. Mom freaked out after that incident and always came upstairs to close my door. She also made Dad install a swinging wooden gate at the top of the front stairs, a glorified, super-embarrassing baby gate.

I tried to calm myself down at this moment, and, per my therapist's advice, I tried to think of a time when I felt brave.

The night we celebrated the completely uneventful event of Mikayla's coming out to her parents and the end of term came to mind. We'd gone to Chirpy's, a bar full of obnoxious frat boys, but good music and a dance floor. Mikayla, Hannah and I danced until we were sweaty and thirsty, then moved to the bar to order our sodas. We stood there, black X's adorning our hands, when the scent of men's body spray nearly suffocated me.

"Hey there, what position do you prefer?" sneered a nondescript white guy in a polo shirt, his eyes landing on Mikayla's chest.

"Umm, I don't know what you mean?" she responded in a polite, clipped tone she reserved for these kinds of encounters, of which there were too many.

"Well, you play basketball right? I mean you look like you should play basketball, so what position?" *Does he really think he is being clever, or engaging?*

"I don't," Mikayla replied. She turned away and continued waiting for her drink, discreetly holding Hannah's hand under the bar.

"Really? Hmm, volleyball then, what do you play?" *Man, this guy is just not giving up.*

"She doesn't *play* anything. She's pre-law if you must know," I interjected, putting my small frame between them.

"Huh. I would have never guessed." He hovered there uncomfortably like a gnat flitting around your face in the summer.

"Why? Why would you have never guessed that?" I could hear the edge in my voice creeping up.

"Well, no reason."

"Yes, there is a reason. Why don't you illuminate for me why you assumed *she* played basketball, when her girlfriend sitting right next to her is just as athletically built but you said nothing to her? Huh? You wanna explain that to me?" My voice was verging on shrill as my anger got the best of me. It *may* have also been the shots of tequila I'd had prior to coming out.

● ● ●

"I was just trying to be friendly. You don't have to be such bitches about it," he grumbled, then sauntered off to his group of similarly dressed friends near the pool tables.

"Well, you don't have to be such a racist prick either!" I yelled after him. Mikayla and Hannah nearly died laughing, and Mikayla hugged me tight before we headed back to the dance floor.

Why was I only brave when tipsy and defending other people? That had been nearly two months ago, and Mikayla and Hannah were now traveling up the East coast, visiting different beaches and towns along the way until they got to Boston, where Hannah had family. They were in love, and it was a beautiful thing to watch, but it left me a bit lonely. I had no one around right now to talk to, and while Dad tried, I knew he would never understand the helplessness I felt in that dream.

Memere and I were talking, but not like before. I'd come to the realization, again with the help of my therapist, that while she reacted poorly in the moment, she couldn't control the actions of someone struggling with depression. I was beginning to see the adults in my life through a clearer lens than the rose colored ones I always viewed them with in the past, and slowly realizing that the idea of adulthood was possibly a myth. Adults were just as likely to strike out in anger, and to struggle with emotions as much as anyone else.

My parents enjoyed a loving relationship for years. I only saw them argue a few times. Usually about chores that should have been done but weren't, or tasks that were not completed up to the other person's standards. They genuinely loved each other, and more often than not resolved their disagreements without an excess of yelling or anger. I wondered if I would ever find anything like that. Who was going to want to be with a girl who felt panic at the idea of someone on top of her, and talked to her dead mother with a surprising frequency?

Beside the bed, my phone dinged with a voicemail. I picked it up and a familiar voice washed over me, my anxiety over the dream floating away as I listened.

• • •

"Hey, Jo, it's Luke. I was going to take the girls on a hike at White Oak. I thought you might want to join. Just let me know if you do. We'll probably leave around nine, and we could pick you up along the way."

Luke and his sisters were great company. As a guy accustomed to being outnumbered by women, he took their constant gentle teasing of him in stride, and it always made for a fun outing. Cynthia, Luke's mom, worked two jobs, and Luke often took Rebecca, Mary, and Sarah out to do things on weekends while she was on shift to get them out of the house.

They were all vibrant and fun, and clearly adored their older brother. It was no small wonder. Luke hadn't shared all the gory details of his past, but I knew their father had been physically abusive to their mom for years. Cynthia felt divorce was an affront to a marriage blessed by God, and stayed with him for far too long. Until Luke's father nearly blinded Cynthia with a blow to the face that broke the bones around her eye. Luke intervened, managing to lock him out of the house and call the police. It was the final straw, and Cynthia finally filed for a divorce and restraining order. After that, he was out of their lives for good. I called Luke back and left a message, letting him know I'd love to join them. A day in the woods with Luke and his sisters would be just the thing to clear the dark dream from my mind.

We arrived at our picnic spot around eleven after hiking from the parking area. Sunlight bounced off the surface of the water as we dipped into our favorite pool on the trail. Rebecca had packed sandwiches, and Luke and Sarah sat on a rock nearby, eating and relaxing in the dappled sunlight. Mary and Rebecca were wading up the stream barefoot, picking up small stones and watching fish in the eddies. The water was a comfortable respite from the oppressive heat of July in Virginia. I lounged on my stomach in a shallow rock pool, the stones smooth and slippery beneath me.

"You look happy, like a hound wallowing in mud!" Luke teased from his rock.

"Haha, how flattering!" I responded, splashing water toward him.

• • •

"Well, it looks so nice I think I'll join you." He took his t-shirt off and stepped into the pool, lying down next to me on his back, looking up at the trees over our heads.

"This is the life, isn't it?" He grinned as he turned toward me.

"It is. Nothing better than cool water, sunshine, good company and yummy food." I sighed, feeling happy and relaxed. The three girls were now splashing in the water near us, and occasionally at us. I stood up from the water, dripping, and stepped toward the shore. I was starting to get hungry and wanted one of those sandwiches. As I stepped forward, my foot slipped on an algae-covered rock and my body lurched forward. I tried to correct but failed, my body dropping toward the water's surface. Luke scooped his hands under me and caught me just before I hit. He wrapped his arms around my waist and set me back on my feet, holding my hand as I made my way onto the sandy bank.

"Thanks," I puffed, trying not to think about how it felt to have his arms around me. Trying to not think about how good it had felt. When I looked up at his face, it was flushed, and he quickly glanced down at the rocks just under the surface of the water.

"That would've hurt if you hit those." Luke stepped out of the water and handed me a towel before grabbing one for himself. He draped it around his shoulders and sat down on the rock he'd been eating on earlier.

"Hungry?" He pawed through the backpack with food and water in it. I felt my stomach rumble in response to the prospect of peanut butter and jelly sandwiches and potato chips.

"Definitely." I sat beside him and took a foil-wrapped sandwich as he set the bag of chips down beside us. I unwrapped it and bit into the soft, gooey comfort of the flavors. His sisters made the jam from blackberries in their yard. It was deliciously sweet against the salty peanut butter. Luke handed me a napkin, and I promptly dribbled jelly down my front.

"I thought you didn't read minds?" I said as I wiped jelly off my stomach.

"I don't. You're just a super messy eater," he said, grinning at me and laughing as he leaned away to dodge a swat I directed towards his shoulder.

● ● ●

"Haha." I mockingly glared at him. "Hey, at least I enjoy my food!"

"I didn't say it was a bad thing. I'm just saying it's an observation I've made." He bumped me gently with his shoulder, and his warm skin brushed mine again, filling me with a heat that had nothing to do with the sunshine filtering through the treetops.

Neal

Jo's birthday weekend arrived again, and she and Luke were coming for dinner tonight with Mikayla and Hannah. Celestine was joining us as well. My Dad had thrown his back out earlier that week lifting something he shouldn't have, so they couldn't make the drive but sent a card and gift ahead. Jo's birthday was bound to be better this year than last. The specter of last year hung around us, but was hopefully being pushed out by the process of making happier memories to replace the old ones.

I headed out to our favorite local bakery to pick up a cake. For dinner, I had chili ready in the slow cooker, and would put some cornbread in the oven to go with it. I was very proud of myself for thinking ahead. Nora would have been proud of me as well. I'd prepared all of Jo's favorites, all by myself. Well, with the help of a professional bakery.

Jo always loved cornbread and chili. Even as a toddler, she would scarf it down, dropping chili-soaked crumbs everywhere. Nora always made a huge mess while eating as well. The woman could go through three or four napkins easily if tacos were on the menu. I loved it about her. The way she would grin at me from across the table, laughing at my 'ridiculously clean plate' as she called it. I was just careful. I never overloaded my taco, or burger bun, or whatever else I had. Nora, meanwhile, would load as much food as possible into whatever vehicle she was using, then bite into the whole thing. Juice, meat, vegetables, everything would all come spilling out the other side, onto her increasingly messy plate. I always teased her that she was the only person I knew who was messy enough to need a fork to eat finger food.

At least cake was relatively neat, I thought to myself as I stepped up to the familiar bakery counter. Nora and I had frequented this place for years, and the large sunny windows and ancient wooden counter were a familiar comfort. A girl a bit younger than Jo greeted me with a cheery smile.

"I ordered a cake for my daughter's birthday. It should be ready. It's a nine-inch coconut cake."

"Ah yes, Mr. Brooks, we have that ready for you! I'll just go into the back and grab it." She hurried into the back and I started to ponder the selections in the case.

"You're not going to tell her it's Dr. Brooks?" a familiar voice came from behind me.

"Ha, no, I don't really worry about that anywhere but work." I turned to see Janet, a previous resident sitting on a couch by the window. She'd always had a wicked sense of humor. I had tried and failed to get Janet and her husband out to our house for dinner several times. She and Nora would have gotten along well. She walked over to me and placed a hand on my shoulder. I backed up. No woman had touched me, other than Mom or Jo, since Nora's passing and the awful funeral. It felt strange and uncomfortable.

"How are you, by the way? I was so sorry to hear about your wife," she said, applying the same blanket expression of sympathy I had seen so often.

"Nora. Thank you." I turned my wedding band with my fingers. The smooth metal was reassuring and familiar.

"It's been over a year now, hasn't it? Gosh, I can't believe I haven't seen you in that long." She brushed her hair back over her shoulder and kept smiling at me. I felt awkward and stilted. This was someone I had worked with elbow-deep in blood-filled abdomens, yelling orders, then bonding after over-hurried meals eaten out of tupperware containers. Amazing so little time would lead to this level of disconnect.

"Yep. It's been a while. What have you been up to? Where did you end up after finishing?" The girl from the bakery nodded to me and set a cake box down on the counter. I handed her my credit card and turned back to Janet.

"Oh, I went up north to a practice in Maryland for a bit, but Mike and I split up, and I moved back down here about three months ago. I'm at a private practice in Charlottesville now."

"I had no idea. Well, sorry to hear about you and Mike, but I'm glad to know there's one more excellent GP nearby I can refer people to. Do you have a card?"

She pulled out a business card and wrote her cell number on the back. "Thanks, Neal. Hey, we should get lunch sometime. Catch up."

"Sure, my office number is the same. I check it daily, so that's probably the easiest way to get in touch." She frowned a bit, then smiled again.

"I was hoping to get your personal number, if that's okay. I've given you mine. It's only fair you give me yours." I gave her my number, and she gave me a quick hug before heading toward the door.

"See you soon, Neal," she called, smiling as she left.

I thanked the bakery clerk and carried the cake home. Later that night, I told the group about it over dinner.

"Dad! She was hitting on you!" Jo exclaimed when I told her how Janet had asked for my personal number. The idea seemed alien to me. I wasn't available. I had no interest in dating anyone.

"No way, I'm not interested. Nora was all I ever needed. I don't want anyone else."

"I know that, and you know that, but this Janet lady doesn't know that. She just knows she wants a piece of that hot booty!" Jo dissolved into peals of laughter after this last statement, with the rest of the group chuckling as well.

"Haha. Well, she is in for disappointment if that is what she expects. This booty is pale and old, and not available."

"Eeew, Dad, we're eating!" she said, still chuckling.

"Right, then let's change the subject," I said, smiling over at Jo, who was now wiping her mouth and shirt after dribbling chili on herself. Nora would have loved this laughter at my expense, a fact that made me miss her more. Conversation drifted along merrily through chili and cake. Jo opened her

* * *

presents. After a while, I felt myself fading and excused myself to my room.

As I left the dining room, I could hear Luke and Mikayla starting to load the dishwasher, admonishing Jo for offering to help. Mikayla's voice rang through the kitchen, "No! It's your birthday dinner. You are not allowed to do dishes. Go sit down and relax!"

Jo came into the hallway behind me. "Dad, thanks for tonight. Just let me know if we get too loud and are keeping you up, okay?"

"Don't worry about me, honey. I'm so tired you could drive a truck through here and I wouldn't notice. I'm glad you had fun. Happy Birthday, honey." I kissed her forehead, and she gave me a tight hug.

"Thanks, Dad. Goodnight."

"Goodnight honey."

The bedroom door closed behind me, and the voices in the kitchen were muffled to soft background noise. Had Janet really been hitting on me? I found the thought shocking but supposed I shouldn't have. To me, Nora was still a presence, a force in my life that wasn't extinguished by the short amount of time she had been gone from it. Nora and I were together for thirty two years. The majority of my life up to this point was spent with her. The idea that I may live long enough to spend the majority of my life without her was daunting and foreign. This wasn't the plan. I was supposed to live with her until I was old and frail, until I was far too old for anyone to consider the idea that I might be romantically inclined. Instead, here I was at fifty-four, with the idea that I wouldn't be with anyone else. I could live another forty years. My parents were in their mid-eighties and still fully independent. They moved slower and my dad complained more, but overall they were in pretty good shape. Was I really planning on being alone for all of that time? I sighed, lying down in the middle of the bed.

Hobbit followed me into the bedroom and hopped up on the mattress. She snuggled herself into my side and purred. I didn't feel quite so alone then and curled up around her little rumbling body, scratching her under her chin. She purred louder and kneaded the mattress beside me. As I lay there, thoughts of what my future would look like swirled around in my head.

● ● ●

Alone with just animals for company, I could become one of those hermits who never left his house except for work. Was that a bad thing? I pulled the card Janet had given me out of my pocket. I looked at her writing on the back and threw it in the trash. I wasn't ready for her attention, of that I was sure.

• • •

Josephine

T he sky through the trees was a bright blue, broken by whispers of cirrus clouds, their texture that of a feather, undulating and shimmering. The mixture of gold, red, and yellow in the leaves stood in stark contrast. I snapped a picture with my phone. This would make a nice painting.

"Getting ideas?" Luke said as we walked along the wide trail. Mrs Norris snuffled along beside me, rooting through leaves and wagging happily.

"Yeah, I like the way the colors play against each other, and the shape of the branches."

"You would certainly do it justice." He smiled over at me. "You are really amazing with color. I love what you do with it every time."

"Thanks. What you do with fabrication is amazing to me. I mean, you turn abstract ideas and cast off items into sculptures."

"Ah, it's just glorified recycling."

"Maybe, but they are something you should be really proud of."

His hand touched mine, and for a moment our fingers intertwined.

"Thanks. Oh, I think we're at the spot." He gestured at a small offshoot of the trail. We walked a short way to an old stone foundation in a clearing. It was one of our favorite picnic spots. During winter, it offered an amazing view of Old Rag.

• • •

With the leaves still mostly on the trees as they were now, it was less dramatic, but instead a secluded and peaceful picnic spot.

We finished our sandwiches and lay back to look at the branches above us. I cut my eyes over to Luke and admired him. His jawline was brushed with dark stubble, and his full lips curved in the smallest of smiles as he contentedly gazed at the trees and sky above. He closed his eyes, and his long dark lashes barely brushed his high cheekbones. He really was beautiful. I turned to him just as he looked over at me. He barely turned his head, but it brought his mouth closer to mine, and I leaned over and kissed him for the first time. He was warm, and just a bit scratchy, with lips that tasted of the salty chips we'd had with our lunch. He kissed me in return and then pulled slightly back.

"Why'd you do that?" He smiled. "I certainly don't mind, but I just thought maybe you wouldn't ever want that to happen between us."

"I think I do. I think I do want it to happen between us. I don't think there is anyone else I would want it to happen with than you." The words tumbled out before I could think, and I sat for a panicked second, afraid I'd ruined our friendship. Then his crooked smile spread into a full-fledged grin, lighting his face.

"Thank goodness, because from that first day you came into the coffee shop, it's been you. You crept into my thoughts long before you walked into Joan's office, and then after."

"Really? That long? I was so awkward though."

"No you weren't." He smirked. "Well, maybe a little."

I smacked him playfully on the chest, and he caught my hand in his gently.

"But I liked that. I liked *you*. I liked that you weren't putting on a show, and I liked your ideas, I liked your creativity, and, well, I always thought you were beautiful." He blushed and sat up next to me. I lifted my body to his and kissed him again, this time allowing myself to immerse myself in the feeling. His hands moved down my body to the hollow of my back, and I arched closer to him. I felt secure and safe in his arms even as my body was set alight.

After that afternoon in the woods, it was a headlong rush. Luke entered my thoughts at all times. Being apart from him felt like part of myself was torn away.

"How do people live like this?" I asked Dad one afternoon. I was home, and Luke had a reading to do, leaving me without him for part of the day.

"Live like what?" He passed me a glass of iced tea as he sat down on the couch next to me.

"I mean. I feel like I just can't think about anything else but Luke."

"Yeah. Love is like that at first." Dad smiled. "But then it mellows out, and the lucky ones, the ones who have built a friendship under all the fire, settle into life together."

"When does that happen?"

"Oh, I don't know. It took awhile for me anyway. I was stupid over your mom for a long time. Way longer than she was over me." He chuckled and shook his head.

"Really?" I sipped my tea and contemplated a love-stricken version of my dad.

"Definitely. Nora was more mature than I was. She'd traveled, dated, and experienced way more than I had."

"Huh. Do you think Luke and I have what it takes to make it?" I was terrified of losing Luke now, and also terrified that maybe I was choosing too early. *Didn't people usually date multiple people before 'settling down'?*

"I do, honey. You guys did it the right way. You became friends first, before all the hormones clouded the picture. You got to know each other, and liked each other before you fell in love. From *my* experience, which may be worth nothing, the relationships that work out the best start out slow, then catapult over the cliff of romance *after* a friendship."

"Is that how it was for you and Mom?" I snuggled into the sofa and wrapped a blanket around my knees.

"Kind of. I mean, I punched that guy at the party, which meant your mom noticed me. But it took a while before I got up the nerve to ask her out. By the time I finally did, she just laughed and asked what took me so long."

"How long did it take you?" I had never thought of Dad as tentative or fearful.

● ● ●

"Oh, only a few months. Your mom couldn't have made it any more obvious what she wanted. I just didn't read any of the signs. It may surprise you, but I was kind of awkward before meeting your mom."

"Really, I *never* would have guessed." I smirked at him. Dad constantly made terrible, nerdy Dad jokes. Mom had always teased him about it.

"Hey now. I can quote your mom here. She would always say, 'Awkward, earnest guys are the best ones to date because they try harder and they're honest.' I like to think she was right about that." He gave me an awkward, goofy smile, thus proving her point.

"So, you think Luke is good? I mean, do you think he's the right person for me? It feels like he is, but I don't trust myself. After all, I thought Colin was charming and sensitive."

"Luke is nothing like Colin." His voice became firm when it touched on Colin and the smile dropped away. Then he softened. "I like Luke very much, and it is very, very clear to me that he loves you and you love him. Nobody is good enough for my only daughter, but Luke is about as close as someone is likely to get." I leaned over and hugged him, relieved that someone who loved me as much as he did didn't think I was crazy for falling in love with Luke.

"Thanks, Dad."

"You're welcome, honey. I promise, if I didn't like him, you'd know."

"I know, Dad, I know." I was filled with a warm flush of gratitude. I was only two years past the hardest year of my life and found myself flush with happiness I thought I'd never feel again, or possibly ever. When people say, 'It's all downhill from here,' they tend to mean things will get worse, but I thought of the phrase differently. We all have our hills to climb. I'd climbed mine, and here I stood at what I hoped was the top, ready to let life carry me along down the other side.

● ● ●

Eleanor

S unlight filtered through old stained glass windows and lit Jo's face in an amber light as she married Luke. There was so much intention, joy, and grief held in the old stone walls of the small church that I felt anchored by them, allowing me to watch the ceremony with relative clarity. Luke's mother had insisted on a church wedding, and I was grateful for her insistence. Jo and Luke were finally where they belonged. Together. Luke proposed two years into their dating, and I watched the planning that went into this day over the following year.

Tears filled Jo and Luke's eyes as they recited their vows, hands clasped together. The small crowd frequently needed tissues, and there was a loud, raucous celebration as they made their exit after the ceremony. The reception was held at our house, in a rented tent placed in the backyard with friends and family gathered again at my home, this time with unbridled joy in their hearts. It was a long way from five years ago when people gathered for my funeral.

They found a little house and parcel of land not far from Neal and his parents who now lived with him. It was a bungalow that Jo filled with art and cast off furniture from various places. I could see why they chose it. While small, it was bright and airy inside with huge picture windows in the back that

• • •

overlooked the rolling fields behind. It even had some of the craftsman details that I'd always coveted. Little built-in bookshelves to either side of the fireplace that sported original green glazed tile. The front room had a beautiful row of stained glass windows that cast color and shape along the wood floors. It was a perfect combination of warmth and brightness making it feel like it had been made for them.

Jo moved Callie and Briony there to be near her and gave my old mare Georgia to the girl who took care of the horses while Jo was away at college as a way of thanking her for all the work she'd put in over the years. Briony, once a dark dappled grey, was now a snowy white, her back sagging and her joints stiff. She ambled through the pastures instead of bucking through the grass on cool mornings. Mahalo was gone now, passed from his large, solid body like ether. Jo had found him dead in the pasture, lying on his side with grass still in his mouth. I hovered over her as she sobbed over his lifeless body.

Neal would occasionally tug on our connecting line between us as he puttered around the house. Talking to me about his day, blaming me for all his missing items, even though I'd stopped hiding his keys years ago. Sam and Grace were ensconced in the in-law apartment upstairs and used a chair to come downstairs. Sam would fix little things around the house as he was able, or tell Neal how he should be doing it if he was unable. Grace cooked, and the warm aroma of her meals would fill the house, greeting Neal when he came home. They still functioned well but moved slower each day. I fully expected them to come over to me first, but instead my mother arrived, panicky and chaotic.

Her energy crashed over me like a powerful wave at the beach. I was reeling from it when she came at me again. I tried to wash myself over her to calm her down, but she was fighting this process strongly. Finally, Dad came to help, blending his energy with mine to envelop her like a blanket. Her thoughts were scattered, images of her bedroom at home, then bright flashing lights, then unfamiliar voices all around her. But overall she mostly conveyed fear. I tried to give her images of myself, and Dad did the same. Then her energy moved away from us,

• • •

and I could tell she was pulling herself back into the physical world. However she died, it was sudden and surprising to all involved.

I felt for the threads attaching me to those I loved and found Neal first. He was at home, on the couch in his sweatpants and a t-shirt, working on course plans with a cup of coffee steaming beside him. I stayed with him in that space watching, savoring the normality of this moment. He ran his hands through his now mostly silver hair and then stretched his arms up with a groan. His newly acquired reading glasses sat perched on his nose, and as he got back to work, he adjusted them with a finger. I found it surprisingly sexy. Jesus. What was wrong with me? Neal's phone rang and reminded me I was not here simply to leer at my husband like some supernatural peeping tom. I knew what would be on the other end of that phone call.

"Okay, just let me know what you need me to do. Has anyone told Jo yet?" A pause as Neal paced the room while talking.

"Right, okay, I'll call her now." He ended the call, sat back down, and put his face in his hands, letting out a long sigh. I realized this must be bringing up feelings of having to call Jo when I died. It would always be up to Neal. He would always be the one to give her bad news, about me, Mom, his parents. I lay my nonexistent hands on his shoulders as I hovered behind him on the couch. It was something I had done in life when Neal needed me, and the gesture was familiar and comforting to us both. He reached his hands up to where mine should be and relaxed slightly, before picking up the phone to call Jo.

"Jo? Hey honey, it's me, Dad." He paused. "Are you at home? Oh, okay, good. I have news for you about Memere." A longer pause, and then, "She passed away this morning." His face was drawn, and Mrs. Norris wriggled over to him on the couch, putting her now grey muzzle in his lap. He put a hand on her head and stroked her long, soft ears.

"Yes, it was sudden. It may have been an aneurysm. Obviously they don't know yet. What I do know that it looks like she was found by her friend Idina, in her bedroom. They were meeting for a sunrise yoga session, and when Celestine didn't answer the door, Idina let herself in with the frog key."

• • •

My mother always kept a spare key in a small iron frog statue near the house. When asked about it, she always chirped, 'You never know when you will need a spare.' Looks like she was right. It's just too bad Idina hadn't arrived a bit earlier.

"No, I don't think she suffered. No, she had a plan in place, so we shouldn't have too much to do other than show up when and where we are told. Flora will be meeting with the lawyer when she gets in from New York. We'll know more then. Alright, I love you too, honey.

"Well, I suppose we better get ready for this day," he said, patting Mrs. Norris, who was now curled up next to him on the couch snoring. She hopped down and padded slowly along behind him as he went into the bathroom to shower and dress for whatever was to come.

Josephine

I hung up the phone and pressed my face into the coolness of my palms. Luke came out of the bathroom, still damp from showering, and sat beside me.

"I felt her, Jo. Memere. I felt her in the house for an instant," he said, knowing already what I had been told on the other end of that line.

"Oh, Luke, why now? She seemed so healthy. I mean, I know she was older, but she wasn't sick. I was going to tell her next weekend." My hand went instinctively to the small swell of my stomach. "I was going to tell everyone. Now what do I do? I can't announce anything now. Not with this going on." Luke wrapped his still damp arms around me and held me, letting me cry into his shoulder.

"I'm sorry, I really am," Luke said, his voice full of concern. I sat back and looked at his shoulder.

"Oh, I'm sorry too. I got snot all over you," I said with what I hoped was my most charming smile as I wiped at his slimy shoulder. He smiled at me.

"Eh, it's a hazard I'm willing to deal with." He grabbed a tissue and wiped his shoulder off as he handed me another for myself.

"I love you. I just wish I could have shared this with her," I said, touching my belly with my hand.

"I know. She'll still be there. She'll still know our child as long as you want her to."

● ● ●

195

"Yeah, I know, but she will never hold our baby, and our baby won't know her, or my mom, not really. I just feel so alone in this. I have Grandma, but she's frail, and she won't be around forever. I feel like there aren't any women for my child to look up to like there were for me. I mean, except your mom."

"No, it's okay. I love my mom, but she isn't exactly the model I want for our possible daughter either. Jo, you are an amazing woman. If we have a daughter, she'll have *you* to look up to, and Mikayla, and my sisters. Maybe our baby won't know your mom or Memere in a physical sense, but through stories and memories, our child will know them all the same."

"Thanks, I needed to hear that. I'm glad I married you, and I'm glad you are going to be the father of our children."

"Children? Is there something you aren't telling me? I thought there was only one little blip on the screen." There was a hint of genuine concern in his tone.

"There was only one, I promise. But we won't know if we are going to be done with just one. Will we?"

"Let's get the first one out and potty trained first. Then we can decide, huh? I'm going to get dressed. Have you done the horses yet?"

"No, I was getting ready to go out when Dad called." I got up, kissed Luke, and headed out the door.

Walking down to our little shed, my thoughts felt detached from the moment and focused on Memere. I filled buckets with grain and called the horses up. They had clearly given up any hope of ever being fed and were grazing down the hill from the run-in where I fed them. After I whistled, Briony's head shot up and she whinnied as she came trotting up to me. Callie squealed and kicked her heels up, following Briony to the fence. Once they were munching happily, I grabbed a brush and gave them a quick groom. Pulling Dad's trick of keeping my body busy to quiet my mind.

After a quick brushing of their sleek summer coats, I put on their fly masks, then leaned on the gate to watch them eat. Briony finished quickly but licked the bottom of the bucket hopefully for a long time after finishing her tiny amount of grain. Eventually she came over to me and nuzzled my hand, looking for treats. I breathed in, smelling the heavenly, sweet, earthy smell of her, and opened the gate to let her back out into the

● ● ●

pasture. She ambled over to the water trough and drank, lifting her head after and letting water dribble out of her mouth into the trough below, bubbles forming on her chin. Still at her bucket, Callie pinned her ears and kicked out at the wall with a loud crack of hoof against wood. I looked around, expecting to see a horsefly. When I didn't see or hear one, I let her out into the field. She tore through the gate and past me, nearly knocking me over. She trotted out, tail high over her back, and stood a few feet away, trembling and snorting at the run-in. I glanced around again, hoping there wasn't a snake or other threat to deal with. I saw nothing and soon both horses were grazing peacefully in the shady paddock like nothing had happened, the only sounds an occasional swish of their tails and the loud drone of cicadas.

The cloying scent of honeysuckle drifted from a vine nearby. I stood for a moment, aware of the life around me. The grass was still shining and wet from thunderstorms the night before. The field stretched down to a small copse of trees, where a fox vixen and her cubs emerged. She lay in the grass as they hopped about tackling each other.

I placed a hand on my belly to rest my hand on the slight fullness that wasn't there before. I felt warm and happy for the life beginning inside me, but sadness for the lives that had ended before they would get to share any of this joy. Memere wasn't here in the physical world any more, but I hoped she was still around, the same way Mom was with me in moments like this. Tangible, but unseen.

Neal

Celestine had a very detailed will and an organized funeral plan. I shouldn't have been surprised. We attempted vacationing with her once as a family, and it was awful. She had itineraries planned and activities for each day sorted by which family member might be most interested in them. If she'd known how to use Excel, I'm sure there would have been a spreadsheet involved.

Nora and I both preferred to throw schedules out the window while on vacation. Both of us had jobs that were very task and time oriented, which meant when we were not working, we liked to just go with the flow. When Jo was old enough, we sent her off to places with Celestine on her own, knowing she would come back exhausted but happy after the whirlwind of activity dreamed up by her Memere.

That attention to detail made things like death much easier to deal with. Every step of her funeral arrangements had been prearranged. All we had to do was show up. Her memorial service was held at a gallery she ran in DC with many faces I didn't know. I'm sure most of them were from the surrounding art world. Jo knew far more of them than I did. There was a portrait of Celestine hanging over her urn that she'd commissioned several years back. It was a beautiful rendering of her in an armchair in her living room, flattering to be sure, but still her.

● ● ●

There were also several photo albums out on the table surrounding the urn, along with a notebook for people to sign. I looked at the photos and marveled at the life she'd led. Black and white photos of her as a child, posed stiffly with her parents in France, were juxtaposed with vibrant photos of her smiling broadly as she hosted galas and events. One photo caught my eye, and I lingered over it for a while. It was of Celestine with Nora at a horse show. Nora smiled as she held the ribbon-laden reins of a pony, face alight with joy. Celestine was looking down at her with an expression of softness rarely caught for long. I looked at Nora's beaming face and felt tears well up, which I quickly wiped away.

This death was so different from Nora's. Nora's death was such a blur of hurt, shock, and anger, the idea of looking back over her life in that moment felt overwhelming. Celestine's ceremony was so well orchestrated, even her sudden death allowed a genuine reflection back over her life.

Weeks later, we met with Celestine's lawyer in an old building in downtown D.C. The street was narrow and lined with ivy-covered brick buildings holding various businesses from burger places to law offices such as this one. Jo, Flora, and I sat across from Celestine's attorney around a worn, wooden table in a book-lined office. His white hair and lined face belied his age as advanced, but his eyes were sharp, and there was a matter-of-fact nature about him that set me at ease. Light streamed in through the wavy glass in the old windows, casting interesting patterns on the walls of leather-bound books. I was pondering these patterns when Flora's voice cut through my peaceful private moment.

"Just sell it. I don't want anything to do with that house," Flora huffed.

"Well, what you do with the property is your decision, Ms. Turenne. I am simply here to complete the reading of the will." Flora turned and looked out the window, her arms crossed over her chest. Jo leaned forward and listened intently. He continued reading, listing Celestine's many assets and their dispensation. I was brought to full attention when he read that I was to receive half a million dollars from a trust.

● ● ●

"Wait, *I* get what? How much?"

"You do, Dr. Brooks. She was very clear. Mrs. Turenne was always very detailed, as you know. She didn't leave things to chance." He smiled.

When he read out that Jo would get the contents of the house, Flora sighed and shook her head.

"Is there something you would like to say?" Jo asked.

"Who, me? No, I hold no affinity for anything that woman owned." She paused and sipped her glass of water. "There are a few photos I might want though. If you find any of my dad, I would appreciate some of him. Other than that, I don't want anything else." She pushed her chair back and began to stand.

"Ms Turenne, if you would please stay until the full reading, please?" She sat back down.

"Typical, the old bat still trying to control things even from the grave."

"Have a little respect. She was your mother," Jo snapped at her, still protective of her grandmother.

"Oh, honey, you have no idea who that woman was. She was no mother to me. I'm sure she was perfectly lovely to you and Nora, but me? No. She was no mother to me." Her voice was full of venom, but there were tears in her eyes.

"I'm sorry you felt that way, Flora," I responded. "We've invited you down every year. Nora always wanted to be closer. You just had your own thing going in New York and always seemed too busy. I'm sorry you feel isolated, but it isn't by our doing that you feel that way." I watched her lip twitch and her eyes narrow at me.

"Oh, I never had a choice in the matter thanks to the old bitch. Besides, Nora never meant those invitations and you know it. They were just so she could keep being the good, selfless sister, and I could keep being the selfish sister, the villain. Just like when we were kids. Mom always took Nora's side because she was the baby. She always needed protecting."

My pulse quickened as I felt anger course through me. It was one thing to attack Celestine, but Nora was off limits. "Hey now. Let's not insult the dead here. Neither of them are here to defend themselves. It's a bit unfair to attack them. Also more than a little hurtful to those of us who loved them both."

• • •

"Well, I'm so happy for you that you got to have such a perfect family." Her hands waved around in the air, her bitter sarcasm filled with pain. Her voice was barely audible as she said, "I never had *that* luxury."

Jo's face was splotchy red at this point, and she was chugging her water. She set the glass down with a loud thunk, startling everyone. "Look, my family is none of your business. If you ever cared enough to be involved, you could have been, but you didn't, so stop insulting two people I loved, especially my mom." Her voice was quiet, but I recognized the sharp edge in it. There was a steely resolve in that tone. Nora used to do that. She would become deathly still and quiet before exploding. Some of our worst arguments started with that tone. It was eerie to hear it now from my daughter.

"I think I need to step outside," Jo said as she slid her chair out and turned to walk out. Flora wasn't long behind her and left through the opposite door, closing it with a thud that shook the old windows in their frames.

"Huh. Are all will readings this emotional?"

"Most are way worse," the attorney replied with a chuckle and a shake of his head. "I'll miss her, you know."

"Celestine, you mean?"

"Yes, I always respected her. She looked fragile and willowy, but inside, Celestine was made of iron. Looks like she passed that quality on, I'd say." He patted me on the shoulder. "Good luck."

I stepped out onto the street and found Jo sitting by the car, drinking a soda and eating cheese-covered french fries out of a cardboard to-go container. She looked much more relaxed now that she was eating.

"Ready to go home?"

"Yes. *So* ready. You're driving right? I'm sleepy."

"You're sleepy? After that?" I was amazed at how quickly she oscillated from angry to yawning in the sun.

"Yep, I'm ready for a nap. I'm tired all the time now, with the baby and everything."

The sentence sunk in slowly.

● ● ●

"Wait, the what?" Wide eyed and mouth pinched, Jo groaned.

"Oh shit. Did I say that out loud? Sorry, Dad. This is not at all how I planned on announcing it, but yes, the baby. Dad, I'm pregnant." Joy flooded my entire body as the reality began to hit me. Nora and I struggled so much with fertility, I was afraid Jo would have the same difficulty. The possibility hovered ever since Jo and Luke got married, but I never brought it up to Jo. It made me happy to think of a little grandchild, but it was bittersweet. Nora always talked about how much she was looking forward to a grandbaby, and how much she would spoil one if the opportunity arose. Now here we were with no Nora.

"I'm happy honey, so happy. How far along?" I brushed a tear from my eye.

"Nearly twelve weeks." A wide smile spread over her face as she buckled in. "We were going to announce it after the next ultrasound, but I kinda bungled that one." She shot me another, more impish grin.

"Oh, it doesn't matter. Congratulations! Let's get you home then. Safe and sound, the both of you." I leaned over and hugged her close.

"Thanks, Dad." She leaned back against the headrest and rubbed her belly with her hand. There was a tiny smile left on her lips, and she closed her eyes as we drove off. There she sat. My baby, warm and full after french fries, looking much like she did as a child, but now she was a woman with a child growing within her.

● ● ●

Josephine

I stepped out onto the sunny brick sidewalk and felt blood pulsing rapidly through my body. I took several deep breaths and tried to calm myself down. I got my phone out and called Luke. He picked up after two rings.

"Hey there, how'd it go?" His voice wrapped itself around me and my heart slowed some.

"Oh boy, wow. It was, well, it was strange."

"Okay, you are going to have to give me more than that, hon."

"She was so cold and angry about something, but I don't really know what."

"Who, Flora?"

"Yes, Flora! I mean she insulted Mom and Memere, and basically acted like she didn't care at all that they were dead." I could feel the hurt of it welling up inside me as my voice broke. Mom once told me anger was just hurt that went ignored for too long. Maybe there was some hidden hurt that made Flora so detached and angry. As always, Luke picked up my wavelength and mirrored my thoughts without trying.

"Well, she was kind of estranged from the family. Maybe she has her reasons for feeling detached," he said with a sigh. I pictured him running his hand through his hair as he always did when faced with a problem without a real solution.

"It was just strange. I'm feeling all sorts of things. I'm not even sure if I can even process all the emotions I'm feeling,

• • •

and there she sat just insulting my family and acting like none of it even mattered. I don't know." My stomach grumbled, and I felt a gnawing of hunger. I'd been barely able to eat the past few weeks, with persistent nausea, but now I found myself ravenous. "Wow, am I hungry."

"Okay, that's a sudden change of topic." Luke was patient, but my fluctuations in mood were definitely giving him a challenge. "Well, is there any food around you?"

"There's a burger place up the street." I could smell the aroma of fried food wafting through the air, and my stomach growled loudly in response.

"Okay, well go get yourself something to eat and we can talk it all over when you get home. By the way, what did Memere leave you?"

"Oh, she left me all the contents of the house, and gave the house to Flora. My dad got money from a fund. It's a ton of money for each of us. The lawyer said Flora and I would each have about a million dollars in inheritance." There was a long pause and a small choking sound.

"Holy shit. Wow. That's…wow." Silence.

"I told you she was wealthy."

"I know, but I didn't think it was anything like that. I mean. I thought, I dunno, normal wealthy."

"Normal wealthy?"

"I don't know, like, she has a nice house, and a few antiques, but I, wow. That would allow us to pay off the house, and set up a fund for college, and retirement for us. Jo, this is major."

"Well, mine is only worth that if I sell all of it. I will most likely sell a fair amount of it, but some of it I do want to keep. There are some paintings and a few pieces of furniture that I definitely want, but to be honest, I don't even know what all is in the house. It has to clear probate, and once it does, it will all be packed up and moved into storage closer to us so I can sort through it more easily. It's going to be a process for sure. I just miss you and want to get home."

"I miss you too. I'll see you when you get home. I was going to make some corn chowder for dinner. Does that sound okay?"

"That sounds perfect. Love you. Bye."

● ● ●

"Bye honey, love you too. Get home safe."

Five minutes later, I sipped on a cold soda and let the fizzy sweetness soothe me. I'd cut out soda since finding out I was pregnant, but I figured I could allow myself to indulge just this once. It paired perfectly with the greasy warm goodness of cheese fries. By the time my dad came back out, I had calmed down and was rather sleepy.

Disarmed by the grease, the stress of arguing with my aunt, and the warmth of the sun, I managed to awkwardly blurt out the news of my pregnancy. Dad was thrilled, of course, and wiped a tear from his eye as he started the car for home. I rested my head against the headrest and tried to put things into perspective.

I was growing a living continuation of both Mom and Memere, and all the other people who came before me. I'd never really thought about lineage or bloodlines before this. My parents had a big family tree framed on one wall in the living room. Over the years, they had pointed out different members of the family, giving me tidbits about their lives. Up to now, it seemed like an abstract concept, a history lesson. But now, I was keenly aware that all of those people were a part of me, and now, all of those people, plus all of Luke's people, were part of my baby.

I woke up at home in my driveway as Dad turned off the car.

"Good nap, kiddo?" Dad took the keys out and smiled over at me.

"Yeah. Thanks for driving. Do you want to come in for dinner?"

"No, I wish I could, but I've got a ton of work to do that has backed up, and I have to have it done by Monday when I go back to lecture. Plus, I want to be sure to check on Mom and Dad."

"Okay, can I send you with a container of corn chowder at least? Luke said he was making some for dinner. It's delicious."

"Oh alright, but just that."

I worried about Dad. He often got so busy taking care of his students and Grandma and Granddad, sometimes I think he let himself slip by. The screen door slammed shut behind

• • •

Luke as he came out with a container of soup and bread wrapped in foil.

He grinned and handed it to Dad. "I hope you like it. I didn't have any carrots since *someone* fed them all to the horses." He nudged me and put his arm around my shoulders, kissing my temple.

"Congratulations, guys," Dad said, clutching his soup in both hands. "You are going to be great parents. And Luke, your kid will never be able to get away with anything! It's really a little unfair."

Luke glanced at me, then turned back to Dad. "Thanks, Neal, I appreciate it."

Dad hugged me goodbye and headed out, a plume of dust rising along the driveway as he drove away.

"Sooo, we are announcing it now?" Luke asked with his eyebrows raised in mild surprise.

"Well, I *may* have let it slip. I'm blaming the french fries."

"You know it's fine with me either way. I just want to make sure you are okay with whatever we do." Luke leaned over and kissed me, holding me close against him. I leaned my chin against his chest, listening to his steady heartbeat and inhaling the scent of him.

We walked into the house, his hand protectively against my back as I went up the steps. "I'm not made of glass, you know. I remember how to do steps," I teased.

"I know that. I just, I don't know…"

"I know. I love you, Luke, and everything you do for me." I leaned my head against his shoulder.

Luke knew all too well how fragile this life inside me was. I'd been pregnant before, only to awake in the middle of the night with cramping, covered in blood. I ran to the bathroom where I was faced with blood and tissue that had once been a tiny promise of a baby swirling in the toilet. I flushed and collapsed on the floor where Luke found me. He carefully lifted me off the floor and ran a bath for me. I sat in the water as he washed my hair and body. He wrapped me in a robe and put me back into bed, where I bled into a maxipad for ten days. We closed the shop and he stayed with me. The first morning, when

● ● ●

he went out to feed the horses, I screamed into my pillow with the rage and grief that consumed me.

After my body emptied of that dead child, a void opened up within me. From then on, I made it my mission to fill it, controlling everything I could possibly control. I bought ovulation predictors, peeing on them twice daily. The idea of intimacy and bonding as a part of sex were gone. Luke obediently did everything he could, knowing I needed to fix this emptiness inside me, this vacuum left by a bundle of cells that had never finished forming. I would see mothers yelling at their children out in the park and feel a sharp pang of jealousy and anger. *Why is it so easy for them? They don't even seem happy to have those children. Do they even know how hard it is for other women?*

Months went by, and when we consulted with the doctor, she consistently assured us that if we could get pregnant once, we could do it again. It felt like an empty reassurance every month when my period came like clockwork.

Then, finally, after nearly a year of disappointing periods, I missed one. I hesitated to take a test. So many times I was excited by a period that was a day or two late, only to feel bitter disappointment when I saw the tell-tale flush of red in my underwear the next time I went to the bathroom. I waited a week. No period. Then I took a test. Two blue lines. I felt elation mixed with anxiety. What if this ended like last time? I wasn't sure I was strong enough for another loss like that.

I was terrified there would be something wrong. Two weeks later, as I stared at a little blob of grey and a flickering pulse on a dark screen, I finally saw the beauty in ultrasound images that my mother so often spoke of. Tears ran from my eyes with the sheer joy of knowing this time there was indeed a little life there, holding on and doing its job.

That was my baby. I taped the printed-out image to my bedside table. I looked at it each night before bed, touching the glossy surface of the paper in amazement. This little swirl of grey would one day be a full-fledged person. I thought the heady rush of falling in love with Luke would be the strongest feeling I would ever have for someone, but I was wrong. This wasn't even a person yet, and still, I loved that little blob more than I ever thought possible.

● ● ●

With every wave of nausea that followed in the next few weeks, I felt better about holding on to this one. I still checked my underwear with a surprising amount of neurosis, terrified I would find blood in them, but no. This time things were going differently. I could already feel the strength of this life. Now that the worst of the nausea was over, I was craving cheese and Ethiopian food. I couldn't stand the smell of red meat, and pesto made me gag, but I didn't really care as long as this little person continued to grow and offered a glimpse of a future filled with life rather than death.

Eleanor

My mother was a planner in life and did not react to sudden changes of plan with joy. Her sudden death must have been the ultimate in unpleasant surprises. Her energy, which at first was a bright pulsing flash that nearly knocked me back when it flowed over me, ebbed to a pulsing gold. I could smell the familiar scent of her spicy perfume, and coffee. I inherited my love of tea from Dad. My mother was a consistent coffee drinker, and had a steaming cup every morning. Her favorite was roasted with hazelnuts and had a lovely scent. Unfortunately it never tasted quite as good as it smelled. I let the familiarity of it wash over me and selfishly felt happy to have her with me.

That first day of her passage, I found her with Jo on their property. Jo was feeding the horses and looking out over the fields. I watched Jo brush her cheek lightly and wondered if she had been crying. Mom, who had never really been a horsewoman, tried to move through the run-in shed toward Jo. Of course it completely spooked Callie as she emerged through the wall of the shed, seemingly from nowhere. Callie kicked at the wall, and Mom moved away and toward me in the grass.

"Does she know yet? About me?" Mom asked me. It struck me that she still used words to communicate, having only

● ● ●

just passed over. It was strange to have a one-on-one conversation with her after so long.

"I think so," I replied.

"Nora, I'm dead, right? This isn't some dream I'm trapped in?" This was the most unsure of herself I had ever seen Mom.

"Yes, Mom, you're dead. This isn't a dream. I'm sorry." Mom always had incredibly vivid dreams, and sometimes she would sleepwalk and end up in Flora's room or mine. We would carefully guide her back to her own room. Sometimes she would wake up, sometimes she wouldn't, but either way we would point her to her room and leave her there. I think both of us were afraid of waking her up directly. Some of her dreams seemed like they must be frightening. She would yell, or swing her arms as if fighting off something. Jo had inherited her crazy sleepwalking and dreaming. My dreams, in contrast, were always in black and white. Fitting that I later built my life around black and white images. Mom spoke again, pulling me from my thoughts.

"Thanks, Nora. I'm so sorry you had to do this before me. I should have been the one to guide you here, not the other way around." I could feel her guilt and sorrow wash over me, tinting everything around us grey and somber.

"No, it's okay, Mom. You couldn't help it. Besides, Dad was here for me. He helped."

"He did?" Mom asked softly.

"Yeah, he did. He's still around. He just didn't want to upset you more by coming forward too much. He felt it might be hard for you."

"Can I see him? Talk to him, like I am talking to you?" she asked hopefully.

"Well, he hardly talks and he doesn't really come across to the physical world much at all, but he gives me memories, and images, and we just kind of exist together. I don't know how to explain it, but we can just kind of feel what the other one is feeling. We can mix our energies to know each other better than in life. It's really beautiful once you get accustomed to it." She blinked out of the physical world, and I stayed behind with Jo for a moment

● ● ●

Jo definitely felt different. I knew she had been feeling very sad for a long time. When I was pulled in by her over the past few months, it was almost always into a cloud of grief. I knew it had nothing to do with me, because this grief wasn't aimed at me as it had been when I passed. It was aimed inward, at herself. I suspected she was grieving the loss of a child yet unborn. I longed to comfort her and reassure her that it would happen for her. In the past few weeks, this grief had lifted some. Now, although she was awash in grief for my mom, there was a little kernel of joy, funneled inward. I hoped that this joy was what I thought it was. I reached toward her and felt it, a pulsing tiny light of energy within hers. It was amazing. This tiny little life, in part, was a continuation of my own. A new beginning for all of us.

Jo's belly grew larger over the following months. I hovered around her much more than before, wanting to be near her and this new life, reveling in the joy of it. More and more I could feel the separateness of her baby growing ever stronger and more whole. It filled me with joy and expectation, tethering me more closely to her than before. I was there for every ultrasound and sat with her at night when she couldn't get back to sleep after going to the bathroom for the third time, or when she was awakened by the sharp pain of a charlie horse. I longed to share with her that I had suffered from those while pregnant too. I wanted to tell her to drink more water and take her multivitamin, to rub her feet and dote on her until she kicked me out.

To his credit, Luke did his job as Dad-to-be as well as he possibly could. He helped fix up their spare bedroom into a nursery. It had windows that looked out onto the wooded portion of their property. Even on the sunniest day, the room held a dappled filtered light. Jo painted a large tree with birds, squirrels, and chipmunks on the largest wall, opposite a wooden crib. They had clearly decided on a woodland theme for the room, and it was adorable. I recognized a low chest of drawers, a rocker, and a side table from Mom's house. They were trying to be as ready as any couple can be, which is, in all honesty, ready at all. Nothing can prepare you for the crazy mixture of absolute bliss and terror that bringing a baby into this world entails.

● ● ●

I thought back to bringing Jo home from the hospital, her tiny body strapped into a preposterously huge baby seat. Her little form crumpled between straps and padding, a tiny pink hat covering her perfect fuzzy head. I remember getting into the backseat of the car and staring at her sleeping form the whole way home, panic and joy fighting for domination of my emotions, tears streaming down my cheeks. It seemed impossible that after the long struggle to have her they would simply send her home with us. How were we possibly qualified to care for this little person? Sure, we were both doctors. Sure, we both read the latest pediatric articles on best practices for raising an infant, along with pretty much every baby book available. But now here she was in our car, under our care, and I felt completely at a loss. I watched as Jo voraciously read every parenting book and took advice from everyone who offered it, hungry for the key to how to master parenting. I longed to tell her the key to good parenting is simply to do your best and go easy on yourself.

Everyone fumbles through and tries their best to maintain their sanity while keeping this fragile little creature entrusted in their care alive and thriving. That is the big secret. At the end of the day, it doesn't matter whether you go all organic, cloth versus disposable, breastfeed or formula feed. It doesn't matter if you forget the words to nursery rhymes, or fall asleep with your baby on your chest (which is absolutely the best thing about newborns). The thing is, there are no perfect parents. There are just parents who care enough to try, and parents who don't.

● ● ●

Neal

The alarm buzzed and I awoke dazed and weary, the burden of last night's shift creeping in as I came to full consciousness. The beeping monitors, crying people, and shouted directions always echoed long after a shift was over. As if the normal emotional drain of an ER shift wasn't enough, now, after that fateful shift nine years ago, they always felt more personal. Every DOA made me think of who this person might be leaving behind. Before Nora, it was easier to detach from my patients enough to protect myself, but now when I looked into the tear-filled eyes of children worried about their Mom, I thought of Jo. When I told partners the love of their life may not survive the night, or may wake up a shadow of who they once were, I saw myself. Nora's death changed everything.

When Nora was alive, she would immediately know my night was rough when I walked in the door and shepherd me into a hot shower right away. While I was in the shower, she would whip up a mimosa and something warm and comforting for breakfast. It always helped to balance out whatever horrors I had seen while on shift. Now, many years older, with no Nora to help balance me out, I was struggling.

Since Nora's passing, I backed away from floor shifts in favor of more classroom work and pretty much lived in a lecture hall or my office. However, there was a nasty stomach thing going around the entire campus, and they really needed another set of hands for a Friday overnight. When they asked if I could

● ● ●

take a shift, I said sure, not really considering how different I was from the twenty-something that once relished the focused frenzy of a busy ER night.

The light through the window was pale and muted. I rose and looked out the window to find the silent softness of snow falling outside. The fields were blanketed in white, and the pine trees sagged under the weight of the heavy snow. A bird feeder stood outside, and cardinals, juncos, and towhees hopped busily on and around it, plucking up seeds. Mom dutifully filled it all winter, and the birds were clearly appreciative. The snow must have started early this morning after I'd gone to bed. The soft light through the clouds and muted sound outside didn't help my feeling of being suspended in time after an overnight shift.

I stretched and reached down to pet Hobbit. She stood up and chirped, purring and rubbing against me. I glanced at the clock. 3pm. She was probably expecting dinner. I heard my parents' voices in the kitchen, so I roused myself with a groan and stretch.

My parents had been with me ever since Dad fell on their porch steps and fractured his pelvis in the process. Now, he had healed enough to walk, but used a cane and was at risk for a second fall. Mom was the one to finally convince him, arguing quite accurately that if she hurt herself picking him up off the floor, they would be in quite a bind in Maryland. Here, they had someone to help in the event of another fall. It took convincing, but finally his pragmatism won out over his pride, and they sold their home in Maryland and moved here. We installed one of those chair lifts on each of the back sets of stairs so they could live in the third floor apartment and retain privacy and mobility. They rarely came downstairs unless Mom wanted to putter in the garden or use our kitchen to cook. I threw on a robe and came out of my room to see what had brought them down from their nest above.

"Sam. It was starving, poor thing," I heard Mom say to Dad, to which I could hear an indistinct mumbled reply.

"What's starving?" I asked as I entered the kitchen. I looked down and saw my parents standing over a small, skinny animal of some sort. I bent down to get closer and identified the poor creature as some sort of dog. However, its coat was so matted it really didn't have a recognizable dog shape. It was more akin to a large, dirty mop head.

"Where did this come from?" I asked, looking up at my parents, who seemed a bit unsure themselves.

"Mrs. Norris found it out in the snow somewhere and led it to the porch," Dad grumbled. "It's probably someone's dog. It came right up to us and seems friendly, but it's a mess."

"I'm sorry we brought it in without asking, but we didn't want to wake you, dear. It's just so cold out there," Mom said as she bent to pet its head.

"No, no, we couldn't have left it out in weather like this. Mrs. Norris brought it in?"

"Yep. Silly dog started barking her fool head off, so I came down to let her out before she woke you up. When she came back up on the porch, this thing was with her."

"Well, if it's owned, it hasn't been cared for very well. I'll call the vet and see if we can get in to be seen."

"Umm, honey, it's three in the afternoon on a Saturday, remember?" Mom reminded me.

"Oh, right. I suppose we are going to have to take care of it until I can get it into the vet on Monday. They'll know what to do with it. Until then, I guess the first thing to do is to try to get it cleaned up if we can."

I put on some boots and trekked down to the barn to try to find some clippers. The fields around me were silent. The only sound was the swishing of my tall winter boots as I moved through the snow. I opened the barn door, peering into the darkness as I stamped the snow off my boots onto the worn brick aisle. I flicked on the lights, and their warm glow made the interior look almost cheery despite the cobwebs and disuse. I hadn't been down here since Jo moved out, and it was strange to enter the silent space. I went into the tack room and found a trunk of excess equipment Jo had left behind. I dug through until I finally found a pair of clippers. I brought them into the house and set them down on the counter.

"Honey, I made you a bowl of soup," Mom chirped as I came back in.

"Come sit down and eat while I set a towel out for your dog grooming session." Mom set out a bowl and glass of water on the dining table.

● ● ●

"How was your shift last night? Or do you not want to talk about it?" Having a mom who had once been an ER nurse was nice and, in no small way, the reason I pursued medicine to begin with.

"It was pretty rough. You know how it is. It was a sunny Friday, with a winter storm prediction, and a full moon, so…"

"Oh, wow, yeah. Here, hang on a minute."

She set a cold beer down on the table beside me. Now, ER staff are all highly trained, generally scientific people, so naturally we are also incredibly superstitious. You never comment to a nurse about the quality of a vein prior to catheter placement, you never, ever say out loud that it's a quiet night, and you know, without a doubt, if you have a weather change on a full moon, it is going to be crazy. We all talked about it, even though the evidence showed otherwise.

Studies showed the only thing that made ER trauma cases go up was nice weather. Likely due to people doing things they shouldn't, like climbing ladders while intoxicated, for example, which was one of my cases from last night. A guy got completely wasted, then decided he needed to clean out his gutters before the predicted rain and snow storm moved into the area. It did not go well for him. He fell, fracturing several ribs and giving himself a nice hemothorax for his troubles. He was in all likelihood going to be fine, but was spending today in a hospital bed with a nice tube in his chest to drain the blood out of it. He was lucky not to have punctured a lung, giving himself a frothy mixture of blood and air around his lungs, the oh so desirable hemopneumothorax.

I looked down at my bowl of tomato soup, savoring the warmth of it in my stomach.

"Mom, did you make this?"

"Of course, honey. I canned a bunch of it this summer to use up all the tomatoes. There's plenty more in the pantry if you want more." Mom was happy to be taking care of me. It didn't sit right with either of them to be a burden on anyone.

I had to admit, having them home had been much more pleasant than I thought it would be. Mom resurrected Nora's garden plot and supplied the family and any visitors to the house with a cornucopia of tomatoes, squash, eggplant, and cucumbers. She was also an excellent cook, and I'd eaten better

* * *

in the past year than I had in ages. Plastic containers regularly appeared in the fridge, containing a variety of delicious items. I say plastic because they were not always actual Tupperware. In fact, most often, they were not. Sour cream containers might contain sour cream, but more likely they would have soup, or cooked green beans, or spaghetti sauce. It was a bit like an Easter egg hunt in my fridge now, opening containers to see the surprise within. It was like being a kid again. Jo had bought a set of fridge storage containers for Mom this past Christmas, thinking she just didn't have any. Mom had looked puzzled when she opened it but thanked Jo anyway. They still sat unopened in their tidy little kitchen upstairs.

I turned my attention to the dog in my kitchen. Dad was cleaning and lubricating the clipper blades while Mom set out a towel and a bag for hair on the kitchen floor. I finished my soup and walked over to the staging area, prepared to make my first attempt at dog grooming. I could suture nasty wounds into near perfect closures. Surely I could shave this dog.

I sat down cross-legged on the floor and the bedraggled thing came over and checked me out. I turned on the clippers and it just lay down on the floor, seemingly ready for the process. Shaving a matted dog turned out to be much harder than I thought. Under all the matts, the poor dog was terribly thin, and I kept catching the clippers on bony prominences and skin. Dad kept spraying the blades with cooling spray, and Mom cleared hair as I cut it away. They were like a pit crew in some kind of deranged sporting event. The dog, for his part, as his anatomy revealed him to be, was very cooperative and nearly fell asleep several times as I worked.

When I was done, we had a roughly dog-shaped creature of brown and white. I suspected if he were a healthy weight, he would be about twenty pounds or so. He had a square face and was probably some kind of terrier mix. He could be cute if taken care of. I carried our new charge into the bathroom and bathed him. The water that ran off of him was brown and gritty, and he looked much better after I finished. He would still need some professional attention, but he looked more comfortable and was recognizable as a dog now. He wagged his tail as I dried him off, and I started thinking of what to name him. Clearly he was staying. I would call the shelter and notify

● ● ●

them that I'd found him and have the vet scan him for a chip, but I was not going to work too hard to find his owner if they had allowed him to get in this kind of condition willingly.

"Wallace?" I tried out loud. He cocked his head to one side. "We'll see. Don't worry, bud, you're safe and warm now. A name will come soon enough."

He dragged his slightly damp body against me, then against the bathroom rug. When let out into the living room, he displayed the familiar 'zoomies' that dogs always seem to get after a bath. Maybe he was not as old as I initially thought.

As it turned out, he was not very old. In fact, the vet estimated him to be no more than two or three. He was an intact male with no microchip. Dr. Sorenson assured me that I should feel no guilt over my lack of desire to find his owner.

"Look, he's unneutered, unmicrochipped, and has no collar on. You have contacted the shelter, and we will put up a notice here, but honestly, this guy is lucky to have found you. I doubt very seriously that anyone is looking for him." She patted him gently on his nearly bald head and looked across the table at me. "You are going to keep him, aren't you?"

Dr. Sorenson had been our vet for years, and I always respected the breadth of knowledge she possessed. While I had the luxury of patients that were verbal on many occasions, she never had that help. I had respect for veterinarians because of this. The medicine was amazingly similar, but the pay and respect paid to our veterinary counterparts was not nearly adequate for what they were capable of.

"I think so," I replied to her question of his future ownership. "Mrs. Norris loves him, and he seems very gentle. I think he might be housebroken too. He didn't have any accidents over the weekend."

"Well, he couldn't find a better home." She smiled. "Good job with his shave, by the way. He looks pretty good. If you ever want to leave medicine and start a career as a dog groomer, I'd hire you!" She laughed.

• • •

"Thanks, I will take that under consideration, but it was more stressful than I'd care to admit. Satisfying, but tricky for sure."

"Yeah, these matted guys can be tough. Just be glad it wasn't summer and you didn't find nests of fleas or maggots under all those matts."

"Oh, yeah, that would have been unpleasant to say the least."

"Yeah, they hide under the matts, and sometimes as you shave, you find them in big clusters. It's disgusting, but satisfying once you kill them all and get the poor animal nice and clean." She had a look of mixed satisfaction and revulsion shared by doctors of many kinds. I recognized the same glint in her eye I had when patients came into the ER with abscesses that needed draining.

"He'll need to be neutered," she continued. "We can set up an appointment for that. We can even align it with his booster vaccinations in three weeks if you like, to make it more convenient. It wouldn't hurt for him to gain a little weight prior to anesthesia anyway."

I found myself looking forward to seeing Dr Sorenson again, then found myself glancing at her left ring finger to find it empty. Why was I checking? More importantly, why was I happy to find it empty?

● ● ●

Josephine

Once everything cleared probate, I filled my free time going through Memere's things. After many dust-filled weeks, I had organized and cataloged all items of value. I parceled out items for the shop to sell, things we would keep, and things we would store. Yet the things I found most fascinating held almost no monetary value. There were newspaper clippings and photos that Memere had kept for reasons that remained unknown. There were dried flowers, leaflets from art shows, and tons of Mom and Flora's drawings, paintings and assorted art projects. There were two huge boxes full of them, labeled Eleanor and Floraline. Many were sorted into paper file folders, and within them I found a progression of life in drawings. From scrawled lines in crayon to charcoal sketches and watercolors. I mailed the one labeled Floraline to her address in New York and included several pictures of Charles and Memere, along with a few of Flora and my mom. Then I slowly perused the box labeled Eleanor. I was surprised at how talented Mom was. Another assumption proven wrong.

I longed to talk to her as an adult, to gain a better understanding of who she was as a woman. Mom had died before I understood what she really offered other than being a mom. Now that I was facing motherhood, the appreciation of an identity before children and after children was beginning to dawn on me. I knew my mother from stories and as a mom, but I didn't really know who she was as a woman. Not truly. Grief

• • •

washed over me anew, this time tinged with a loss of the parts of Mom I didn't know rather than the parts I did. After weeks of living in the past, I decided to go visit Mikayla and remind myself of the women who remained in my life, and who would be in my child's.

Light streamed in through the old warehouse windows of Mikayla's DC apartment and cloaked the room in an amber glow. She had a view of the tide basin from her balcony, which was beautiful at this time of year. The cherry blossoms were in full bloom and reflected off the water below. We walked out onto the balcony and watched people strolling along the water's edges hand in hand. Luke was at home with the horses, and while I missed him, it was nice to have a girl's weekend before the baby arrived. I was due next month, so this was my last chance to do something on my own for a while.

We came in from the balcony and I sat down on her velvety green sofa.

"Mikayla, this place is amazing! It has everything you'd want in a hip single lady professional apartment." Vaulted ceilings, exposed brick details, and an open concept design that made the most of her huge windows and phenomenal view. "I'm a little jealous."

"Nah. Your house is perfect for you and Luke. It's so cute. Plus, you have your horses and quiet space. You know you wouldn't actually trade it in." Mikayla handed me a warm mug of tea and plopped down on the sofa next to me.

"You're right, I wouldn't give up my status as a country mouse. But this place is perfect for you, my city mouse best friend." I sipped the warm tea and looked over at her beaming face, dimples as deep as I'd ever seen them.

"It is. I'm close to Mom and Dad. I love the city, and Nicole is, well, she's really great. She should be here any minute. I'm excited for you to meet her."

"She lives in the complex, right?"

"Yeah, we met while I was taking out the trash one day. My bag broke open as I tossed it into the dumpster. She helped me get the garbage into the bin and then picked trash out of my hair for me. It was the first of many acts of kindness." Her face alight as she told me the story.

"So, you've been dating for about six months now?"

● ● ●

"I know, I can't believe you haven't met her before this, but my job at the new firm has been kicking my ass and I've barely had time for anything."

"Well, you've had time for *some* things." I grinned as I said it, and Mikayla and I both burst out laughing. We were still giggling when Nicole let herself in a few seconds later. She was gorgeous, with long lean legs cloaked in dark jeans, amber-colored eyes, and long dark hair that cascaded down her back. While I was still not attracted to women, it was obvious why Nicole had drawn Mikayla's attention. They made a stunning couple.

Nicole lifted her hands and beamed at me. "So this is the fabled Jo! I've heard so much about you!" She was even more stunning when she smiled. I poked Mikayla with my elbow and replied, "Hopefully all good."

"Yes. Definitely all good." Nicole kissed Mikayla on her cheek and nuzzled her neck. Mikayla's face lit up and she smiled happily. It was the most at home and happy I'd ever seen her with a partner. Mikayla had dated several people over the past eight years, all lovely people, but she always held back a tiny part of herself when with them. Already in the first thirty seconds of meeting her in Nicole's presence, it was clear Mikayla found it easy to be herself with her new partner.

"So what's the plan, ladies? Dinner?" Nicole asked, getting up from the sofa.

"Oh, goodness yes." My stomach rumbled. "I am always hungry."

"So, where do you want to eat, country mouse?" Mikayla nudged me with her shoulder.

"Ethiopian. I've been craving berbere spice for months now with absolutely nowhere to get it near me."

"Indira's it is then!" Mikayla exclaimed.

After freshening up, we walked a few blocks to a small restaurant that smelled delicious from half a block away. It was on a small but bustling side street with brick sidewalks and intimate, dimly lit restaurants intermingled with boutiques closed for the day.

"My cousin Haile works here. I texted him to let him know we were coming and he saved a table for us," Nicole said

● ● ●

to me as we reached the door. She waved to the very handsome bartender who came up and hugged her.

"That's her cousin," Mikayla whispered as Nicole and Haile chatted. He had long, perfectly tended dreadlocks down to his waist and the same caramel tone of Nicole. His eyes were a brilliant green.

"Geez, Mikayla, is her whole family this hot?"

"All the ones I've met have been." Mikayla snorted, and Nicole turned and came back to us, giving Mikayla a quizzical look. "We have the best booth! They weren't too busy tonight and we were able to get it." Nicole beamed.

The restaurant was completely full, with one empty table in the window, which made me wonder what 'busy' would look like compared to this.

We settled down at our table. I was supremely grateful for this seating rather than some of the other tables with low woven stools. I was afraid I might tip off of one with my now ginormous belly if I tried to crouch that low. We settled in and discussed our food and drink order. Nicole and Mikayla both ordered sweet white wines. I stared at their frosty glasses with longing.

"So, Mik tells me you guys were college roommates. It's nice that you guys are friends. Most people hate their college roommate."

"Well, we got lucky, I suppose," I responded.

Mikayla smiled at me. "We most certainly did."

"My first roommate at Howard was a mess. She was always coming in wasted. She puked on my notes more than once." Nicole wrinkled her nose and shook her head. The server came up a moment later with our appetizer of lentil Sambossas, and I lost all focus on conversation. They were warm, savory, and delicious. The meal that followed was just as good with tangy soft injera to scoop up the spicy dishes with. We'd gotten the vegetarian sampler and all ended up stuffed and happy.

After, as we sat digesting, the baby got the hiccups for the first time. I placed my hand on my belly and started to laugh at the little jerky movements.

"What is happening over there, you two?" Mikayla asked, grinning.

• • •

"Oh, she has the hiccups," I responded, warm with food and good conversation.

"I am so happy for you, Jo. Honestly, you're going to be such a good mom." Mikayla reached over and held my hand.

"Am I? I worry about that all the time. What if I'm terrible and mess everything up?" I squeezed her hand and she squeezed back.

"Jo, you have been nurturing and protecting things your entire life, including me. You've got this." She let go and leaned back in her chair, placing her arm around Nicole.

"I don't know. How have I ever had to nurture you? You're so strong, you never seem to need help from anyone," I said after taking a sip of water.

"Ha! Do you not remember constantly coming to my defense while we were in school?" Mikayla said, waving her hands in confusion.

"I remember losing my temper around racist dicks. That's not being a mom," I said, after which Mikayla leaned forward and became very serious.

"No, that was not you just losing your temper."

Nicole raised an eyebrow at Mikayla.

I attempted an explanation. "While Mikayla and I were at UVA, she was asked constantly if she was there on a sports scholarship. People just assumed she couldn't have gotten in on her academic performance. It pissed me off, and I went off on people a few times. It always made me angry, because no one ever asked me if *I* were on a scholarship. Why would they even think they could ask her that? Fucking racists." I felt my face getting hot and really wished I could have a sip of cold white wine.

"See what I mean? You still get mad about it." Mikayla was smiling at me, laughing softly.

"Well, I love you, and it makes me angry when you have to put up with bullshit from frat boys who assume things."

"Exactly. You defended me, even though it scared you, because you love me. I'm your grown ass friend. How are you going to feel about your child? Plus, how many animals have you rescued, fostered, or cared for?"

"Well, yeah, but that's different."

● ● ●

"Is it, though? To me, a good mom stands up for her kids when they can't stand up for themselves, and she cares for them when they can't care for themselves. She gives them guidance and protection at the same time. You have always done that for everyone you love. Plus, you are creative, smart, and beautiful. Your kid is going to be lucky to have you!" Mikayla took a sip of her wine and leaned back in her seat again.

"Thanks for that. Everyone keeps reassuring me, but I still feel scared that somehow I'll fuck it all up and she'll need therapy later on." I sighed and placed my napkin on the table.

"Well, I can't guarantee you she won't need therapy, but I *can* assure you it won't be you or Luke who sends her there. Just the fact that you are worried about being good enough means you'll be good enough. Nobody has perfect parents, but we forgive them as long as they're trying, right?" Mikayla tipped her head at me, knowing she'd made a winning argument. This is what happens when your best friend is a lawyer.

"Yeah, I suppose that's true. I am going to have to stop cursing, though. Which is hard."

"You come by that one honestly, though. Your dad said your mom had a mouth like a sailor before they had you. I'm betting there is a lot more of her in you than just that." The server came and Mikayla snatched up the bill before I could.

As I lay in bed that night, watching flashes of light move across the ceiling from cars on the street below, I hoped Mikayla was right. Mom and I did share many traits, both the good and bad. I could thank her for my practicality, my love of horses, and my sense of humor. I could also blame her for my temper and my potty mouth. Hopefully the good would outweigh the bad, and I could pass Mom's best attributes on to my daughter.

The next morning, I emerged from my room to find Nicole and Mikayla snuggled on the pull-out sofa, Nicole rubbing Mikayla's feet. We had breakfast of toasted bagels and cream cheese, and then Mikayla walked me down to my car.

"I'm glad you found Nicole. She seems really great, and you seem genuinely happy around her," I said as we hugged.

"Thanks. Your opinion matters to me. I love her, and it feels different this time. I'm glad you approve."

"I do approve, and I better be invited to the wedding one day!"

● ● ●

"Haha. I think that's rushing it a bit." Mikayla grinned and finished, "You'll be my maid of honor."

"I better be. I love you," I said, giving her another hug.

"You too. Drive safe and let me know when you get home."

"Will do." I got in the car and looked back at my waving friend as I drove off.

Luke was just coming in from feeding the horses when I got home that afternoon. The grass was starting to flush with the fresh brilliant green of spring, and birds sang from bare branches festooned with tiny buds.

"Hey, hon. How was your trip?" he said with a soft crooked smile, putting his arms around me. He was pleasantly warm and smelled of horses, hay, and grain. In a word, home.

"It was really good. Thanks for letting me go."

"Letting you?" His eyebrow raised and he laughed. "Jo, I would never keep you from Mikayla. Plus, did I really have a choice?" True. He didn't.

"Well, how were things here?" I asked, picking a stray piece of hay from his shirt.

"Good, but we need a bunch of stuff from the store. I was going to try to sneak off and buy groceries before you got home, but you beat me to it." I was torn between my desire to curl up on my couch and my desire to be with Luke after three days apart. My desire to be with Luke won out.

"I'll go with you."

"Okay, you sure?" I nodded and hugged him closer, letting his body wrap around me and trying to sink into him, an effort impeded immensely by my enormous belly.

The brightly lit, noisy grocery store in Orange was a far cry from the bistros and markets I'd just visited in DC. I was strolling down the bread aisle when I saw another figure with a cart and stopped in my tracks. Cece was there, in strategically torn jeans and a loose sweatshirt, her hair in a messy bun. It wasn't the first time I'd seen her since the day in the cafe, but in other cases I'd been able to dodge actually talking to her. There was no dodging this. She was pushing a cart filled with food and three children of varying ages straight toward me. It was one of those carts that looked like a race car, and one wheel was sticking. I could hear it from all the way down the aisle. Was this a glimpse into my own looming chaotic future? Her face initially registered surprise when she saw me, then fell into a controlled smile.

"Hey, Jo, how are you?" she said, pushing a rather large child back down into the cart seat, telling him that he had to share the cart or else.

"Good. How about you?" I responded, feeling the desire to turn and run away. The baby crammed in the seat with the attempted escapee turned toward me and gawked at me with a drool-covered face. There was a smear of something red on his cheek. I wondered briefly what the nature of the substance might be, then decided I didn't really want to know.

"Busy. You know, kids and stuff. Me and Micah got married right after school, you know. I was lucky and started having babies right away. I have three boys and a girl now. How about you? Is this your first?" She nodded to my swollen belly. I felt an odd mixture of inadequacy at my lesser fecundity and relief that I still bore a single completely contained child.

"Oh, yep. It's my first, a girl." Luke walked up behind me and put his hand on my shoulder.

"Hi, I'm Luke. Are you an old friend of Jo's?" If only he'd known how much Cece lusted after him when we were high schoolers going to Roystons coffee, he would have understood how much it must hurt her that he didn't have any idea who she was.

"Yeah, me and Jo go way back." Her mouth pinched, and her face started to flush.

"Luke, this is Cece."

"Oh, Cece!" His face shifted slightly. "Jo has told me tons about you. You guys were best friends for a long time." He smiled and leaned forward to shake her hand.

"We were, weren't we?" Her eyes softened.

"We have so much to catch up on."

"How is Micah?" I asked as Luke began to deftly distract the kids with silly faces and questions.

"Oh, I left him two years ago, but I've got a new man now, and he's much better than Micah ever was." She smiled, gesturing toward the baby. "Isaac here is his." Isaac started

● ● ●

wailing loudly before spitting up a large volume of foul-smelling white fluid. Cece pulled a towel out of her bag, deftly wiped the baby and cart off, then deposited the towel back in the bag. "Well, I better get them moving. Otherwise they'll go crazy. Good to see you Jo. Maybe we'll find time to catch up sometime."

"Maybe. That would be good, Cece. Later!" I called after her now retreating form. I touched Luke's hand and watched her go down the aisle before turning and walking the other way.

My encounter with Cece lingered in my mind that night. I wondered about our separate trajectories in the years since high school. It was obvious to me that I would go to college after high school, and I thought she would, too. Was it obvious to her that she *wouldn't*? While I was dreaming of galleries and art openings, she was simply trying to get out of her parent's house. There was never the financial promise of tuition or housing for her. Her opportunities were far fewer than mine by simple virtue of what family she was born into. I suppose marriage was her way out, and college was mine.

It was a privilege that I never really considered before now. I had the benefit of being an only child, with well-educated parents. Cece's family had been broken and repaired several times. Cece was one of an eventual total of eight children, of which she was the oldest girl. Three of her siblings were from her father, and four were from her Mom's second husband. Cece's dad left them when she was eight, and I remember her calling our house that night crying. She stayed with us a long time after that, most of that summer. I thought it was fun to have a playmate, never considering what it would take for someone at the age of eight to want to leave home for that long. I talked to Luke about it over dinner, and he, of course, immediately gave me a rational and empathetic response.

"Jo, not everyone finds happiness the same way. Her life may be fulfilling to her, and while it's not what you would envision for yourself, maybe it's what she wants. Robbing yourself of happiness with guilt won't make her any happier." I leaned my head against his shoulder and rubbed my swollen belly.

"I suppose I just feel bad for her because I'd be overwhelmed and unsatisfied with that as a life. I'm not even sure I'm ready for one baby, let alone three." I sighed, looking down at my swollen feet.

"We'll figure it out," Luke said, placing those swollen feet on his lap for rubbing. I groaned and leaned into him.

"I'm happy to be home."

"What, Mikayla didn't rub your feet?" Luke laughed.

"No, she did not, and this is why I love you." I closed my eyes and relaxed further.

"I love you too," Luke replied.

● ● ●

Eleanor

Little Leona Grace, all dark lashes and rosy cheeks, slept in her bassinet next to Jo and Luke's old double bed and filled me with a bittersweet tenderness. I watched her little chest rise and fall under a swaddle adorned with chubby ponies. I leaned in close so I could hear the soft whisper of her. I could only imagine that sweet, milky perfume only the most newly arrived babies have. I longed to feel the soft fuzz of her dark hair against my cheek, or to feel the warm squish of her cheeks against my lips as I kissed them.

Jo had been my only chance at maternal intimacy with an infant. I adored her, and savored every moment of her as a tiny newborn, chubby baby, unpredictable toddler, creative child, and sensitive teenager. I always told myself a grandchild would be my second chance at the whole wondrous process. As it was, I could watch Leona grow, but I would never be able to touch or hold her. The idea brought me great sadness, tempered only by the fact that at least I could watch from the sidelines. The tactile world had stopped holding much interest for me years ago, but now that there was a baby to hold, I missed it again.

Leona stirred in her sleep, grunting and moving her tiny head from side to side. A little hand escaped her swaddle and probed the edges of the fabric. Her pink tongue came probing out of her mouth and she began to grunt and wiggle more vigorously. She was hungry. Jo heard her and began to stir as well. She sat up in bed with a tired groan and reached over for

● ● ●

Leona. Leona was now awake, dark eyes open, and hungrily grumbling for milk. Jo scooped her up into the bed and within a moment got her to latch on. I heard her let out a little cry at the ferocity with which the tiny creature fed. Soon after, I heard the happy sounds of a nursing child, and an occasional snore from Luke, who slept blissfully through all of it. I suppose having a psychic for a husband didn't change how oblivious most men were to a waking baby.

I remember feeling irrationally angry at Neal for sleeping through many of Jo's nighttime nursing sessions. Nursing went well for me after a month of absolute hell. Jo was tongue-tied and had trouble latching in the beginning. By the time we had that corrected and her latch improved, my supply had dropped, so I had to pump, give a bottle, and nurse for a while. It was unbelievably hard. I hoped things would go more smoothly for Jo.

There were so many things I wanted to share with her, mother to mother. Things I wanted to say to her that I couldn't. I knew the pressure being a new Mom brought. The judgment from those around you for everything you did, and the self-criticism that was often harsher than anything anyone else could say. I wanted to tell her it was okay to not be perfect. That it was okay to do whatever made her sane and happy and kept her baby safe. I wanted to give her a safe place to land, to cry, to yell, to sleep. Whatever she needed, I wanted to provide for her.

I hovered for a moment longer as Leona finished nursing and dropped off Jo's breast, mouth agape and blissfully asleep again. Jo was able to carefully replace her in the bassinet after a quick sniff test of her diaper. Jo sighed and slipped nearly immediately back to sleep. I had no doubt Jo was going to be a good mom. It was true she had my temper, but she also had a strong desire to nurture and protect. I would like to think she got that from me, but Neal was pretty nurturing in his own way as well.

We'd made a beautiful little family, he and I, and now that family was growing. I thought about all the family members who connected to create one tiny little person and felt amazement at the idea. Now that I was dead, I could feel my lineage as a tangible cord running through me. Memories from long-dead family members would often wash over me, allowing

● ● ●

231

me to glimpse the most amazing moments in their lives with a level of detail and intimacy I could have never known in life.

My maternal grandmother often chose to show memories of my mother as a child to me. One of the most clear memories was my mother at the beach in France, running along the sand, being chased by my grandmother. Mom was giggling and looking back at my grandmother. She fell over in the sand, and my grandmother's hands reached out and tickled her. They were the hands of a young woman, smooth and strong, with tanned skin and neatly trimmed nails. I could feel her happiness flooding through me as she shared it. Most memories shared were like this, brilliant in their clarity, but unimportant in the larger view of a life lived. I thought back to my own life. What memories would I want to share? Which ones were most vibrant in my mind? They were made up of moments that were pivotal and moments that were inconsequential in equal measure. Many were moments that caught me off guard in life, where I experienced blinding happiness quite unexpectedly.

One of my favorites was during a car trip we took when Jo was around three or four years old. I have no idea where we were going, and it doesn't matter now anyway. We were driving on a country road, and she kept putting her bare feet up on my seat back. I would turn around and grab them, pretending to eat her toes, sending Jo into screaming fits of laughter. I just had to place my lips to her wiggling toes and she would belly laugh until she snorted, sending all three of us into another fit of laughter. It was a lovely cycle of joy, and one of my most distinct memories from her childhood. I suppose life is like that. We drift between big events marked on a calendar thinking that they are what our life is for, only to realize later that living is really all the small moments in between.

● ● ●

Neal

Jo gave birth the day I dropped Wallace off to be neutered, which meant I was late picking him up. Graciously, Rebecca agreed to meet me at the clinic that evening.

"I never got a chance to tell you how sorry I was about Nora," she said, laying her hand on my shoulder. "You know, I lost my husband Paul to cancer five years ago. It's not a club anyone wants to be in. The club of people left behind."

"Thanks. It's true. It's often hard for most people to understand." I felt a surprising wash of gratitude to see not pity, but respect and understanding in her expression.

"Well, if you ever want to talk to someone who does understand, give me a call." She handed me a business card with her personal number written on the back.

Three weeks later, I sat across the table from Dr. Sorenson, now known to me as Rebecca. We'd chosen a little sandwich shop tucked away in Charlottesville. It smelled of grilled onions and baking bread. My stomach grumbled as soon as I stepped inside. It had heavy wooden doors with brass handles and booths of wood and dark green vinyl. Rebecca waved me over to one with a radiant smile.

• • •

"So, how is Jo doing? She had a girl, right?" Rebecca asked after ordering our sandwiches.

"She did. Leona Grace is her name, and she's perfect." Pride welled up in me as if I had given birth myself. I pulled up some pictures on my phone and showed her.

"She's a beautiful baby." Rebecca nodded as I scrolled through pictures.

"Do you have any kids?"

"No. Paul got sick for the first time when I was finishing up my internship. We planned on having kids once I settled into a more regular job with steady hours, but it didn't really work out that way." She looked down at the table and fiddled with her napkin.

"I'm sorry. Children are a joy. I'm sorry you missed out on that."

"It's okay. I have my horses, cats, dogs, and chickens. My life is pretty full. I have really wonderful friends here, and my parents moved to Culpeper to be closer." There was a pause, and she inhaled. "Paul had testicular choriocarcinoma. He had the affected testicle removed and underwent chemotherapy. We tried to save some of his semen prior to treatment, but it was deemed non-viable later when we tried to use it for in-vitro. He went into remission for nearly five years, but then it popped up in a regional node, and during screening they found it in his spine. We tried another round of chemo, but it never responded like it did the first time. We lost him a year after he came out of remission. It was a long, hard year, and looking back I wonder if we even should have tried. Hospice may have been kinder to him, but at the time, we just really wanted to hope he would beat the odds."

"I'm so sorry. I suppose it was a blessing Nora didn't suffer at all. It was sudden for us, but at least it wasn't a long process. She died of an aortic dissection secondary to trauma from a car crash."

Rebecca nodded. "It's hard either way. I had years to prepare myself for his loss. We knew his moments could be limited. While a long death is hard because of the suffering, at least you can prepare and make sure that you don't leave anything unsaid. With a sudden loss, you never have that chance. They are just…gone."

● ● ●

"True. I go over and over in my mind the last time I saw Nora. It was a normal morning, and looking back, I wish I could have fixed it in my mind better, said the things I wanted to say. I really wasn't attentive enough, everything was routine so I ignored it. I have Jo, though, and we can share her memory with each other without feeling sadness now. We're both just grateful that we had her to share." I felt lighter sharing myself so easily with someone who actually knew what the loss of a spouse meant.

"Having a child would have made things a bit easier. I felt guilty for putting things on hold for my career, for putting off a family until it was too late, thinking we had so much time. You never have as much time as you think you do, though. At least I have my animals. They keep me company, and busy!" She gave a little laugh and shook her head.

"Yeah, when Nora died, the animals were a comfort, and now that Jo is out of the house, I appreciate their company more than ever. My parents live with me, but they can't come out to the fields when I check fences, or hike along the stream with me. I tell you, Wallace has been a real joy. I don't know how he ended up at my house, but I'm sure glad he did. Mrs. Norris loves him, and he keeps her active."

"That's good! She is getting up there, isn't she? What is she, thirteen now?"

"Well, we got her Jo's sophomore year of high school, and that was twelve years ago, so yeah. You wouldn't know it to watch her, though. She romps around with the little guy like she's a puppy."

"I like that you enjoy your animals so much, and pay close attention to them. Some people around here just think of them as something to have around, or as a tool for hunting or farm work. I have always felt that they were part of my family. They just make the world better, don't they?" She smiled over the table at me.

"That they do," I agreed.

We finished our lunch with much conversation and eventually headed out to the parking lot. When we got to our cars, there was an unwelcome awkwardness between us. I wanted to see her again. I'd enjoyed her company, but I wasn't sure she didn't just look at this as an obligatory good deed.

● ● ●

"I had a really nice time, Neal. We should hang out again. Maybe next time we could watch a movie or something."

"I'd like that. I'll look over my schedule and call you?"

"Definitely. I have a fairly open schedule. I work some Saturday mornings and have a trail ride or two I'm going on, but otherwise I'm free most weekends."

"Okay, will do. See you later, then." I wanted to hug her goodbye, but I pushed the urge down. I didn't really know her that well. Instead, she hugged me, her body pressing against mine until I could smell her perfume, and I realized I was aware of the softness of her stomach and breasts against my chest. I pulled out of the hug and smiled at her, unsure of the strange rush of emotions I was feeling.

"Thanks for the talk, and understanding," I said.

"Any time, just give me a holler!"

She waved bye and got into her car, and I into mine. I sat in the car for a moment. It was really nice to talk to someone so freely, and it made me aware of just how lonely I'd been.

That night, I dreamed of Nora. She was standing across the bedroom, next to the window, looking out at the pastures. Through the window, I could see the grass, silvery and undulating in the evening glow. The moonlight came in through the old panes of glass, draping itself over her body through a thin old t-shirt.

I could trace the curve of her breasts and the rise of her hips. The shirt ended at the top of her thighs, and as she turned toward me, I followed the shape of her legs as she crossed the room toward the bed.

"I've missed you," she whispered in my ear as she straddled me. The warmth of her body pressed against mine. Her hands moved over my shoulders and down my sides until she pushed them under my back and pressed me into her. I awoke with a jolt, my heart pounding and an ache in my groin.

Confused and frustrated, I got up and took a late night shower. I wasn't sure how to move forward. Nora was the only woman I had ever been truly intimate with. There was a drunken one night stand, and a few make out sessions, but as far as a real relationship, Nora was it. Was I even capable of another relationship? Clearly my dreams were holding on to Nora's

● ● ●

image, but I found myself already looking forward to the next time I could see Rebecca. It wasn't the same all-encompassing desire I had felt for Nora, but more of a yearning for someone who understood. Someone who I could talk to, or watch a movie with, or go to dinner with. I wasn't sure I even wanted anything physical, but just the idea of consistent adult companionship was appealing.

Josephine

My fingers traced the extra fold in Leona's left ear that looked like a heart. Exhaustion in the first few months was only tempered by small intimacies when it was just the two of us. Days and nights became a blur of sleep, nursing, and diaper changes. Gradually Leona began to sleep for longer stretches, but I found I would snap awake thinking I heard her crying, only to find her sleeping peacefully. I would then relax and be able to go back to sleep just in time for her to wake up a few minutes later.

Luke was supportive and caring, but since *we* were breastfeeding, I did most of the work. Often at night I would look over at his sleeping form and fight the urge to push him out of the bed. It wasn't his fault he couldn't lactate, but man, it certainly would have been nice if he could.

I felt isolated and alone, most of my time spent with a person whose dark grey eyes held unfocused pupils like those of a baby kitten. During those first few weeks, she really was more of a little animal than a person. She worked on instinct, sensation, and the base needs of hunger and sleep. Gradually, a tiny human began to emerge, and one day she looked at me with a truly focused stare.

Those eyes, which had remained unfocused and often barely aligned, gazed into mine. She just stared at me, and I at her, for the very first time. I smiled and cooed at her and she just stared, fixed on my eyes. Over the following weeks, she began

● ● ●

to smile, and coo, and gurgle more and more. She finally resembled a person, and I could see her personality blooming each day.

Soon she was lifting her head, rolling over, and trying to crawl. Time seemed like it was flying by, and there were many moments when I felt completely lost. Since Grandma was so close, I called her often for advice, and she often came over to help me navigate the bewildering land of burps, diapers, nursing, and sleep habits. Without hesitation, she would head over and give me whatever I needed. She helped me with the art of burping, having me sit Leona on my lap and bounce her instead of draping her over my shoulder like most people did. She told me my dad had to be burped like that too, that the shoulder thing never worked for him. She was always willing to hold her for me while I took a shower, or ate food, or tried to dress myself in something other than a milk-stained pair of pajamas.

Sometimes she would tell me about my dad when he was a baby, but other times she would just share her nursing knowledge with me. I found it reassuring, and it brought us closer, giving me an appreciation for her that I'd never really felt before. When I was younger, she seemed boring in comparison to Memere, who took red eye flights to places like Milan. Memere's life was dramatic and exciting, but her skill set was not what I needed now. I still missed her but found that in her absence, Grandma filled a void I didn't know existed. Nurturing and care was what I needed as I poured out nurturing and care for my child. Luke tried his best, but there were things he couldn't fully appreciate, like sore nipples, blocked ducts, and hemorrhoids that made sitting painful. Grandma had helpful tips for all of these things and gave me space to not be okay all the time.

Luke was running the shop for me while I was home with the baby, and he assured me that things were going fine. Our sales were steady. I could take as long as I wanted. When he came home in the evenings, he would help cook dinner and do the dishes without complaint. He changed diapers and did laundry, and overall was a perfect, supportive husband. Even so, after months of being home, I found myself jealous of his days in the shop. He would tell me about different customers who came in, what he'd ordered for lunch, or some funny joke someone told. Basically, normal adult life. Life that didn't revolve around poop, pee, and milk. I felt like bodily fluids were basically all I ever thought about anymore and, with guilt, wanted to have some time away from home. I approached Luke about it as we lay in bed one night.

"So, hon, I was thinking, I've been home for three months now and Leona is doing well. Maybe we should start introducing the bottle so you can be home with her some? We can trade off days at the shop, and it would give you more time with her."

"Whatever you need, I'll do it. I would love more time with our girl. She is definitely all about Mama right now, and it would be nice for her to want me too." Luke smiled at the little angelic face sleeping in her bassinet a few feet away.

It was a solid plan, but Leona clearly thought plans were pointless. She refused just about every bottle known to man. We bought every type of nipple available, tried warming the nipple, making sure I was never around when he offered it, all the tricks people said worked. She flat out refused. It was the boob or nothing in her book. I was distraught. I wanted to try to go back to work, but I certainly couldn't have a starving baby at home.

Finally, after two weeks of struggle, Grandma saved us all. She suggested we try a slow feeder sippy cup. It was unlike the breast, but was new and novel enough that maybe she would go for it. It seemed wrong, but it worked. She would take warm pumped breast milk from a sippy cup, but not from a bottle. Our mistake was clearly in trying to fake the boob. She was too smart for that, but this new fancy thing called a cup did just the trick. Finally, I started to go back into the shop three days a week, and Luke went in three days a week. We decided we would close the shop on Tuesdays since it was our slowest day. Life regained some level of normalcy, and the months flew by.

In a blink it was Leona's first birthday. We had a butterfly-themed party with balloons, cake, and family. Leona loved it and didn't seem overwhelmed by all the activity, until she fell asleep in my arms.

• • •

Her long dark eyelashes fluttered, and she snored happily with her sweaty cheek stuck against my chest as I sat in a rocking chair tucked in the corner next to the fireplace. A portrait of Mom hung above it, and an old photo of Memere and my granddad on their wedding day sat on the mantle.

Mikayla and Nicole were chatting on the couch opposite me, and light from the windows caused the ring on Nicole's left ring finger to sparkle while she gestured to Grandma and Grandad as they sat on the couch opposite. Nicole was telling a story about one of her early days in college when she fell down on the sidewalk and couldn't get back up because her backpack was so heavy. Granddad had tears in his eyes laughing as she described being stuck like a turtle rolling around on the sidewalk. Joan, Luke's long time mentor and second mother figure of sorts, was chatting with his mom and sisters at the kitchen island. Jacklyn and Lucian sat in the bay window seats, eating pieces of cake. When they'd visited a few months ago, Jacklyn confided in me that she held out little hope of a grandbaby of their own from Mikayla, so they might as well enjoy Leona. I tried to reassure her that same sex couples had babies with donors all the time, but she didn't buy it. Which meant she instead bought an inordinate amount of adorable outfits, toys, and books for Leona.

It was a varied, strange mix of people, but it worked, and it was a family. My daughter's family. I had worried so much that Leona would miss out with Mom, Memere, and my grandfather passing before she was born. It was true, she was missing out on that side of the family since my aunt was distant at best, but she wouldn't be lonely. This little group was exactly what I wanted her to have. There were strong, loving people around her who would support her and serve as good role models for all kinds of life paths. I breathed in, and there it was: Mom's perfume, wafting over me.

Tucked in my little quiet corner, I knew she was the only one paying attention to me at the moment. "Hi, Mom," I whispered, looking down at Leona, who smiled in her sleep. Perhaps she was dreaming of a grandmother she had never met, but who would always be there.

● ● ●

Neal

I'd once thought happiness was over for me the day Nora died. Yet here I was, full of bliss, holding Briar Celeste Forest in my arms and kneeling to let Leona kiss her brand new baby sister. Leona had Nora's wide green eyes, and they peered at this new tiny bundle with both amazement and a touch of fear. Leona was almost three years old now, and terribly excited about becoming a big sister.

"Papa, can I hug her? Will she cry?" Her little voice would turn her "R" sounds into "W" sounds for only a bit longer, I was sure.

"You can touch and kiss her, but maybe no hugs just yet." She smiled as she brushed the tiny, wriggling little toes, and Briar moved her foot around in a herky jerky attempt at escaping the tickling sensation. While Leona had been born with dark, thick hair and an enviable tan, Briar was fair, with reddish-gold fuzz and a pale complexion. Her eyes were pale greyish-blue at the moment, and although there was no telling what color they would end up, my bets were on blue. She snuffled and turned her head toward my chest, grunting and shifting in her swaddle.

"Uh oh, I think it's time for mommy, little piggy." I handed her back to Jo, and she deftly took her from me and just as easily put her to her breast to nurse. I had never seen a second-time mom in action, and the difference from the first go round was immediate. Jo was more confident and relaxed already, resigned to a lack of sleep, but not afraid of it. Luke refilled her

• • •

water and got her snacks before she asked, a perfect one-man nursing Mama pit crew. I watched as he tucked a pillow under her back and made sure she was comfy before distracting Leona with a new toy they had given her "from the baby."

I thought of Nora, and how we wanted to have two, with the fates aligning against us. Would we have been this good at it a second time around?

I turned to Jo, planning on making my exit. She would need this opportunity for sleep. "Well, you guys seem to have things sorted pretty well. I'm glad they let you go home from the hospital a day early. You've got such a nice little setup here." Their bedroom was on the shady, wooded side of their little house, and felt cool and secluded even on this bright sunny day in June.

"It *is* nice to be at home rather than the hospital." As she said this, Pushkin, their fluffy orange tabby, hopped up on the bed and plopped down, purring extremely loudly, making biscuits on the bed and drooling.

"Does he always do that?" I asked as I looked at this slightly cross-eyed cat, who had clearly not gotten the feline elegance memo.

"What, the drooling? No, only when he's super happy. In fact, it's why his previous owners got rid of him. They said he drooled too much and they didn't like it."

"Wow. So they essentially got rid of him for being too happy?"

"Yeah, humans suck. He's the best cat. Not the smartest, but so sweet, and he lets Leona do anything to him. He'll even let her dress him up without fussing." Pushkin's tongue was now slightly protruding from his mouth, and his eyes were closed as he furiously kneaded the bedspread.

"So you're glad Rebecca told you about him?" I asked, placing a towel over their thin antique quilt in an attempt to save it from the steady drip of drool that was now pouring from Pushkin's chin.

"Oh yeah, we love him, and he's blended in really well. Even with the other two who are definitely a bit more grumpy." Jo gave me a wry grin and patted Pushkin with one hand while holding Briar with her other.

● ● ●

I had been dating Rebecca for a little over two years now. It was nice to have someone around who didn't need translation from medical jargon to normal speech, and we could talk freely about work and life in equal measure. But the main thing that made me appreciate Rebecca was our mutual understanding of what we were to each other. Both of us agreed we had lost our greatest loves in our spouses, but needed company sometimes. We could provide that for each other without the expectation of a grand, sweeping romance.

Rebecca was also perceptive and sensitive, which helped ingratiate her to Jo. When we first began to really date, moving things from friends into something else, Rebecca asked if she could talk to Jo personally and assure her that she was not trying to replace Nora. Jo gave me the thumbs up after their meeting, and they had gotten along really well ever since.

"She should come see the new baby. She'd love it, since Leona was already over a year before she met her. She wanted kids, right? This might give her a chance to at least sniff a newborn. They do smell amazing." Jo leaned down and brushed Briar's reddish fuzz with her lips and inhaled, eyes closed.

"I'll tell her you have requested a visit." Briar had finished nursing and was now blissfully asleep in Jo's arms, her little mouth gaping open with a tiny rivulet of milk in the corner. I believe it was what Jo referred to as a 'milk coma.' "I'm going to head out. Do you need me to do anything before I go home?"

"Nope. Thanks for coming by, and especially for bringing the casserole. We'll eat that for dinner tonight."

"Well, you can thank Rebecca for that one. She made it, but I'll make sure to let her know. I love you, honey." I bent and kissed her on her head, gently touching Briar's soft tufts of hair before heading out of the cocoon-like room. I went out into their comparatively sunny living room where I found Leona and hugged her while swinging her around, then set her on the floor to pepper her face with kisses until she squealed.

"Papa! You so silly." She laughed and plopped back on the floor with her blocks.

"You make me silly!" I responded. Leona's dark ringlets fell back from her rosy cheeks as she laughed and shook her head.

● ● ●

"I love you, munchkin. I'm going to go," I said, wishing I could sit on the floor and play with blocks with her all day.

"Nooo, stay and play with me, Papa!" She reached up and hugged my leg tightly.

"I have to go. But I love you and I'll come back soon."

Leona detached herself from my leg and huffed back on the floor. "Okay, Papa. I miss you." Her bottom lip stuck out some and she sniffed and rubbed her eyes. I felt surprisingly teary-eyed myself and took a deep breath.

Luke came in from the kitchen with some blueberries and set them down next to Leona. "It's okay, Neal. I won't judge you. I feel the same way sometimes."

"Yeah, you guys really have a beautiful family here. I'm happy things turned out the way they have. Things could have easily gone in a completely different direction, and I think you helped steer Jo towards this. Thank you for that."

Luke put a hand on my shoulder. "You don't have to thank me. Jo has been the greatest joy in my existence—next to the girls, of course. I'm just thankful she came into my life, and we found each other. Not many people can accept me for who I am and not find it frightening. Most people just think I'm crazy." He bent and tickled Leona until she was rolling around, snorting and squealing for him to stop. He laughed and picked her up onto her feet. She promptly ran off giggling down the hall into her bedroom.

"Where is the new one going to sleep? This is only a two bedroom, isn't it?" Their little bungalow was the perfect cozy retreat for two adults but was rapidly looking a bit cramped with a child and baby added to the mix.

"Well, we figured they'd share a room until we can find something a bit bigger."

I thought of my huge house, with its empty rooms looming around me all the time. Mom had recently developed dementia and had moved into a facility near us with a memory care unit. Dad was in a rehab unit after a second fall, and I doubted he would be out of his wheelchair and would likely join Mom in long term care. Our house would never be able to accommodate their increasing needs again.

"I have more house than I can use at the moment, and we have that in-law apartment on the top floor. I'd be happy to

• • •

move up there. Before you look at too many houses, consider whether you guys might want to move in there." Luke smiled and tilted his head, considering.

"I'll talk to Jo about it. It's a beautiful house, but are you sure you want to share it? You could probably sell it for plenty and buy yourself a nice place."

"I'd rather not let it go. Nora's there, and it would be nice for it to stay with family."

"I get that." He nodded. "Alright, I'll talk about it with Jo, I promise. She might not be able to make any decisions at the moment, though, Mom brain and all." He smiled and then turned as there was a crash and squeal from the other room. "Hmm, I better check that out."

"Yep. I'll be by sometime this weekend with Rebecca and another cooked meal."

"Okay, sounds good." He gave me a quick hug and headed off toward Leona's bedroom, which was now ominously silent. As I slipped out the door, I heard Luke's voice down the hall. "Now what have you been up to in here?" With a wild giggle in response. I shut the door with a click, leaving for my silent home.

Eleanor

A movie made some time after my death was on the TV, and the old blue and white porcelain lamps to either side of the sofa cast a warm glow in the living room. Rain pattered on the porch roof and, judging from the light filtering through the curtains, it was close to dark. Our vet, Dr. Sorenson, was shirtless and sitting atop Neal. I was so startled by the scene that I knocked into the lamp beside the couch and made it wobble. Neal sat up like a spooked deer and nearly threw the poor woman on the floor.

"Neal, are you okay?" she said as she stood up, looking for her shirt. Clearly this woman had never had children, because certain things on her body were not where gravity had taken my best attributes after breastfeeding. Either that or she'd paid someone for some very nice repair work.

I was pondering this great mystery as Neal rose and started to apologize. He seemed conflicted. I didn't want that for him. She seemed like a good choice and I had no right to complain. After all, he had plenty of life left. He shouldn't live it alone. I withdrew from the room and vowed to visit Neal less often. However, the irony of giving my living husband 'space' when I didn't actually take up any physical space was not lost on me.

I didn't really feel any jealousy over Neal moving on. In life, I was admittedly quite a bit more jealous than Neal was. He was always completely oblivious both to women's attempts at flirting with him, and impervious to feeling threatened by men making advances at me. He was confident—not the arrogant kind of confidence that most men carry, but a quiet, steady confidence. He trusted me, and he trusted himself in equal measure.

Instead of stalking Neal in a potentially pervy way, I hovered around Jo and Luke more often if I longed for time in the living world. Plus, with two grandchildren to watch, things over there were much more fun. Leona was raven-haired and the spitting image of her father with the exception of my green eyes. Leona was a quiet and creative child. She drew and painted constantly, and her big green eyes watched the world around her with avid fascination. The first time Leona saw me, I think it scared me more than it scared her.

I was in their shared bedroom about a year after Briar was born, watching Leona play with her toy ponies. The girls' room was painted a sage green with the woodland mural Jo painted adorning one wall. It was a happy, if crowded room with Leona's twin bed on one side and Briar's crib on the other. Leona sat up and held a pony out toward me.

"Want to play with one?" she asked, looking straight at me. I was so stunned I couldn't even form words. Jo came in a moment later to check on her.

"Mama, I'm being good. I'm sharing my ponies with grandma." Jo was as stunned as I was, and tears rolled down her cheeks as she failed to form words.

"Why are you sad, Mommy?" Leona spoke in the small voice of a four-year-old worried about her mom for possibly the first time ever.

"Oh, honey, I'm not sad, I'm just…You can see your grandma?" Jo replied, wiping her cheeks.

"Yeah, I see her. She's pretty. But Mama, you're crying. When people cry, that means they're sad."

Jo crouched down and held Leona close for a moment. "Not always. Sometimes people cry when they're happy too. If I feel something really strong, whether I'm happy, or sad, or scared, or even mad, sometimes I cry. It's okay. Sometimes feelings are so big they just spill over and out in tears."

"Okay. Mommy, I'm hungry, can we have a snack now?"

"Yes, we can have a snack. I was actually coming to get you for one. Briar already started hers." Jo smiled as they walked into the sun-filled kitchen with her hand on Leona's head.

Whereas Leona was naturally a bit introspective and reserved, Briar proved to be a pure fireball of energy. I think she was too busy to see me even if she could. She was a constant blur of blonde hair and sound. She had bright blue eyes that flashed every emotion she felt, of which there were many. She had a passionate nature that could flare into fireworks at a moment's notice, but that same energy made her magnetic and engaging to everyone around her.

One day a two years or so after Leona first saw me, Briar painted poor Wallace with polka dots. By this point, Luke and Jo had moved back to our house, and Jo was in our familiar kitchen making lunches while the girls were supposed to be painting at the dining room table. When she turned toward the dining room, Briar and the dog were under the table, the dog and carpet now bedecked with multi-color polka dots. For his part, Wallace looked thrilled as he wagged his tail, flinging wet paint all over the table legs. Jo lost it. She yelled at Briar and carried her into the bathroom to strip her down and wash her off before placing Wallace in the bath with her and hosing him down as well. She dried them off and then set about the task of cleaning the carpet and dining room table. Because my daughter thinks ahead, it was washable paint and came up with relative ease. However, during the cleaning process, there were many words said that need not be repeated. When Luke got home from the shop later that evening, Briar lamented, "Mommy yelled at me and was mean." With a sigh, Jo threw up her hands and shook her head. Later, when the girls were in bed, I heard them talking about it. With Luke uttering the fateful words, "It was just paint."

It's never *just* paint. It was the cleanup of both living things, the cleanup of items, the delayed lunch that then delayed naptime, leading to a cranky three-year-old who then wouldn't

● ● ●

nap because she was overtired, and a six-year-old who felt ignored because her little sister was taking up all of Mom's attention. One seemingly small thing can careen an entire day off course, leading to a mother who feels that somehow all of it was her fault.

Let me just say it, kids are hard and they can nearly break you. Yes they are a blessing, yes they light up your world, and yes you love them. But let's face it, they are self-centered little creatures that take up parental energy, time, and care without ever seeming to notice all the sacrifice, yet never miss a slight.

I had only one child, and an easy one at that. Watching Jo juggle two very different children gave me a new respect and admiration for her. I conveyed this as best I could, but encouraging words from a dead mom just didn't suffice. After the paint incident, Jo took a shower and cried alone. I didn't miss being alive all that often, but in that moment I certainly did. I wanted to take the kids for a weekend, buy Jo a riding lesson, and make her join a book club. She had very few ways to give herself time off. Neal's parents had passed within a month of each other after Briar turned two. Neal watched the girls but not as often as Jo really needed. I should have been there more for her. Living was hard. The afterlife was relatively easy by comparison.

By this point, my in-laws were happily settled on this side of the afterlife, my mother and father had finally reconciled, and we had become a surprisingly happy family unit. Things were relatively peaceful on this plane. Until Flora came over, bringing with her a wave of anger, isolation and loneliness that I never expected.

Josephine

B riar was running through the front hall when my phone rang. As she turned the corner into the living room, giggling wildly, I made the decision to let it ring. After all, she was holding Dad's reading glasses, and her hands were covered in peanut butter from lunch. She was a supremely creative, completely unpredictable tiny force of nature that made our lives richer and more chaotic in equal measure. She also created plenty of messes. I heard the front door slam shut, and Leona hurried in with a handful of lilies from the yard. Lilies being toxic to cats, I needed to get the flowers from her before any kitties could chew on them.

"Leona, please put those outside," I said more sharply than I intended. I softened my tone. "They can make the cats sick if they eat them, so we can't bring those flowers inside."

"But Mom, they're so pretty, and I picked them for you." Her little face turned down and her bottom lip trembled. I could see tears brimming in her eyes.

"Okay. We can put them in a vase, but we'll put them on the table on the patio. How about that? Then we can see them from the dining room and kitchen windows, but the cats can't get to them." I watched her expression slowly lift, all the while wondering where Briar had gone with the double threat of peanut butter fingers and potential for broken reading glasses looming. I couldn't hear her any longer, which worried me.

● ● ●

"Okay Mama, we can do that." I went into the pantry to find a vase and saw Briar sitting on the counter with her hand in the peanut butter jar I'd foolishly left there. She was covered in goo and appeared to have attempted to use it as shampoo while she ate it. She grinned at me, and I plucked her off the counter.

"Stay there, and don't touch anything," I told her uselessly as she ran off again.

Finally, hours later, after putting the flowers in a vase, bathing Briar, helping Leona with a project, making dinner, and helping Luke get the girls into bed, I checked my voicemail.

"Mrs. Forest, this is Robert Mulgrave. I am unfortunately calling to inform you of Floraline Turenne's death. She named you as sole beneficiary of her estate. If possible, it would be best to meet in person to go over her estate holdings." He left a number to return his call and expressed his condolences for my loss.

"Who was that?" Luke asked, a look of concern on his face when he saw my expression.

"A lawyer. My aunt Flora died, and I'm her beneficiary."

Luke's eyebrows furrowed. "Huh."

"Really, that's all you've got for me, huh?" I smiled at him, teasing him for his lack of his normal oracle-like wisdom.

"Well, yeah. Huh. She really didn't have anyone else in her life?"

"I'm surprised too. I barely spoke to her, and the last time we did, it was not friendly." I thought back to our argument during the reading of Memere's will. I thought back to the hurt and animosity she had hurled at both Memere and Mom. It had been over six years since that exchange, and Flora and I had minimal communication. I sent her a card each year for Christmas, and she sent a card back, each with generic greetings. Still, I suppose I was her only living family member.

I arranged a flight and arrived in New York a week later feeling both excited and nervous. It was the first time I had traveled alone since my trip to see Mikayla before Leona was born. Luke was home with the girls and sent regular texts with pictures of the controlled chaos. The bustle of New York City was nothing compared with the effort of trying to get a four-

● ● ●

year-old and seven-year-old fed, bathed, clothed, and ready for bed on your own.

It poured rain as I made my way to Flora's apartment building and I was soaked to the skin by the time the doorman greeted me. Water dripped from my clothes on the shiny white elevator floor as I rode up to the 24th story and let myself into her apartment. I felt like an intruder. The lawyer had assured me that I was her sole beneficiary and gave me a copy of her very simple will. This apartment was now legally mine, but still, something about it felt wrong.

It was surprisingly bright, even on such a dreary day, with a sweeping view over the Hudson River. The black and white modern architectural detail of the apartment was a contrast to her well-worn furniture, which was primarily made up of various antiques and soft fabrics.

There was a shelf holding several dying plants in pots by the window. I found a watering can and watered them, then trimmed off the completely dead leaves with the small pruning shears left next to them on the shelf. Most of the pots were plain clay pots painted in various colorful patterns. I wondered if Flora had painted them, or if she'd bought them that way. Again, I was struck by the thought that I barely knew this woman, and here I was in her most private of spaces, dismantling a life I had no part of.

I cleaned out the fridge, throwing away old milk, takeout containers I dared not open, and sadly outdated smoked salmon. I threw it all into a trash bag and was getting ready to take it out when I saw the envelope taped to the back of the front door. It had my name on it in neat handwriting. My aunt's handwriting, which, with a jolt, I realized looked eerily similar to Memere's and nothing like Mom's nearly unreadable scribble.

● ● ●

Neal

A week after my routine checkup, I waited in my doctor's office for lab results, knowing they were bad. If they were normal, I would have simply gotten a call from a nurse. The shelves around me held familiar medical texts and a few generic paintings on the walls. The space was neat and impersonal. I waited, listening to nurses walking by as they discussed lunch orders and patients, until finally I heard a rustle and the click of the door to the office.

Dr. Michak was an excellent clinician, which is why I went to him. He may be impersonal and drab like his office, but he was a brilliant man with a razor sharp mind.

"Dr. Brooks, it is nice to see you again. How are you feeling today?" He sat across from me at the desk and flipped open the laptop, presumably to pull up my results.

"I'm fine. How are my labs?" I couldn't stand this waiting much longer.

"Well, there were some abnormal results that we would like to confirm, and a few further diagnostics we would recommend." Oh boy, here we go.

"So what are my results? May I see them?" I leaned forward as he turned the computer screen to me.

"Well, on your initial labs, some of your base hepatic enzymes were elevated, and we added on a total AFP which was elevated. When compared to your AFP-L3, this is highly indicative of hepatocellular carcinoma. I'm recommending that

• • •

we get you in for a CT so that we can see exactly what we are dealing with here." He looked across the desk at me, his sharp, hawk-like eyes piercing mine.

"I understand. Let's get it scheduled, the sooner the better." I tried to appear calm and resolute, but fear was creeping in from all around, closing down my ability to remain objective and absorb any new information. I was stupid to not bring someone else along when I knew there was a high likelihood of bad news.

I was alone again when I went in for my CT a few days later. Jo had gone up to New York after Flora's death, and Luke would be busy watching the kids while she was away. I already decided to not burden Rebecca with any medical worries. Once was enough for a long illness and a sad ending to a relationship, if this was really bad, I wasn't going to make her do that again.

So I sat again in that drab office to be told that, despite having none of the common risk factors for hepatocellular carcinoma, I had it. They believed it to be operable, and my prognosis was good if they were able to remove it all surgically, but it would be a long road, and there were no clear answers as to what my future would be.

When I got home that evening, Luke invited me to join in on dinner with himself and the girls downstairs. Since Jo and Luke had moved back into the house, I tried to take my dinners mostly upstairs to give them time together. Tonight, though, I was happy for the company.

"Neal, please join us. I made mac and cheese, and there's no way we will eat all of it," Luke said encouragingly.

"Sure, I'll just feed Wallace." I knelt down and patted his scruffy brown and white head. He was now the only dog. We'd put Mrs Norris down at the ridiculously old age of seventeen when we were no longer able to keep her comfortable in her old body.

"Oh, I already fed him." Luke's expression clouded for a moment as he put a hand on my shoulder while I stood.

"Thanks. I'll just go in and see the girls then." I smiled at him, and saw that his face was full of worry and concern. He

● ● ●

knew something was up, but I wanted a little more normal. One more night of happiness unclouded by worry before I exploded this news on everyone.

That's the main problem with having a psychic in the house: you can't bullshit them. If something is up, they know. Luckily Luke also knew when to not push someone into talking about it. I turned and walked into the living room where the girls were watching a cartoon about talking ponies. I knew a difficult conversation would come, but for now, I just hugged my granddaughters and kissed them on their sweet-smelling heads.

"Papa, are you going to eat dinner with us?" Briar asked, a huge grin on her face. "Pleeaaase!"

"Of course I'll have dinner with you. I have been sent in here by your dad to get you to come into the dining room and eat." I was nearly deafened by the screams of joy that erupted in response. Their joy was buoyant and easily conjured, but did nothing to shake the lead weight I felt in my belly. What did my future hold, and how much time did I have? The ability to focus on the here and now rather than what was yet to come was a skill I'd honed in my years on the ER floor. There's no use worrying about a case you haven't seen yet. I just hoped I was up to the task now that it was my life that needed the focus on the present without the worry for the future.

Eleanor

My father walked down the street with the same man I had seen in that most intimate memory he shared with me so long ago. They strolled along across a slush-covered street, huddled in their pea coats, shoulders touching. They were smiling and laughing as they walked and talked, their breath coming out in a mist that swirled and combined. They appeared to be oblivious to my presence. They turned the corner to a narrow side street and stopped beside a nineties BMW. I heard the beep of the car unlocking and the other man leaned back on the car door, inviting my father to lean into him. Dad glanced around quickly before kissing him on the lips. They embraced for a moment before he got into his car and my father walked away down the side street. I stood frozen on the salt-covered sidewalk, watching his form disappear into the shadows of buildings.

It was my sister's memory, which meant she knew about my dad. I could feel her relief at finally getting this secret out. It filled me with sadness for her. How long did she keep this inside? Was this why she had been so distant? She then showed me another memory that made my non-existent blood run cold.

My mother was in the living room of our DC townhouse, and Flora was sitting across from her. Garlands were hung on the mantle, and a huge tree stood in the corner. It was decorated in ivory and gold with doves as a theme. Mom never recycled tree decor, and you could chronicle the years by what

• • •

our tree looked like in photos. This was the first year I'd gone off to college. Flora would have been home on winter break from her senior year at N.Y.U.

"I don't know what you think you saw, but it wasn't your father. There are so many men in wool coats. It could have been anybody,"my mother spoke in a hushed tone.

"Mom. Seriously? You think I don't know what my own father looks like? It was him. He kissed another man on the lips." My mother raised a silencing finger and glared quickly at the dining room door, shushing my sister.

"Well, even if you do think you saw your dad canoodling with some other person, keep it to yourself. We don't need rumors running around about him, now do we?"

"Mom, I don't care about rumors. What does this mean for us? Is Dad gay? Is he cheating? Do you think that is why he is so unhappy all the time? Shouldn't you at least talk to him about it? Should I?"

"No!" Mom yelled out. "You most certainly will not talk to him about it. It probably wasn't even him anyway."

"Okay, but Mom, if he is closeted, outing him could be traumatic if done the wrong way. I have tons of gay friends in drama school right now. It's not easy. He might want to leave."

"Oh, honey, you're so young. Adults handle things differently. I promise, things will be alright. Just don't say anything to anyone, okay? You can't even be sure of what you saw. There is no reason to upend Christmas because of what you may have seen." Mom's tone left no room for discussion.

"Okay, Mom, I promise." Flora sighed. Mom patted Flora's knee and moved into the dining room to supervise what I assumed was the setup for our yearly Christmas dinner. Flora rushed up to her room, still set up for her to come home from college. All her favorite posters hung on the garish pink walls. The Clash, Joan Jett, Culture Club. She lay on her bed and cried, knowing things were not going to be the same, no matter what Mom said.

Dad died that spring.

I wasn't sure when the conversation I'd seen between Mom and Dad had occurred. But the trees through the windows

● ● ●

in Dad's memory had early green leaves on them. Their fight most likely occurred almost immediately before his suicide. Anger coursed through me. Flora clearly showed she was ready to deal with this problem the way it should have been dealt with all along, out in the open. It was Mom who suppressed everything yet again. With her ultimatum, she pushed our family further apart and contributed to Dad's death, which took him from us all forever. He wasn't innocent either, cheating on Mom for who knows how long. That hurt and betrayal could break any family apart no matter the gender of the other person. So many lies. Lies had destroyed what could have been a very different life for all of us.

Josephine

Josephine,

If you are reading this, I'm dead. I developed inflammatory breast cancer and opted to forego treatment. So, here we are. By the way, you should get yourself screened because it can be genetic.

You don't know me well, and sadly I don't know you well either, but that doesn't change the fact that we are family, you and I. I thought you should know something about the family you come from. I loved your mother. Despite all appearances, I really did. I'm sorry I missed out on so many things, but that is my regret to hold, not yours.

I want to tell you about your grandparents, and why I stayed so far away. Your grandfather killed himself. He did not have a heart attack as my mother said. I know he killed himself because I found my mother in his room after it happened, cleaning up a pill vial and bottle. She still insisted it was his heart, and maybe in a way she was telling the truth. See, your grandfather was gay, and had to hide it from the world. I think the pressure of hiding it drove him to end his life. I think my mother drove him to this in her denial of his truth. She threatened to cut me off completely if I ever told anyone of his suicide or sexuality. The irony is that because of my promise to never tell anyone, I cut myself off from my family anyway. Money is a twisted motivator. I regret this, and I regret not knowing you, but old habits die hard, and once I decided to leave, coming back was too hard for me. Perhaps if things had gone differently, we could have been friends. I think we may have had more in common than you think.

Do what you want with the apartment, and the items in it. There is a notebook in the secretary with my contacts. I have highlighted the ones

• • •

that would care to be notified of my death. You would like them. They are all creative people, some former students, some colleagues, and a few friends. They are the family I made after I left the one I was born with. They knew I was sick, but I didn't want them to suffer through things with me, and I opted to forego all that chemo crap. I told most of them I was going away for a while. I didn't want to be remembered as a burden, or pity party. "Better to burn out than fade away," am I right? Ha, you're probably too young to even get that reference. Oh well. Call my lovelies up, and throw a party in my honor. They'll tell you some stories, I'm sure. They can paw through my stuff if they want, but don't let them kill my plants.

With love,
Floraline

I was floored. Not only had Flora known about my grandfather's death, but she knew why. It must have been a huge secret to keep all those years. Memere threatening to cut her off financially must have made her mother's love feel very conditional, which I suppose drove her away from all of us. I thought she was running toward a fabulous life, which may have been partly true, but she was mostly running away from secrets and the people who made her keep them.

I went through her contact list, and every person I called dropped everything to come to an impromptu gathering at her apartment the next day. Thus I found myself surrounded by an eclectic group of about twenty people crammed into her small apartment. They ranged from a broadway producer who extolled Flora's talent, to a former student of Flora's who made a living busking on subways. Several had known her since days together at NYU. They knew my aunt better than I ever did, and it was fascinating learning about her life.

One in particular was a small, pixie-like man who had that strange ageless quality some men have when they are very well groomed. He could have been in his forties or his sixties for all I could tell.

"Man, once the old lady kicked the bucket, Flora was sure happy to get this place. Better than the rat hole she used to live in," he exclaimed while looking out the windows. "Sorry, I probably shouldn't have said that about her. She was your

● ● ●

261

grandma, I suppose." He offered me a sheepish smile and took a long sip of his wine, then shook my hand. "I'm Gabe."

His hands were smooth, and his nails perfectly manicured. I looked at my rough, calloused hands with short broken nails then slid them into my pockets.

"Well, I think your perspective of her was a bit different from mine. I saw her as my Memere, but I now know she was also the woman who drove Flora away from her family. Tell me about Flora. Help me know her better."

He grinned again. "Well, let's see. There was that one New Year's Eve." He yelled over his shoulder, "Hey, Roni, do you remember New Year's of 1999?" A very tall woman came closer and leaned in. She smelled amazing.

"Oh yeah, how could I forget that one?!" She started cackling. "So, we decided to drive out to the shore to Gabe's parents' summer house, and we were all drunk, except Gabe here." Roni nudged him with her shoulder.

"Flora and I were in the back seat and totally hammered when we got pulled over by a cop. Now, I was in full drag, and Flora was all done up too, which meant she was very nearly in drag herself." They both laughed softly, and Roni put her hand on Gabe's shoulder, showing long oval nails in a vibrant fuschia. "Gabe here was driving. Who was in the passenger seat, though?" Roni tilted her head in question.

"Oh, it was Mark." Gabe lifted his nose in slight disgust.

"No wonder I don't remember. Ugh, he was always so boring, but probably a good thing for a traffic stop. Anyway, we get pulled over and it takes forever. We were hoping to do midnight on the beach, but instead listened to Prince's 'Party like it's 1999' and kissed Flora in the backseat as he gave you a speeding ticket. It *was* memorable, though." They both dissolved into giggles at the shared memory.

"Did you finally make it to the shore?" I asked.

"Oh yeah, we sat out on the beach most of the night, drinking, smoking, laughing. It was a good start to the 2000's, despite the underwhelming magical midnight moment." Gabe smiled, tears started to fall down his cheeks, and Roni rubbed his back.

● ● ●

"Sorry, I miss her, and those times. She was great, you know. I mean really great." He sniffed and pulled out a beautiful handkerchief from his pocket to wipe his nose.

"Obviously, you two have known her for a long time."

Roni smiled and spoke, since Gabe had his face buried in his handkerchief still. "Ever since she came to New York for drama school. She walked in that first day with her sunhat and floral dress, and I knew I needed more of that in my life. She was *so* southern." She smiled again. "We all landed in different places professionally, but stayed close as friends."

This was a window into a life that was very different from mine, but in some ways similar. I suppose we all build a network of people to support us, and those people aren't always family. It's the memories of a shared life that make people your family, not blood. Flora's life made that realization clear to me as her friends shared stories of a life spent well. At the end of the evening, when everyone left, I felt a sadness for missing out on this part of my family. Flora wasn't the demon I had made her out to be. She just built emotional walls and protected herself from a family she felt isolated from. I knew where the blame lay, and it wasn't Flora. Memere, again, had driven a wedge between members of her own family, all for the appearances of perfection. By stifling the true nature of those around her, she drove them away. Only my mother stayed by her side, blissfully unaware of the truth until her death. Why hadn't everyone just trusted each other with the truth?

I vowed to myself to never, ever do this to my own family. I wanted to go home and hug my children. I wanted to go home and make love to my husband, then fall asleep against his warm body. Instead, I changed the sheets on my dead aunt's bed and tried to fall asleep to the sounds of car horns and sirens.

Over the next few days, I cleared out Flora's apartment, giving items to friends who came forward for certain things, odd trinkets mostly. No one wanted anything for its monetary value, and almost everyone that met me to take something home had a story about the item and why they wanted it. This left me with several large pieces of furniture to deal with. I contacted a moving company, and they were able to take the remainder and place it in the same storage unit where I kept some of Memere's items. Finally I was able to go home.

● ● ●

It was like coming up for air after being held under water. I got out of my car in the late afternoon and reveled in the space and greenery around me. New York was a vibrant place of life, but filled with concrete, man-made noise, and people. Virginia, specifically my lifelong home, was filled with sound and life as well, but in a completely different way.

It was late July and the cicadas permeated the air with their raucous buzzing. The air across the pastures was alive with insects flying back and forth in streams of light. I breathed in the fresh, grass-scented air and released all the residual tension I had been holding since the start of my trip. The front door screeched open and I heard the best sound of all: joyful cries of Mama and Mommy as my daughters crashed out and tumbled to me, both embracing me and squealing with delight at my return. For a moment, I felt pure golden joy at the unbridled love being given to me just for being home. I looked up at Luke as he lifted my bags for me, but noticed his smile didn't reach his eyes.

Neal

The following year of my life was the hardest since the year following Nora's death. I underwent treatments and tests, surgeries and trials. It was exhausting and sometimes painful, but I pushed through it to be with my girls. They were the beacon that kept me going when I wanted to just slip away into the darkness that pulled at my periphery.

Rebecca and I remained friends, but she agreed that one cancer treatment in a partner was enough, and while she provided support, she distanced herself. I understood. This was not a process anyone wanted to go through once, let alone twice.

Eventually, after more medical procedures than anyone would ever want to endure, it was over. For now. I was in remission. They'd removed the bulk of the mass in my liver surgically, and I had completed both radiation and chemotherapy to eliminate as much microscopic disease as possible. At the moment, there was no sign of it on any of my scans, and I was a free man. I couldn't feel my fingertips and my hair was now thin and oddly curly. I couldn't eat many foods without horrid indigestion, but I was pretty much functional and determined to enjoy this body I fought to bring back from the brink of destruction.

I decided to use some of the money Celestine left me to take Jo, Luke, and the girls to France. Nora and I never traveled there after her grandparents passed away, and even then

• • •

we'd only come once before Jo was born with Celestine as a tour guide, largely avoiding her family. Exploring where Nora's family had come from might help Jo deal with some of the revelations that had come about after Flora's death.

It seemed that Nora was the only one in her family who never knew the truth during life. Obviously she knew that truth now, but that didn't change the turmoil left behind. I wanted to make sure Jo had a full idea of her roots. Plus, the idea of traveling to the south of France was an entirely more pleasant idea than the past year spent in drab hospitals and waiting rooms.

Three weeks later, we were on a plane flying over the Atlantic. I thought back to the last (and only) time I'd made this trip. One of the biggest fights Nora and I got into during our time together occurred during our one trip to France together.

Nora flew often as a child and was admittedly more comfortable in a plane than I would ever be. However, it made her annoyingly sure of her prowess at navigating an airport. I studiously looked up NSA guidelines since we would be flying post September 11th, and Nora had flown only prior to September 11th at that point. She insisted she 'knew what she was doing.' This was always a bad sign, as generally when Nora said this, she did not in fact know what she was doing.

As it happens, in this case we got into a huge fight over shoes. Yep. Shoes.

Anyone who has been married for any length of time will understand. Nora wanted to wear lace up sneakers, as this was what she always wore when traveling in the past. I tried to convince her to wear slip on shoes, and failed. This meant that at every airport, Nora had to lace up her shoes every time we went through security. Now, this doesn't sound like a big deal, and in the grand scheme of things it isn't. However, our layovers were very short, and both were in sprawling airports with shuttles to each terminal. Therefore, I spent our trip standing next to my beloved spouse as she sat on a bench carefully lacing her shoes, watching as other people seamlessly moved through security slipping shoes on and off with ease. That trip

● ● ●

culminated in a near screaming match at our last airport and a very quiet final flight to France.

Now the five of us sat in our slip-on shoes, in a plane over the Atlantic, also quiet, but for different reasons. Briar slept curled next to me, her head resting on my lap as she snored softly. Luke, Jo and Leona sat in the row across the aisle and were watching a movie on a tablet. The grey clouds outside the windows revealed little about where we were, and I drifted into a soft dreamless sleep, happy to have this respite after long months of fear and dread.

● ● ●

Josephine

After a long flight with two first-time flier children, and a first-time flier husband, I was exhausted by the time we arrived in Lourmarin, France, where we were staying at Memere's childhood home. My great aunt, whom I'd never met, lived there, and this would be the first time I met any of my family in France.

The first view of the home was straight out of a painting. The house was sprawling and grand, built of pale sand-colored stone with large mullioned windows and a complex clay-tiled roof with multiple chimneys, smoke drifting from one. It sat amidst rows upon rows of lavender bushes, currently a pale green in color. Inside, the front hall was large and welcoming, with huge dark beams spanning the two-story ceiling, and a wide central staircase leading to a landing with a large leaded glass window overlooking the fields.

The home was now set up as an inn and farm, open for tours, with a little shop and tasting room set apart from the inn and private rooms. It had been in the family for over three-hundred years, and was now run by my great aunt Christianne and her husband Philip. Christianne was a small bright woman in her early seventies, whose fast-moving hands, pixie cut hair and flickering smiles gave her a birdlike quality. She was the youngest of the four Bujeron children and the only one interested in taking over the family home. Normally the task

• • •

would have fallen to Memere, as she was the eldest, but she had chosen to move to the US with my grandfather instead. The middle two brothers seemed equally eager to make their own way and left for larger cities within France as soon as they got the chance. The elder of the two brothers had already passed away, and the surviving one lived in Normandy and no longer could make the nine hour trip without good reason, and we did not count as a good reason.

After setting our luggage down in our respective rooms, we went downstairs for dinner. The beautiful but austere formal dining room was reserved for paying guests of the inn, so we ate in a much less formal but much more cozy dining area adjoining the kitchen. The old wooden table set for dinner was solid and long enough for all seven of us to eat comfortably, and the worn terra cotta tile floor made me worry less about food dropping onto a precious antique rug. February in this region was not a high tourist season, and we could enjoy the place in relative privacy. A fire was lit in a large fireplace, warming the room nicely. While it wasn't bitter cold, the air held a crisp chill that the fire kept away.

"It is so nice to see you here after so long. I only wish Nora and Cele could have come once again before we lost them, but that is the way, is it not?" Christianne noted as she settled down to the table.

"It is. I'm not really sure why we went so long without visiting," Dad said as he began eating the soup Christianne had given everyone to start their meal. I took a bite of my soup and the creamy, salty, savory flavor filled my mouth. It was an amazing stew with greens, pasta, and beans. I rapidly became too absorbed in the flavors to focus on the conversation around me until I caught a thread of conversation that drew my attention.

"Oh, well, they never really got on very well. Celestine tried so hard to be everything and never seemed to realize that she couldn't be. That of course didn't stop her from trying," Christianne said, dipping her crusty bread into her soup as she talked, sucking the juice from the bread as she put each piece into her mouth.

"Was it really so hard for her?" Dad asked, his brow furrowing.

"Oh, well, our parents were, how is it? Perfectionists. Everything always had to be just so, and if it was not perfect then no one in the house would rest until it was. They would be horrified to know strangers are now regularly staying in their family home, but it was what needed to happen if we were to keep a home like this. This is a place built for another time. One really does not need fifteen bedrooms anymore, unless you are letting them out for sleeping." She got up and cleared our empty bowls as Philip went into the kitchen and got clean plates for our main course, which he set in front of each of us. Briar yawned hugely and leaned against Luke, her eyes closing heavily as she did. I shot a glance at him and he nodded.

It was now half past eight French time, which put us at 2pm Virginia time. However, after a ten-hour flight to Marseilles from DC, followed by a two-hour overland trip here, the kids were absolutely done in, and I was right there with them. Luke leaned over and whispered to Leona. She looked up at him and nodded, rubbing her eyes.

"I hate to be rude, but I really think we ought to get them to bed. I 'm not sure they have the energy to finish dinner. Would it be alright if we tucked them in and one of us came back down to join you?"

"Of course! They must be completely exhausted, certainly. Do what you need to, dear. I'll keep a plate for anyone who needs it in the refrigerator for later. Bonne nuit mes amours." She smiled over the table to the girls as they readied to go up.

"Mama, what'd she say?" Leona asked as she took my hand to go upstairs to our rooms. Luke was carrying Briar off up ahead, her head heavily resting against his shoulder, arms and legs draped over him loosely.

"Oh, honey, she said, 'Goodnight, my loves.'" I told her, prompting Leona to give Christianne a hug.

"Goodnight, auntie," Leona said as Christianne smiled and held her close before placing a kiss on her head.

The sun seeped in through the pale floral curtains and cast a soft glow over the room. The walls were clean white plaster adorned with old oil paintings of multiple landscapes. Luke was still asleep, arms sprawled across the bed and one foot poking out from under the linens. The girls were in the adjoining room still quiet, and I got up to peek in through the doorway.

● ● ●

Briar had crawled into bed with Leona at some point during the night and was sleeping with her head at the foot board, feet on her sister. Leona was curled around her stuffed bunny Bun Bun, head resting on her pillow. I dressed quietly and slipped downstairs for some food. After having only soup for dinner, I was starving.

Christianne was in the kitchen, baking something that smelled delicious.

"I'm sorry we left dinner so early. The girls were beat, and once we got up to our rooms, we just didn't have much energy left ourselves."

"Oh, don't worry about it. Those transcontinental flights are rough, especially with little ones. Half our guests don't even make it to dinner, let alone through it that first night with us." She pulled a beautiful loaf of fresh bread from the oven, then set some jam and butter on the table. I buttered a fresh warm slice of the crusty bread and sat down on a stool by the counter.

"So, you are the youngest of Memere, sorry, Celestine's siblings?"

"Yes, my parents would never admit it, but I'm pretty sure I was an accident. I am six years younger than Jean, the next youngest, and he, Luc, and Cele were each roughly three years apart. I got away with much more than they ever did. I think Maman et Papa were too tired to care by the time I came along."

"So, they were hard on Celestine?" The name felt foreign and strange on my tongue as I said it, not aligned with the woman I knew.

"Oh yes, she got the worst of it as the oldest. They fully expected her to take over the running of the chateau, and to marry someone of adequate status and wealth to ensure the survival of the family as it was. She tried to please them, but then she fell madly in love with Charles, and it was all over. The saddest part is that even early on, he did not seem to be as much in love with her as she was with him. She could not see it, of course. When a heart is blinded by that kind of ardor, there is nothing that will dissuade it. It is really a bit tragic to think she left behind her entire family for a man who never seemed fully committed in the same way she was."

● ● ●

"So he didn't love her?" I asked. Christianne sighed, taking a long sip of her tea before answering.

"It is complicated. I do think he loved her in the very beginning, and he clearly admired her in a way. But his love for her just faded over time. Charles himself faded over time. He receded from those around him. Celestine compensated by trying to make everything as perfect as it could be. It didn't really matter. He had a sadness that she just could not fix. He genuinely loved your mom and Floraline, though. That much was apparent when they visited."

"Did they visit much?"

"Not as much as we would have liked. They split their trips home between Charles' family and ours. My parents could be difficult people to be around, especially for Cele. Nothing was ever good enough for them, and that included Charles, but they doted on Nora and Flora. Grandchildren were not included in their criticism."

"What was my mom like when she was young?" Christianne smiled and leaned over the table to pat my arm.

"Your mother was always so funny and sweet, easy to be around. She was creative, sensitive, and always made the funniest comments. Oh, her timing was perfect, even from a young age. And Floraline was just so vibrant, always with a story or song she had made up. The imagination on that one was amazing. They were a lovely pair of girls." A smile lit on her face, then faded.

"It is such a shame that they are both lost to this world now."

"I know. I miss Mom so much. I wish she could see my girls, and know them in life."

"Ah, your Leona is very much like her, you know. So sweet saying goodnight to me. It is something Eleanor would have done, I'm certain." Briar came in, still in her pajamas as we were speaking.

Christianne's face brightened and she bustled about, offering her all sorts of pastries, fresh bread, and milk. Which Briar gladly accepted. After everyone emerged from their rooms and ate breakfast, we set off to see the estate. By midday, the day warmed to a perfect temperature for light sweaters and jeans, and the sun was shining in a perfectly bright blue sky. The

• • •

cream-colored stone walls of the chateau were surrounded by lavender fields, groves of olive trees, and a small vineyard, all of which we enthusiastically explored. We walked through one of the groves of trees, their branches still bare, revealing angular trunks and branches. It reminded me of a Van Gogh from one of my books back home.

"This one is the oldest on the property." Phillip lovingly rested his hand on a gnarled, thick tree and gazed at it. "It was the only one that survived the freeze of 1956, and it is believed to be one of the original trees planted when the chateau was built in the early 16th century."

"It's beautiful." I took several photographs. It would make an amazing study in oil.

"We think so. It has survived wars and famine, so many changes, becoming bent over the years, but still faithfully producing fruit for us to share with the birds, and holding our soil with its strong roots. It will be here for our sons when they come home to take over for us when we are too bent and gnarled to run things. It is not even old as olive trees go. Elia vouvon, in Italy is the oldest olive tree known. It is over 2,000 years old. They are quite remarkable, these trees." He patted the trunk and revered the tree before turning to show us the vineyards.

We finished our tour, and after a snack of bread and olive paste we went into town to look around. Dad walked ahead with the girls, one on each hand, their voices floating behind the trio as they walked. Luke put his arm around me and kissed my cheek as we ambled behind.

It was a moment of perfect lazy happiness after months filled with anxiety and pain. Dad never complained. It wasn't in his nature to complain or burden anyone with his problems. Still, he struggled to remain positive while enduring treatment upon treatment. His tenacity paid off.

We spent fourteen days total in France, based in Lourmarin, and side trips to Marseilles, Cannes, and Paris. Memere and I visited Paris once when I was in middle school, but we'd never gone to her home. It struck me as strange at the time, but now, knowing her relationship with her family, I understood. Seeing the city as an adult was a completely new experience.

● ● ●

Whereas my trip with Memere so many years ago felt like an education, this one felt like an expedition. Leona and Briar found treasures such as interesting stones, pretty leaves, and a broken earring in a park. These were added to the suitcases with equal importance as clothes, books, and gifts purchased during the trip.

Eventually everything was packed in suitcases and we began the long journey home. I fell asleep on the plane and awoke to watch the sun rise over the navy blue horizon. Leona slept with her head in my lap. I stroked her dark hair and looked over at the other row, where Luke, Dad, and Briar were sitting. Briar was sprawled across both of their laps, snoring softly. Dad was dozing against the window, his head resting on a pillow. Luke was displaying his talent for falling asleep sitting bolt upright. France gave us fourteen golden days of light and joy, while delivering insight into Memere and her relationship with my grandfather. The trip also gave me glimpses of a happier time in Mom and Flora's life, before things became so complicated.

Neal

I came out of remission just over a blissfully uneventful year that followed our trip to France. My bones ached and throbbed, leading to scans, which led to the grim discovery. All the treatments had bought me this time, but now I had multiple metastatic lesions in my spine and pelvis, which led to constant pain. At risk for pathologic fractures should I fall, I was confined to a wheelchair and Jo and Luke moved me into my old bedroom downstairs. I entered hospice care at home, preparing to die.

The pain my body was going through was minimal compared to the pain I saw reflected in my daughter's eyes when she came to sit with me. She covered it when the girls were around, but when they left, it showed itself to me without her knowledge. It hurt to know I was causing her this pain and could do nothing about it.

My best moments now were when I could wheel myself out onto the patio. It was harder to feel sadness with light and life around me. It was late April, and the fields were a vibrant green once again. The horses were shedding, leaving swathes of fur in the grass where they rolled and patches of sleek summer coats under their dry winter fur. Purple, white, and pink hyacinths Nora had planted along the edge of the patio years ago were blooming, and their thick, sweet fragrance filled the air. Pollen-laden bees buzzed around, busily unaware of anything but the heady perfume and its promise of nectar.

● ● ●

The girls often played out here in the afternoon, blowing bubbles, drawing on the slates with chalk, or running and chasing each other. Their voices filled the air with the music of their joy. They knew I was sick, but in the way of children, they lived in each moment. Strange that those in the beginning of their lives should know best how to handle the end of a life. They never focused on what was to come, but instead picked bright daffodils, drew pictures for me, and threw the ball for Wallace, who still dropped it at my feet each time he returned proudly from fetching it.

One evening while I was outside with them, a baby rabbit hopped out into the grass. The sun was low over the mountains, casting shadows of trees across the yard. The rabbit sat in the shadow of one of those trees and froze when it heard the girls. They stopped playing and watched the little rabbit. It crouched low and slowly lowered its ears to its back, attempting to blend in and disappear. Briar couldn't resist the temptation of the soft brown fur, walking closer until it finally broke and bolted with a flash of its white tail across the yard to the safety of a blooming forsythia. It was then hidden among the bright yellow branches, causing a disappointed groan from Briar and a taunting "I told you it would run" from Leona.

The world was coming alive just as I was dying. My body, once wiry and strong, was now withered and weak. My hands shook when lifting a water cup to my mouth. I had a prescription for marijuana to help me with my appetite. I was on fentanyl for pain and multiple medications to help slow down this process that was now so obviously unstoppable.

As a doctor, I always felt frustrated when people said they were foregoing treatment. I always judged them and thought they were simply giving up. I now understood they were not giving up. They were just making a choice, a choice to cross sooner but with less suffering. I was no longer afraid of crossing, and this endless pain was almost unbearable without those I loved to keep me here. As much as I wanted to stay, eventually the pain grew to be too much, and I knew I was ready to leave this cancer-riddled body behind, even if it meant leaving my family behind.

● ● ●

Eleanor

When Neal passed over, it was nothing like my passage or my mother's passing. It was a slow, gradual process, allowing all involved to prepare themselves as best they could. Every moment collected in their minds and held onto tightly. His body weakened and he began to slip in and out of consciousness, balancing on the edge of life and death.

In Neal's final days, he lay in our old bedroom in a hospital bed, surrounded by people who loved him. Luke and Jo were taking turns holding vigil, making sure he was never alone for more than a few moments. As he approached his death, he reached out to me more often. His body was small and weak. He could barely sit up to eat or drink, and toward the end he was unable to even lift his head. It was hard to watch his body fail around him, knowing how strong he once was.

It was late one evening and the girls had gone to bed only a short time before. They'd come in and gently hugged Neal before heading upstairs for bedtime as they did every night. They didn't notice the tears in his eyes as they let him go. After they went up to bed, Neal looked right at me, and I knew he was coming. Luke was sitting beside him and knew as well. He called out for Jo in the kitchen and she came rushing in, tears streaming down her face already.

"Daddy, is it time? Are you going?" She reached out and held his hand, wiping her tears with the other. Luke sat beside her and held her close.

• • •

"Mmmhm, I'm going." Neal's voice was weak and scratchy, but he turned to look at our beautiful daughter and smiled. "It's okay, I'm not alone. She's right there waiting for me. I love you." He closed his eyes, and his breathing became more shallow as he started to fade away from her.

"I love you too, Dad. I love you, and I'll miss you." Jo held his hand with hers and sobbed beside him as I watched his energy slip away from his body. Gradually his chest stopped its rise and fall, and his body lay completely still.

Then he was with me. Whole and clear, his energy flecked with green and gold, swirling around mine of coppery red. He was happy to be free of his failing body, and happy to be with me again. There was sorrow for our daughter, temporarily left behind in the living world, but more overwhelming was a feeling of elation and freedom. Our energies mixed and encircled each other as a rush of memories and emotions flowed through us both. We were completely connected again. I felt less alone than I had ever been, even in life. His parents came to him, as did his grandparents. They created a flashing, pulsing sea of light that encircled Neal. My own parents were nearby, and I felt a strong pull away from the physical world.

The fog that separated me from the physical world was thick and only parted when Jo reached out for me, tugging me back to her and the physical world. With more of my loved ones now here with me, their pull to leave the world completely was stronger than ever before. I remained tethered, a kite against the wind, my line held by Jo, her love alone holding me fast against currents that threatened to lift me away forever.

Acknowledgments

First and foremost, I must thank my dedicated editor, Tory Hunter. With your guidance and practiced hand, this book has improved beyond measure. You encouraged me, guided me and made me capable of telling this story.

Erich, you read a terrible first draft, and listened to me muddle through story lines, character traits, and above all, you gave me time. Time to write, re-write, edit, revise, brainstorm and on and on. Thank you for your never ending support in all of my endeavors. Jessie, you read my very first draft and helped me with my first revision and from then on you offered advice, encouragement and inspiration. I am forever grateful that your family decided to live a block away from my family, you have been and always be my surrogate sister. Josie, I am glad to call you friend and the best beta reader a writer could hope for. You helped make this book richer more beautiful through your insightful reading and I am grateful for you.

To the many writing workshops, writing groups, both online and in person, and of course the Moms with a DVM Book club, thank you to every person who took the time to read what I've written and help make it better. Thank you all the members of the Bumble Book Club-Cville, your critiques and insights on books proved a guiding light for me during my writing process.

Mom and Dad, thank you for fostering my love of books, reading that first draft and being kind enough to tell me it was good (we all know it wasn't very good). Mom, I don't think you'll ever know how much all those trips to the library meant to me.

Thank you to my beautiful girls for insisting that I will make the NY Times best-seller list, thanks for dreaming bigger than I do and believing in your mom, you are both more of an inspiration to me than anything else in this world. And finally, but not least, thank you to every author of every book I've read, both good and bad. It takes a special kind of courage to put your inner world out there in the world for all to see. Thank you for

all the stories, characters and places I miss after reading the last page.
With love and gratitude to you all – Devlyn D'Alfonzo

For additional materials including a book club guide, playlist inspired by this novel and author's blog, please visit. https://devlyndalfonzo.com or contact brokentreepress@gmail.com with any questions or comments.

Thanks for reading!